From Faraway Horizons

**David Kimel

DAVID KIMEL

FROM FARAWAY HORIZONS

Travel Notes

WWW.PARAMOUNTBOOKPUBLISHING.COM

This work is published in both electronic and printed editions.

To my patient and ever-supportive wife Valeria, whose encouragement and devotion always created for me conditions for exploring new horizons.

"From Faraway Horizons"
by David Kimel

David Kimel, a charming presence both in life and in writing, belongs to an educated generation that puts its accumulated knowledge to use, nourished by a deep curiosity to understand the world and thus give it meaning. Observant and sensitive, Mr. Kimel takes on a wide range of subjects: from inscriptions on clay vessels discovered in Latin and Greek, to the religious writings of medieval Romanian monasteries, to the modern concerns about individual freedom and the transformative role of technology (which can control both the individual and society as a whole). He writes in a tone that is objective, searching, investigative, with a keen eye for the significant detail—in truth, always seeking meaning, the ultimate sense that may reveal directions for the future. The author adopts a responsible stance, learning from the past and extrapolating its lessons into a future that often appears uncertain.

Of the many themes he explores, I'll mention just a few: *How will our young people learn history?* And what lessons will they still draw from it? Then, the image of a tree at the roadside, damaged by technology without even suspecting it… *Beware!*—Mr. Kimel tells us. Coming into the new world with the experience of Communist surveillance, the writer recognizes a growing and troubling tendency: electronic eyes collecting information about us at every street corner, without asking permission, interfering with our private lives. These are alarm signals, raised with a sense of responsibility, not only drawn from books but also from his own life experience and from those who came before him, from whom he has learned and continues to learn. David Kimel does not forget—more than that, he manages to draw from this act of not-forgetting educated conclusions to meaningful questions, which lead to answers full of substance.

We are speaking here of a man raised in the spirit of truth, honest in his undertakings, who presents even the most unsettling insights about the state of the world with decency, grace, and—let me add—good taste. His concerns stretch from figurative or literal encounters with Dalí (an artist who toyed with our shifting perceptions, pushing the boundary between art and innovation toward strange and unusual creations), from Cadaqués and Figueres, to the author's virtual encounters on Facebook—some of which have proven disappointing. From his youthful memories to the contrasts he observes in a life lived on the North American continent. From revelations discovered on the roads of inner exploration to those found on his journeys *From Faraway Horizons*.

His writing has fluency and charm, it has both content and form; it is gifted, and yet carefully crafted. You feel the attentive care that shapes the material, polishing it to its present refinement.

Although David Kimel presents himself to the world with modesty—and at times even with self-doubt—I know this comes only from his constant drive for self-improvement, or from a desire not to be mistaken. Living by high standards, he strives to remain true to them, in keeping with his expectations of himself. In the preface to the volume, I found a disclaimer suggesting that since the publication of certain articles, things may have changed. Yet I wonder whether any missteps or outdated opinions can truly be found in this book. On the contrary, I am convinced the author will smile across time with the thought, *"I told you so,"* and in most cases, time will likely prove him right. I fear we shall remember his predictions if we fail to take his concerns seriously. More than that—if we fail to act on them.

David Kimel is a name to remember, to read, and to keep close. Personally, I hold him dear, since the few interactions I have had around his books have turned into memorable experiences— ones I gladly recommend to others. When I read him, I try to uncover what else fuels his passion, where curiosity drives him next, and what new horizons remain to be explored. His conclusions have long-reaching echoes, and they urge the reader to learn—and, more importantly, to question.

The author thus becomes an excellent guide in the search for meaning in a chaotic world, for he sheds light on its tender points, suggesting that perhaps, through a kind of acupressure, some of our pain might be relieved. Here we speak of a healer who understands suffering. And more than that, he watches with compassion, offering generously of his vast experience so that we may grow wiser. I discover him with childlike joy, sincerely intrigued by his interpretations and perspectives. A complex personality, acting in the spirit of the highest human values—someone from whom we have much to learn. A delight to read.

The warm recommendations surrounding *From Faraway Horizons* carried the book throughout the community, passing from hand to hand, read by everyone who asked for it. As a result, I have heard nothing but superlatives, along with readers' desire to know more about the writer, to read more of him. This is one more reason for him to step forward with full confidence into new and exciting projects, as he moves on toward a new horizon of age, experience, and artistic fulfillment.

Milena Munteanu

Acknowledgment

It is well known that after a lifetime of work, when a person finally reached the point of being rewarded with his old-age pension, in addition to the freedom of being able to do whatever he wants, there is also the benefit of being able to carry out a number of projects which never could done before due to lack of time. Many people pursue gardening plans, others remember the musical instrument untouched for decades and, with patience and care, begin to retrain their fingers with the finesse required to touch the strings of the instrument. Along with other projects, many return to the technical passions of their youth such as carpentry or mechanics. An old acquaintance used to collect old cars from friends who wanted to get rid of them for free and, in his home garage, buying books and spare parts, he rebuilt the worn-out engine into a new one. Then he would give the car to a young person who could not afford the luxury of a new car, for a token amount which barely covered what spent to buy replacement parts. There are quite a few who develop a passion for travelling and that becomes a dream come true.

If my life had unfolded according to my own planned score, destiny would have taken me along different paths than those I walked. From childhood, teachers discovered in my writings a leaning towards poetry, which was later used by friends and colleagues in their letters to their beloved ones. But poverty, parental authority and social conditions constantly kept me away from my passion for art and writing. For decades – during which immigration also occurred – the pen was completely forgotten in a corner, because more urgent necessities had to take its place. I remembered it when my daughter turned seventeen. Then a few verses flowed from my heart for her birthday. With them, the source of creation began once again to gather in the forgotten riverbed a delicate thread of crystal-clear water, from which I distilled a few poems and later a book.

This book is the result of providence, which brought into my life people of rare moral quality and selflessness, such as Dumitru Puiu Popescu and his wife Anca, who have devoted a large part of their lives to gathering, around the "Observatorul" (The Observer), a Romanian cultural magazine in Toronto, and founders of "Nică Petre" literary circle. Romanian writers with a high level of culture, discernment and great literary talent became members and contributors to its purpose. Under the warmth of their encouragement, my modest literary attempts – articles and commentaries – grew over the years that span along about two decades, and with these lines I wish to express my sincere thanks, gratitude, and respect to their help. I also cannot omit many of the magazine's colleagues whose support and encouragement were and still are deeply appreciated: Veronica Pavel Lerner, Elena Buică, Maria Cecilia Nicu and the poet Ion Segărceanu.

My deepest gratitude is owed to my friend, the writer, researcher, and scientist Gabriel Watermiller (Gavril Iuliu Morariu) who suddenly passed shortly after elaborating this book. His knowledge, covering a wide and varied spectrum in almost all fields – literature, history, and science – has been of real help in creating this volume, eliminating some errors and, no less, stylistic corrections. With the same friendship and generosity, he devoted time and effort to the writing and promotion of my first autobiographical novel, A *Foggy Sunrise*, recently republished. A thousand thanks!

Further thanks are due to Mrs. Victoria Dimonie, who always found encouraging words for what I created and whose opinions and advice have always been appreciated. Special thanks to the readers of *Observatorul* magazine, who on numerous occasions have shown their appreciation through messages to the editorial staff.

At Paramount Book Publishing House, my warmest thanks belong to April Woods, whose candor, response, and diligence were above my best wishes. Similar appreciation and thanks are due to Mr. Garry Miller and Joe Brandon who offered me warmth, understanding and support. Thank you!

This volume includes a number of writings and impressions from journeys undertaken aboard various ships, as well as a series of articles published over the years. Many of these articles tried to respond to the current issues today - partly outdated – but seen from a historical perspective, are still relevant. For this reason, I thought it necessary to include the date of creation for each article, as a means of justifying the theme addressed in its historical context. I do not know to what extent they helped anyone at the time, but I hope that those who come after us find in them a grain of truth that will clarify their doubts.

Contents

About the World

A Day in the Big Apple

Everything began when I received an e-mail from Princess Cruisess. They let me know about an important sale of a 14-day transatlantic crossing, at only sixty-nine dollars per person per day. I don't know how others react to such news, but I was suddenly struck with excitement from head to toe and ran upstairs into the living room, where I found my wife, as usual, very busy talking on the phone.

"My dear, listen to this," I said.

"I can't. I'm busy. Don't you see?"

"Yes, but look, this is important."

"What is so important?"

"A transatlantic cruise, for only 69 dollars a day".

I was lucky she was already on the phone. I know people who need a fortune teller before taking a decision. Others find the answer to a dilemma by tossing a coin in the air, but my wife is different. She has friends:

"Listen dear, what foolish idea crossed my husband's mind: he says he found a transatlantic cruise for sixty-nine dollars a day. Tell me, isn't that crazy?

"And what did you tell him?"

"A conclusive NO! What, am I just as crazy as he? Who knows what kind of ship that might be?

"From what I know, you enjoyed the other cruises you took with him."

"Then you think we should go?"

"I would."

After three more phones and two hours of consultation, the answer came favorable. OK. So, we began preparations for what would be our first transatlantic cruise.

Among acquaintances, everyone looked at us as if we had won the big prize at lottery:

"How can they afford such an expense? It's true they work, but do they really earn enough for a trip like that?"

To be honest, I don't care. I refinanced our house debt, took out a bank loan to make sure we could cover the expenses, and there we were — ready for a transatlantic departure. Only an hour before our Saturday evening dinner, and one day before departure, the phone rang and a lady with a pleasant voice informed us that our ship, **The Golden Princess**, has been delayed due to rough sea, and the boarding would take place not on Sunday, but next day, on Monday.

"What do we do about the flight tickets?" I asked.

"Fly! We will wait for you at the airport as usual and we will provide accommodation in New York, at the company's expense."

"Perfect. We'll be there."

On Sunday, at quarter past six in the morning, the taxi driver we had booked the day before rang the doorbell. The driver — a short Asian man around fifty years old — with a smile from ear to ear to let us know he had arrived. I carried first the two heavier suitcases, thinking that he would come after me with the rest, but it did not happen. Then I asked him to put them in the trunk and went back to get the rest of the luggage. When I returned, my suitcases were in the middle of the road waiting for me to load them into the car. While I lifted them, I heard him saying:

"You are a strong man."

"Thanks. You. always let your clients do this job?"

"I'm old and week," he said.

We hadn't reached the curb of the driveway when my wife said:

"We left the lights on in the garage."

"How do you know?"

"I saw it when we backed into the street."

"It doesn't matter. The bulbs will burn out before we come back home."

"You're right."

A small airplane. The only steward was selling cold sandwiches for two dollars and, before boredom could put me to sleep, we landed at Newark Airport. It was a perfect day with a clear spring sky shining invitingly through the airplane windows like an irresistible call to go out, to run, to explore the beauty of this enigmatic city nicknamed "The BIG APPLE." After finding our luggage on one of the conveyor belts, we headed for the exit, searching for the Princess Cruise representatives to guide us to the buses.

Here came the big surprise: many passengers from Phoenix and San Francisco, who had arrived at six in the morning, were still waiting to be transferred to the hotel. One of the buses contracted for our transportation had just arrived. There were pushing and shoving and suitcases everywhere. Two ladies with lists in their hands were trying to make themselves heard over the hundreds of people crowding around them in the parking lot, and no one could understand a word. Meanwhile two other buses appeared and, I don't know how – out of inertia, luck, or simply because we were being pushed from behind – we suddenly found ourselves standing right in front of the bus luggage opening.

What a relief it was to sit down in the comfortable seats of the coach, thinking about a city tour, a hot coffee for breakfast, a little rest, and a Broadway show in the evening. To our disappointment, we first had to be transported to the Port Terminal to complete customs documents and get boarding registration. After wandering through some outlying areas of this large city, the bus finally stopped below a bridge near the dock buildings. Numerous other buses in front of us were waiting in line full of passengers. Closer to pier number 4, where our ship, The Golden Princess, was supposed to be docked, rows of people came out of the building carrying bags and suitcases back to a nearby bus. Watching them our confusion grew louder:

"Who are these people? Where are they coming from? Where are they going?" No one knew the answer.

We been waiting. Some officials advised us that it was better to wait on the coach than standing in the long lines upstairs. My wife, Vali, had brought two apples and a few oranges that were left in the fridge at home, and she took them out of her travel bag.

"Take an orange," she said.

I went for chewing gum. In front of us, two huge buildings, with large doors and heavy elevators for cargo, flanked a stretch of water that beat against the concrete walls at the base of each building. Behind the building on the left there was a schooner, its white sails rolled up high like wings along the three majestic masts. The coaches' drivers, stepped out onto the pavement, gathered in a small group to chat and smoke a cigarette. Time seemed endless. Officials in greenish jackets were directing people from other buses to the building on the right. Many of our people fell asleep with their heads bent in uncomfortable positions. I was hungry, tired, and disappointed, but there was no one around on whom I could unload the frustration boiling inside me.

At last, it was our turn to go to the second floor. The wide doors of the elevator opened onto a huge gray hall. A mass of people occupied the space in the center between the building's supporting columns, seated on benches lined up in rows across the whole area. There was no one to indicate what we should do and so I approached an official who was standing near a desk.

"Where do we go now?"

He pointed to a door at the far end of the hall, on the left.

"See that lady in the green suit? Follow her."

"OK. Thank you very much."

I didn't realize at that moment that by following his advice, we had passed in front of several hundred people who were waiting to be called into the next hall. After we passed through security, a labyrinth of cords moved us slowly toward the long desk in the center, holding passports and documents in hand to get the cards with the number of our cabin on board.

Finally, we returned to the bus. We were the only ones there. The others were still upstairs waiting their turn to get the cards. When the last person arrived, we were driven to the Sheraton Hotel in downtown New York, passing magnificent buildings glowing in the golden rays of the afternoon sun; yellow taxis were racing up and down the streets, multitudes of cars of every shape and color, and crowds of people filled the sidewalks lined with luxurious shop windows and colorful signs. What we saw from the bus was fascinating, and our heads, hungry for these fantastic images passing before our eyes, turned in every direction, insatiably.

Turning left from 6th Avenue onto 53rd Street, the bus stopped in front of a side entrance of the hotel. A doorman in uniform, with a luggage trolley, helped me carry our belongings to the reception desk. Half an hour later, Vali and I found ourselves in our room on the seventh floor. It was almost five in the afternoon. Vali collapsed on the bed and said:

"Let me sleep. I don't want food; I don't want anything."

I left her and went down to make some enquiries at the concierge desk. Ten minutes later I came back with a list of expensive restaurants in the area. The theater tickets at the hotel for *Mama Mia* and *Chicago* started at $150 per person. I wanted to see a decent show at the Metropolitan Opera or NY Radio City, but they didn't have tickets for Sunday evening. Vali was almost asleep when

I returned to the room. I showed her the list of restaurants and encouraged her to take a walk, which she agreed to. When we stepped out of the hotel onto 7th Avenue, the doorman in his imposing uniform with braid, cap and golden emblem, asked what we were looking for.

"Where could we find a not-too-expensive restaurant for dinner?"

"Oh, there are many, but I recommend this one – two blocks to the right. Tell them George sent you."

Saying this, he pulled out of his large coat pocket a handful of business cards and chose one. Every card in his hand – including the one he gave me – was signed with his name, George.

"You'll like it there," he assured us.

"Thank you. See you later."

We walked in the direction indicated. After turning the corner onto the second street, we found ourselves on the famous Broadway Boulevard. Bright signs and neon advertisements, with flickering changes of color that took your breath away, introduced us into a new world, like a fairytale, familiar but just as unreal as a walk through Walt Disney's Magic Kingdom. Up ahead, we could already see from afar Times Square, showing the latest news of the day on huge screens as large as the façades of the buildings around them, flashing lights and colors that drew us in with a magnetic force. On 49th Street we discovered the advertisement for the musical *Chicago*, at the Ambassador Theatre.

"Let's see if they have tickets for tonight," I said. Vali didn't seem particularly enthusiastic, but she followed me into the theater lobby. The price of $150 quoted at the hotel frightened me. At the ticket counter there was only one person negotiating with the seller. When it was my turn, I asked:

"Do you still have tickets for tonight?"

"We do. Orchestra or balcony?"

"At what price?

"One hundred dollars."

"Do you have cheaper seats?" I asked, embarrassed to ask such a question, yet still feeling I might be pushing my luck.

"Certainly – seats in the back of the balcony are only $67."

"Could you show me on the chart where they are?" He showed me a few scattered seats in the last three rows of the balcony.

"Yes, but they are not together and are too far back."

He looked at me for a moment and then said:

"The best I can do for you is give you these two tickets for $67 each."

He pointed to two central seats in the second-to-last row of the more expensive category.

"Thank you. I'll take them."

Vali pointed to a poster that said the performance started at 6:30 pm. I looked at my watch: it was almost 6:00. I quickly grabbed the tickets and, holding Vali by the hand, went back out on the street.

"Let's find something to eat."

I saw a food little shop nearby at the corner of the street. It was better than expected. For $6.49 I could fill my plate with whatever I wanted from the salad bar, fruit, macaroni, grilled chicken, and other foods. Twenty minutes later we were back at the theater.

A good show always lifts you up and makes you want to share impressions with someone who can contribute with new ideas and good understanding. But whenever it comes to a film, a book or a show, Vali usually looks at it from a controversial angle I don't feel like debating, so I prefer to drop the discussion from the start. This time, Vali seemed satisfied and although we had slightly different opinions about the show and casting, we both enjoyed it and were pleased.

On the way back to the hotel, we stopped once more to admire the nighttime panorama of Broadway toward Times Square, with its glorious luminous panels constantly changing into a fairy-tale of images and colors like a cascade of fireworks on the velvet darkness of the evening. I wanted to inhale these images greedily into the depth of my memory for eternal safekeeping. And that is exactly what I did.

The next day, Monday, 9 May 2005, at 9 in the morning, we woke up in our room on the seventh floor. Around us, luggage, clothes, and personal items were scattered on the chairs and tables in the room. On the nightstand beside me, a glass stood next to an opened bottle of vodka, reminding me that I had watched movies on TV late into the night. Vali got up to make a coffee with the provisions available in the room, courtesy of the hotel, and, still unwashed and unshaven, I had a mug of coffee along with some wafers we had bought the day before at Hershey's. After another mug, I jumped out of bed to get ready for the big boarding day. I already knew the buses would come at 3 pm to transfer us to the port. But we had to check out before 11 am and our luggage had to be put in a safe place in the reception hall. I called someone to come and help us.

"Are you with the Princess Cruise group?"

"Yes," I replied.

"We're sorry. Our staff is currently busy, so we kindly ask that you bring your luggage to Conference Room E, which is one floor below the reception desk."

During this time, Vali had gone to speak with one of the Princess representatives and came back with the news that all the elevators were full and that other travelers were bringing their own luggage down.

"My God, if only I had one of those trolleys to put all the suitcases on," I thought to myself.

I told Vali to follow me and, lifting the two biggest suitcases, I went out the door, carrying them down the long corridors of the floor to the elevator doors area. There I asked her to wait for me, and I returned to the room for the rest of the luggage. After several attempts to find space in an elevator going down, I even called the ones going up. Surprise! Those were just as packed as the others. Finally, we found space in one which was descending. Conference Room E was on the second floor, below street level, but the elevator only went down to the lobby on the first floor.

"Who planned this?" I asked myself.

Around me were infirm people in wheelchairs, some leaning on walking sticks, victims of heart attacks, and couples holding children in their arms. How were these people supposed to carry their heavy suitcases down numerous steps, posing a danger not only to themselves but to others as well? This lack of consideration from companies with long-established reputations was unbelievable. Many of passengers had made important sacrifices to be able to take this cruise and the hotel's lack of understanding was condemnable and shameful.

Eventually we left our luggage labeled for the ship and went outside for a walk in the city. Vali, a great flower lover, wanted to bring one to our cabin and someone had told her there was a florist on 55th Street towards 6th Avenue. It was a splendid morning; you could walk in just a shirt, although I had a jacket in my shoulder bag just in case. We found the flower shop – a small place with beautiful flowers and exotic prices – where two young women, blooming with the most attractive smiles, offered us a bouquet at a two-digit price which was beyond our budget. We left the girls, promising to return after finishing our shopping.

Across the street from the florist, a building caught my attention, without knowing that it was the New York City Opera. I entered the lobby where the ticket desk was and, with regret, I realized that this was all I could see there that day. I have always been attracted to opera, to theater and almost all other forms of artistic expression. I remember vividly, as a child, the first theatrical performance my parents took my sister and me to see. After World War II, in the early 1950s, a new theater opened in our neighborhood. Because it was within a short distance of our house, we learned how to sneak inside unseen on matinee days and we could watch the same performance again and again without getting bored. From "Uncle Tom's Cabin" to Gogol's "The Inspector General" and many other comedies and dramatic plays, I was always captivated by that miracle called theater. I still am today.

Closer to 6th Avenue we found another florist, from where we bought a newly budded flower in a small glass pot. Continuing along 6th Avenue, we admired the buildings decorated with intricate patterns covering their façades, others with statues and Baroque-style ornaments, or stricter appearance of Victorian-style revealing their presence along the entire boulevard.

We had to return to the hotel before three o'clock, but we intended to get there earlier. Nearing High Park, we decided it was time for lunch and looked for a place to eat. I remembered the florist on 55th Street, where I had seen a place with fresh bread and many people eating sandwiches made to order, so we headed to that place.

Good choice. We had a hearty sandwich, drinks and a mocha coffee, and sitting at a table near the window we watched the new customers waiting in line or looking for somewhere to sit. A lady dressed in black, elegantly, with a silk scarf wrapped around her neck and a shopping bag in her hand, appeared in line. She ordered a bagel, then sat at a nearby table. From her bag she took out a tub of cream, which she spread over the halved bagel. Then she took out a steaming cardboard cup of coffee. A few people stopped talking to her. She seemed to be a faded beauty, perhaps one of the former stars of Broadway, trying to keep some of her former stature with the new generation, fighting off loneliness with a walk through the heart of this Big Apple. She looked happy speaking; her smile, lit by the brightness of her teeth, gave charm to the whole figure and especially her eyes seemed to light up again with the sparks that once made her attractive. But behind them, a shadow of misfortune and problems told a different story.

It was now time for us to return to the hotel. The midday sun spread around a gentle and bright warmth. On 6th Avenue, people out for lunch had brought their food outside to enjoy the green of the grass and the sweet coolness of this spring day.

This city has something miraculous in it. It was not our first visit here. On many other occasions we came to visit friends, who took us out – by day or by night – for a tour of the city. It was beautiful and interesting, something for which I cannot find enough words to express my gratitude. But this time, I asked Vali not to call any of them, because the time was too short to be used up on visits, invitations or submitting to other people's plans. Now, alone, just the two of us on such a beautiful day, we felt free and happy, walking along this boulevard among pedestrians rushing to their business, reading the names of the streets we crossed, admiring the elegance of the shop windows and the buildings with all their ornamental details. It was as if everything around belonged to us, as if we ourselves were part of this universe. After we passed 53rd Street, we recognized the buses that had taken us to the hotel the day before and hurried our pace so as not to be late.

The bus took us in no time to the port, in front of the buildings from the previous day. We left our recognized and labeled luggage on the asphalt in front of the building, in the care of porters who would take it to our cabins on board. Moored along the building, a ship towering many times higher than the surrounding apartment blocks rose from the water, white and shining in the afternoon sun. Inside the building, on the second floor, the last boarding formalities were carried out in the usual ritual, including the security check. From then on, we were free to walk to our home away from home that would take us across ocean, seas, and countries in the next two weeks.

The cabin wasn't very spacious, but roomy enough to hold our belongings, with just enough space to move around, write a letter or watch a movie on television when nothing else was more attractive. Two separate beds stretched along the walls flanking a wide window above the nightstands, which was Vali's favorite place to put the flower she had bought. A small refrigerator, a wardrobe with many drawers, a mirror covering the wall above a writing desk, a few chairs, and a television. The bathroom was indeed cramped;

the shower enclosure, covered by a plastic curtain, didn't leave enough room to bend down.

The Golden Princess was, at that time, one of the biggest ships of the Princess Cruise company, able to host, feed and entertain 2,600 passengers, in addition to more than 1,000 crew members. It was a floating island.

From our cabin, passing through the permanent Art Gallery with its rich collection of oil paintings, classical and modern art, we reached an atrium rising over three floors with circular stairs, two panoramic elevators with glass walls and many shops with sumptuous display windows. Down below in the lobby, surrounded by armchairs, an orchestra was playing a chamber music concert. Around the atrium, along all three floors, there were many restaurants and buffets, bars, a cinema, a casino, a library that covered all domains of cultural and political interest, and a theatre. The sports fields and the swimming pools under the open sky were on the upper deck. On this ship, no one could complain about lack of activity.

The crew asked us to take our life jackets and go to the places where they instructed us what to do in case of an emergency. Our drill took place in the ship's theater, which looked like an amphitheater built over two stories, starting from the huge stage with its base on deck six. This theater, equipped with modern equipment, could compete with the most modern ones, allowing all passengers to watch the shows every day in two series.

After the drill, I took my video camera and set out to explore the eighteen levels of the ship. On deck fifteen, where the Lido deck was located, the bar was open and many, with drinks in hand, were beginning to form groups around an oval swimming pool in the open air, flanked by two round jacuzzi baths. Buzzing among the newcomers, waiters in the ship's uniform brought and took orders for drinks to the people spread out on deck admiring the sea, the buildings around us or another ship, the Norwegian Down, docked at the same pier.

I later read its story in the newspapers: most passengers on that voyage had returned to shore sick. There were so many complaints against the company that they had to offer every passenger a future free cruise and other monetary compensation. The captain of that ship seems to have decided to cross the ocean through a hurricane to reach port on scheduled time. The fury of the storm was unexpectedly fierce; waves entered the ship through the decks, spreading across the corridors and even into some cabins. Objects began to fly off the shelves and the entire ship creaked in its joints like a moan in the middle of the night. Passengers were pale with fear, unable to stand on their feet, and became worried that they would not survive this journey. In contrast, the captain of the Golden Princess reduced speed to four knots during the hurricane, extended the trip by one day, and that was the reason why our cruise began with a one-day delay.

From the ship's deck at the height of its fifteen stories, looking around, Manhattan was a spectacle in itself. Shining in the afternoon sunlight, a forest of buildings and towers unparalleled in the world filled the horizon, bounded by the waters that surrounded the island which from afar seemed to have been randomly placed on a tray. Outside of it, a peaceful world of houses and ordinary constructions reigned. From here it was hard to make out the well-known landmarks from past visits or even from movies.

At five o'clock, the ship was due to lift its anchor. Down below there was still a bustle around the ship. A few crew members were swarming around the hold with the last luggage and platforms loaded with various supplies, while the passenger gangway was being lifted. It was a warm day, but here on deck a light breeze blew across our foreheads with the coolness of a gentle wind, prompting some people to go for a jacket or a sweater. Vali was waiting for me on the deck by the railing, watching the activity around us. Not far away, in the open water, two tugboats waited to assist in case of need when leaving the harbor. Slowly, imperceptibly, without noise, *The Golden Princess* detached itself from the quay bordered by the terminal building with a long whistle as farewell. The departure was delayed by an hour, but now we felt the joy of long-dreamed adventures materializing.

Than the sound of Frank Sinatra's famous song "New York, New York" was vibrating loudly on the speakers as we watched Manhattan slowly recede behind us. Many were waving their hands in the air shouting, "Bye, bye, New York!" I, with the camera to my eye, recorded this unique moment in film. It was impressive. Scenes from countless movies seemed to play again in that moment like a transparent layer superimposed on the real picture. Thank you, Lord, for allowing me to live this moment.

Gliding along the middle of the Hudson River, on one side we had the diminishing image of Manhattan's skyscrapers, on the other side stood the silhouettes of other imposing buildings in New Jersey. To the south, fighting the blinding rays of the setting sun, passing the last metal and glass buildings lining the New Jersey shore, an island appeared in front of us, in the middle of which a multi-stored building resembling barracks came to our attention. It was Ellis Island, I believe, famous in its time as the destination and quarantine point for immigrants from everywhere.

At a short distance, the silhouette of one of the most famous statues in the world – the Statue of Liberty – could be seen in the distance. Tall, raised on a stone pedestal, with her arm held up high to spread the light of her burning torch to the world, she came closer to us from the center of Liberty Island. Everyone on deck moved to that side of the ship, while the loudspeakers played one of the most patriotic American anthems, sung here by every passenger. A sublime moment! It was as if an electric current passed through each of us, uniting us in a common voice to celebrate what America and the symbol of Liberty meant to us. Waving hands, clicking cameras, open smiling faces, eyes filled with tears of emotion gave us the feeling that we knew each other, that we were not meeting for the first time, that we were part of the same family.

June 2005

Travel Notes:
New Zealand and Australia

After a long and exhausting 13-hour flight from Los Angeles, we arrived in Auckland at six in the morning and the sky looked just as bleak as our sleep-hungry eyes. We were picked up at the airport by a bus and taken to a hotel in the city center, the Rendezvous' Hotel. The bus driver said that the hotel used to be called Carlton before Asians bought it. Unlike previous arrivals, we were not met here by a tourist guide and, getting off the disoriented from the bus, we start looking for the office that would direct us to the rooms reserved for us. In the end, we discovered a reception desk inside the hotel bar, but the rooms would not be ready for us until three o'clock. So, we decided to leave our luggage in the hotel's care and take a city tour at ten. To kill time, I had a coffee and solved a few sudoku puzzles from a book I had bought in Toronto.

Auckland is a modern city with many interesting buildings, looking cosmopolitan, with wide boulevards that descend all the way down to the harbor, and streets that climb up the mountain, with luxury shops, breathtaking prices, and a television tower of 350 meters high. Outside the commercial area, along the coast, in the residential neighborhoods perched on the mountain, overlooking the ocean, dozens of villas with wide windows and inviting balconies seem to pour down from above like a cascade of terraces, dissipating the fatigue of the day before. Below, near the coast, where a highway winds along rocky cliffs that seem to grow out of the ocean, there is a museum with free admission that continues underneath the road and then under water, at depth, with a glass gallery from which you can admire the real unfolding of marine life. Here, fish of all kinds inspect us, the ones in the glass tunnel, with the same curiosity with which we look at them. It was also here that I saw many penguins isolated in a spacious room with climate control and a pool bordered by large glass windows through which we watched them swimming or scattered in groups on blocks of ice that imitate Antarctica.

The next day, 12 March, rested, and restored, we tried to revisit the places we had seen the day before on foot, and the city did not seem as large as it did from the coach. But this time we didn't go back to the villas. Across from the hotel, at the City Hall, we came across the opening of a modern art exhibition, which didn't say anything particularly interesting, but had very tasty sandwiches and champagne, so we appreciated the "art" with great enthusiasm. Further on, on the way to the television tower, we saw bungy demonstrations in which people were catapulted up and down on a chair using elastic cables. Others climbed to the top of the tower and then jumped down, attached to similar cables. I wonder: if I were sixteen again, would I have the courage to do the same? I like to think reason would have stopped me from such extravagance.

The next morning, around noon, we boarded the *Sapphire Princess*, a modern ship that can comfortably host more than 2,500 passengers and over 1,000 crew members. Our cabin was on deck 12 (Baja), a large room with a balcony in the middle of the ship. The layout of the ship was familiar to us because a similar vessel, the *Golden Princess*, with which we made a transatlantic crossing, was almost identical. Our luggage was brought to our room with some delay – one of the suitcases disappeared and we did not find it until after dinner. But after a good dinner, a modern variety show and a proper bath, nothing could shake the joy that we were finally sleeping in our own bed rocked by the sea, in our home away from home for the next twelve days.

14 March, Tauranga (The Bay of Plenty). We got up early for an important tour to Wai-O-Tapu Valley, a volcanic area with unpredictable eruptions, with a lake formed in a volcanic crater (on which we sailed in a small fishing boat with a guide), with dozens of hot springs whose steam rises into the air forming columns, pools of bubbling mud like polenta in a cauldron on the stove, and puddles where the water boils endlessly. On the way we were greeted by Māori warrior tribes armed with spears and battle cries, like a powerful reenactment of the surprise of the locals at the appearance of the first Europeans in these lands many years ago.. According to the guide, on one morning in 1886, Mount Tara Wera and Lake Roto Mahana exploded as a result of volcanic activity that destroyed a number of settlements and killed more than 120 people. The mountain was split in two and the lake expanded more than twenty times, forming seven new craters and giving birth to Waitangi Valley. This eruption was the largest natural disaster in New Zealand and, as a result, it stands as the only geothermal phenomenon of nature whose exact birth date – 10 June 1886 – is registered and documented with measurements and testimonies from survivors of the event. On the return, in the evening, we visited Rotorua, a thermal resort with a sulfur smell and steam spurting from cracks, frequented by thousands of tourists who come to the sanatorium for treatment.

15 March, Christchurch. In 1850, a group of immigrants from England arrived in the port of Lyttleton and laid the foundation of this city, the most English outside of England, enjoying fertile fields, a temperate climate and good administration. It has a population of 300,000 and many modern and Victorian buildings stretching along the Avon River, on which gondoliers row boats, though without the flourish and songs of Venice. There is an old-style university, Canterbury University, and schools in which children wear uniforms. As in the other cities of New Zealand and Australia, crossing the street is done only at the traffic lights and only when the pedestrian signal beeps, to draw your attention that you may cross. This beeping is important, because instinctively we try to avoid vehicles coming from the wrong direction.

15 March, Dunedin. Passing through this city with an industrial look, we made a stop at the railway station, which looks like a castle when seen from the road and impressed with a tall hall, stained-glass windows, and a sophisticated mosaic floors that you almost feel guilty stepping on. In this hall tickets are sold for the train and from here you exit onto a platform covered by a wide metal awning. The tour then included a visit to Larnach Castle, built around 1870 in neo-Gothic style, on top of a hill with a wide view over the harbor refuge. An immense park, spread over thirty-five hectares, with greenhouses full of flowers and immaculate gardens surrounding the castle.

The castle has a sad history. At the end of the nineteenth century, gold was discovered in the region and many rushed there in search of fortune, which created a new economic boom and, as a result, many became rich. One of the gold hunters, William Larnach, an Australian who worked in a bank, found the treasure he was looking for by marrying the daughter of a banker in the city. He himself became a banker and built the castle; but unfortunately, his wife died. Shortly afterwards he fell in love with a very beautiful woman, much younger than he was, who secretly maintained an affair with a lover. Naturally, the secret could not last forever, especially since during that period William was often away from home, being a member of Parliament. When the news finally reached his ears, the unfortunate man shot himself in the New Zealand Parliament.

Unlike Christchurch, this place was founded by the Scottish, and both the scenery – roads winding among endless hills – and the worn-out dialect have a Scottish flavor.

18 March. A big day on board. Everyone was on deck, waiting for the ship to enter the fjord area. A rainy day with strong winds, after a hurricane the previous night. But the passengers waited patiently at the bow decks, cameras in hand, ready at any moment to immortalize the appearance of a sea animal – whale or shark, penguin, or any other creature along the way. But nothing appeared. Instead, around nine in the morning, the ship entered Dusky Sound, a narrow area between rows of wooded rocks that rise high, on which, here and there, from various heights, abundant streams of crystal-clear water tumble down. Frozen from the wind, I returned to my balcony. From there I could freely film every notch in the mountain and every waterfall, which made my thoughts fly to our famous "Urlătoarea" (The Screaming) waterfall in the Bucegi Mountains of Romania.

At lunchtime, the ship left Dusky Sound for the Tasman Sea, heading towards Thomson Sound. A local specialist, from the height of the commanding bridge, was commenting on a television channel every detail we passed through. Soon after, we entered Thomson

Sound. My wife Vali barely managed to pull me away from the balcony and we went for lunch at the self-service restaurant on deck fourteen. I loaded a tray with everything we wanted and we sat at a table near the window. The show continued. The fog lifted, visibility became clearer, but the view remained almost identical, as we glided close to these giant flint formations, where an 18-deck ship seemed like a lilliputian toy in this majestic landscape.

After Thomson Sound, navigating northward, around four in the afternoon, we entered Milford Sound. This one is the most glorious of all. The flint of the rocks is bare here, revealing fantastic shapes, as if out of a fairy tale. The waterfalls are numerous and the cadence of the water ample. It is a road without an end into the heart of the mountains, but since there is no exit at the opposite end, the ship must turn around, which only leaves you wishing to see more and go further. Soon the evening shadows would cover these witnesses of the beginnings of our world. Time to change clothes for dinner and get a glass of vodka on the rocks.

Hobart, Melbourne, Sydney, and Cairns

20 March – Hobart. Southernmost city in Australia, is located on the island of Tasmania. Hobart is a small city, with a population of 129,000 people, has a two hundred–year history and was created by the English as a place of relocation for deported prisoners, when America refused to receive any more criminals after the Civil War.

22 March – Melbourne. If I wished to be born again, I think I would like to be born there, in this city. After Washington DC, this is one of the few cities created from the very beginning according to a prearranged plan, with streets, boulevards, parks, and its neighborhoods. Along the Yarra River, the industrial zone lies in the east. The commercial zone is in the center on the north bank. On the south bank are the theatres, museums, and the artistic center of the city. In the west there are the stadium, the sports fields, and the recreation parks. All these commercial and cultural areas are connected by a train circuit that completes its loop in 30 minutes – and can be used free of charge.

A modern, clean, and lively city, with large, well-maintained parks, full of historic monuments that impose themselves through their remarkable adherence to Hellenistic classicism, and buildings that color the skyline through their wide variety of majestic styles. A cruise along the Yarra River in one of the many small boats reveals the entire splendor of the city, spread on both banks with its tall, modern, and imposing constructions.

24 March – Sydney. Disembarking in Sydney, I can say we were swept up and taken directly to the airport, because in one hour we had to fly to Cairns. Since our whole expedition in Australia was going to continue for another week, I'll include my impressions of Sydney later.

Compared to New Zealand, which has a total area of almost 104,000 square miles and a population of only four million inhabitants, Australia – with an area of almost three million square miles (slightly smaller than the United States, which measures 3,675,000 square miles) – has only a population of twenty-five million. In this continental country, a single family's property can stretch over tens and hundreds of miles in length, with widths that often reach three digits. The richest family in Australia, the Kidman family (Nicole Kidman is a distant relative), owns property measured in thousands of hectares.

The climate is varied and has no winter, and the center of the country is flat and arid, a red desert bathed in sun, with scorching, dry temperatures, dried-up waters and wells, and vegetation reduced to a few dwarf junipers growing here and there, or a grass that doesn't even look like grass, with narrow, pointed leaves scattered irregularly in the sand. This is the basic food for the millions of cattle that live in this desert – and no less for the groups of aborigines. This people, the aboriginals are still nomadic, scattered in small tribes and once they have consumed everything in a region, they set fire to the land and move on somewhere else. In their belief, fire helps rebirth, therefore, when they return, vegetation and game will be abundant.

24 March – Cairns. After disembarkation in Sydney, out of almost three thousand passengers, only ninety-nine continued the tour of Australia. Our specially labelled luggage was left in the care of staff, who would store it somewhere until our return to Sydney. With only one suitcase per person and just a small handbag, we were divided into three buses, each with its own guide-director.

Our director was Ella, a pleasant blonde in her late twenties, originally from New Zealand. We were taken to the airport and boarded a flight to Cairns. On the way, Ella told us that today was at our disposal, but that our rooms would not be ready before three in the afternoon. As an alternative, she offered an optional tour to the Rainforest Tropical Park and Barron Falls Gorge. It cost $75 per person, and we decided to go. We left the airport in Cairn in two buses headed south of the city and, in 30 minutes, reached a mountain area about twenty-five kilometers away. Climbing the winding road, we arrived at Caravonica, from where we boarded one of the Sky rail gondolas lined up waiting for passengers.

Soon our gentle flight began over the treetops of the eucalyptus and other giant trees in the forest. As we climbed, the soil and the air became more humid, and the lianas revealed their supple forms entwined around the supporting branches. The total journey of the gondola is only 7.5 kilometers, but along the way there are two stations at different altitudes where you get off and walk on wooden walkways in various directions. In open, close contact with this exuberant nature, you discover a fantastic beauty – unique in the richness of shapes and colors created by the variety of plants, flowers, and trees, straight and slender, more than 10–15 meters high.

The first stop was at Red Peak Station, from where we took the second gondola to Barron Falls Gorge Station. But before reaching Barron Falls, over the shoulders of the forest we could see, at one point, the valley where water is dammed by rock, and on the opposite side the railway track snaking along the valley.

As we went forward, the flint of the cliffs grew higher and suddenly the surging waters appeared, split into countless strands between rocks that seemed barely able to restrain them. Just as I was preparing to take a photo from above of this splendid view, the trees filled the vision and the gondola stopped. Again, we descended onto the walkways spreading in several directions around the station and, circling them, we reached a viewing platform over the Barron River Gorge and Falls. A hydroelectric power station was built here around 1930, and above, on the shoulders of the mountains behind, lay the wide reservoir. Then, falling onto the rotor blades, the water shoots from the rock onto the flint edges that appear in its path and slashes its tired body into myriads of arms that do not reunite until further down, where the riverbed relaxes into a wider valley. There, both the turbulence and the roar of the water diminish.

The last stop of the gondola was at Kuranda Terminal. Here there is a village of local artists, many craft shops, and a market with all kinds of folk-art objects and Aboriginal paintings. These are distinguished by two special features: (a) all their paintings are abstract, and (b) they are created entirely through colored dots. In general, the rows of aligned dots can form straight lines or various geometric shapes – square, triangle, circle, etc. – but they do not depict any human, plant, or animal form. The beginnings of civilization in art elsewhere sought, instead, to bring out human and animal shapes in their paintings. That surprised me; the rest of the world had to wait over 5,000 years before arriving at abstract art, whereas the Aborigines (and children) use it as their first step in art.

Kuranda also hosts the Australian Butterfly Sanctuary, which is worth seeing. The variety of butterflies flying all around you seem to tease you, because they never give you enough time to photograph them. But I managed to catch one on Vali's shoulder and it didn't escape me. There is also a wildlife park with animals living in the rainforest, among them wallabies, wombats, and koalas.

The buses were waiting for us at the exit, engines running, and I was glad to find the air conditioning working. We headed back to Cairns on the winding mountain roads, spiritually enriched by everything we had seen and with a huge appetite for food and rest.

Entering the city, we were surprised to discover a particularly picturesque resort on the ocean shore, with elegant hotels, enticing shop windows, many restaurants and even a magnificent casino. Our hotel – the Cairns International – was right in front of the casino. Our room, on the 18th floor, with a balcony facing the casino, was everything we could have wished for: large, modern, with a bar that invited indulgence, and a marble bathroom with mirrors, bathrobes, and slippers for each of us. After a short consultation between us, we decided to postpone dinner for later, knowing that at six in the evening we were to attend a reception organized by the tour directors and it was better to rest. We came down to the reception hall rested and fresh. We were welcomed by Ella, and the other travelers were gathered around a few tables on which numerous trays of sandwiches, fruit and drinks were waiting.

A very distinguished elderly lady from Texas, named Rose, travelling alone and whom we had met on the ship, attached herself to us and, endowed with humor and intelligent remarks, became a pleasant and appreciated companion. The reception aimed to help us get to know one another better in our group, for which Ella had prepared the next day's program. After the reception, Vali and I decided to go to a restaurant for dinner, while Rose preferred to stay alone at the hotel.

25 March – Great Barrier Reef. After a good hotel breakfast, at about nine in the morning we boarded the buses and after a short drive arrived at the port. There, a huge three-deck catamaran was waiting for us. It was a beautiful day, reflecting its azure on the ocean waves and, fearing too much sun, I gave up a seat on the open upper deck and retreated into the shade on the open lower deck. From behind the catamaran, I watched the imposing city buildings receding until they disappeared on the horizon; once out in the open sea, the speed increased and the vessel began to glide over the water with threatening sways that made many people feel sick. The mountains we had travelled through the day before also disappeared, but to the west new landforms took their place. Close to shore, a sailing ship seemed to be trying to race us, but after a short while it remained behind to catch its breath on a beach that appeared at the foot of a mountain.

After about ninety minutes, we approached a pontoon in the middle of the waters – like a floating island entirely covered with a canvas canopy. Here the catamaran anchored. On deck there was a burst of activity: groups of families with children and young people left their clothes on benches and put on snorkeling gear. Vali and Rose wanted to make an underwater excursion in diving suits, but when they discovered that this activity was not included in the price

($150 per person), Vali let only Rose go. Rose also signed up for a 30-minute helicopter flight costing $250. While the crew prepared lunch in the central cabin, Vali and I went out to explore the pontoon.

About fifty metres long, made of wood and shaded by the canvas canopy, with tables and benches along its length, the pontoon had outside an enclosed area with air-inflated buoys, where people could swim or explore underwater with snorkel. At the opposite ends, a submarine and a glass-bottom boat were anchored, freely available to us. We headed toward the submarine, but by the time we reached it, the seats were all taken. Waiting for the next trip, we went to the Tank – a cabin below the level of the pontoon, with a few benches in amphitheater style and a window through which one could look into the green depths of the water. Curious fish came to visit us, and a few corals seemed perfectly at ease on a wooden ledge outside the window.

After about ten minutes we went back onto the pontoon to wait for the submersible. Vali and I took the frontmost seats and, through the round windows in front of our seats, made acquaintance with the fish passing nonchalantly around us. After a short ride, the ocean floor rose on a gentle slope, now on one side, now on the other of the vessel, revealing its multicolored population of trunks and cushions, with the pearly shimmer of the finest porcelain, like a mystical miniature forest lulled by the wand of a wizard. Gliding gently past these creations, we moved from one colony to another, our breath taken by a profound emotion that we had been blessed to admire a world like this.

When we returned to the pontoon, passengers were just disembarking from the glass-bottom boat, so we quickly boarded along with those still waiting. While the submarine allowed us to view the corals from up close without disturbing their eternal silence surrounded by water, this flat-bottomed boat could easily glide over the coral heads and allowed us to peer into the depths, to watch the fish and the underwater world, nesting among the corals or lying in wait for their prey.

Forests of coral – some rigid as porcelain, others more flexible, seeming to breathe with the movement of the water – then dark valleys and abysses, followed by new areas even more fascinating, coming to amaze us with their surprising abundance of shapes and colors without end.

Returning to the pontoon, we went to have lunch in the air-conditioned interior of the catamaran. Rose had just come back from her scuba-diving adventure, wet and a little unhappy, because she had only been allowed to move within a small plank walkway between the corals near the pontoon.

In the evening Rose came to take us for a walk. It was around six. From our balcony on the 18th floor, the city, and Trinity Wharf (named by Captain Cook on Trinity Sunday, 1770, as the first European to arrive here) could be admired at leisure. In front of us, across the road, was the inner courtyard of the Hilton Hotel with its huge swimming pool and white canvas tents, and on the lawn of the garden a large night-time party seemed to be underway. Between us and the Hilton, the large domed casino building shone in multicolored neon lights, like an orchestration of light and laser color. As Rose and I enjoyed the flavor of a vodka on the rocks and Vali crunched a Toblerone chocolate bar, suddenly huge, black birds filled the sky, flying leisurely just above our height toward the ocean. They came in flock after flock, gliding without flapping their enormous wings, as if pushed forward by the evening mist descending over us. The guide had warned us that the area was very favorable to bats, which spend the day hanging in trees, but never could I have imagined that these bats were so large and so numerous. We left the bats to continue their parade in front of our balcony and went out into the city to find a good restaurant for dinner. Tomorrow morning, at 7:30, we depart for the airport.

The Outback

26 March – Ayers Rock. While we were downstairs in the hotel lobby having breakfast, the porters were loading our color-tagged suitcases onto the buses. In a short time, we had to go to the airport for a three-hour flight to Ayers Rock, a settlement in the middle of the desert, in the heart of the continent. Unlike domestic flights in America or Canada – where meals are no longer included in the ticket price except in first class – Qantas, the Australian airline, serves meals and drinks to all passengers. After landing at Ayers Rock, the luggage was taken to the buses, and we were transported to the hotel. The sky was overcast, the ground a brick-red color, and the vegetation sparse and dry. Here and there a solitary eucalyptus tree grew amongst small tufts of grass. A two-lane paved road cut a straight line towards the horizon. And it was hot – very hot. After about 30 minutes, a new road branched off to the left, and the driver explained that this is the town where the people who work in the area live.

Indeed, small houses were lined up along the street, with more greenery around them, some even with upper floors, giving the place a picturesque appearance. On the way we passed the police station, the government offices and even a school. The buses stopped in front of a small square with a large concrete area covered by an enormous canvas canopy, shaped like the wings of a dove.

Around it there were concrete benches and tables, and shops with wide shaded verandas, and a restaurant that also had tables outside. We were left there for an hour to give the buses time to unload our suitcases at the hotel. Rose advised Vali to buy a net she could place over the brim of her sunhat, to protect herself from the flies that attack people with relentless persistence. I tried – unsuccessfully – to find an extra battery for my video camera, which forced me to be very economical with filming. Many queued up at the ice-cream shop. Before one o'clock, Ella came to call us back to the buses.

Our bus driver, Frosty – a man of about forty-five, with the appearance of Yul Brynner and, like him, completely bald – informed us in advance about what we were about to see. After about thirty minutes, the outline of Ayers Rock began to appear on the horizon – or Uluru, as the local people call it. If Alice Springs is considered the geographical center of Australia, then Uluru lies 280 miles north of Alice Springs. From the direction we were coming, Uluru looked like a gigantic tree trunk, cut flat and rising out of the flat desert. It is a red monolith measuring over 5.5 miles in circumference and 340 meters in height, rising majestically above this stretch of sand – trodden for millennia and once the bed of an inland sea. When we got near it, Frosty continued driving westward without stopping. He kept telling us various legends circulating among the local Anangu, about the first Europeans to discover these isolated mountains, and other historical data. His knowledge seemed inexhaustible, although his strong Australian accent sometimes made him hard to understand.

After a few minutes, another massive feature appeared in front of us on the horizon – just as red as Uluru, but different in shape and even higher – Mount Olga. Its indigenous name is Kata Tjuta, meaning "many heads," in reference to its thirty stone domes rising out of the endless flat desert. For the local tribes, these mountains have religious and cultural significance, and they are the traditional custodians of the Uluru–Kata Tjuta National Park. Out of respect for their culture, access to the mountains is restricted for tourists. The distance from Uluru to Kata Tjuta is nineteen miles, and among the stone domes Mount Olga is the highest, rising over 535 meters.

Here the bus stopped and we got off. In front of us a trail marked with stones encouraged us to approach the red massif – just like the surrounding reddish earth. The sun had broken through the clouds and was beating down on our heads, casting mysterious shadows over the domes that looked like countrymen's woolen caps. We moved forward with difficulty along the ascending path in the burning air and the beads of sweat on my forehead and face attracted an army of flies that buzzed around my head without mercy. We were so close to the massif, and I wanted nothing more than to touch with my open palm the smooth rounded stone surface like the curve of a breast. But the climb became harder and the flies more shameless. Vali came a short distance behind me with a bottle of water, and behind her several fellow travelers were surrounding Frosty. I stopped waiting. To the left of Mount Olga a valley opened, separating it from another formation. The trail led into that valley – the Valley of the Winds – but our schedule and the flies did not allow us to go there. Up close, the mountain didn't look like a monolith at all, but more like a conglomerate created by successive layers of rock and sand. When tectonic movements reshaped these formations, the horizontal layers shifted to almost vertical – and this could clearly be seen here. Back in the coach, with the engine working hard and the air conditioning at maximum, Vali was still struggling to push out the swarm of flies that had gotten inside. Frosty assured us that the air conditioning would eventually put them to sleep. I was still trying to dry the continuous stream of sweat from my body.

After making a full tour around Mount Olga, we returned to Uluru. Frosty drove to the base of the mountain, and as we circled around it, new views unfolded – grottoes and valleys, empty cave openings near the top where eagles and other birds of prey had their nests. Abrupt shapes on the surface looked as though they had been slashed by a gigantic axe. The bus stopped at the beginning of a grassy area – a green meadow amid the red desert. Many small trees with fresh green leaves, and older ones with black, coal-colored bark. Frosty led us along a path bordered with wooden beams. We stopped in front of a small cave, and further up at a larger one. A large slab of stone forming the ceiling of the cave appeared, from a distance, like the head of a gigantic snake with its mouth wide open and neck bent. This is one of those natural wonders that often amaze by their resemblance to real creatures. In this case, Liru – the snake above the cave – has a special significance in Anangu culture.

We entered the cave. Traces of fire had blackened the stone walls. Numerous white engravings or drawings in red and green paint left an amalgam of markings on the walls and ceiling. The Aboriginal people do not have writing; their culture is passed on orally. They used a range of symbols to convey information. A small circle indicated the presence of water. A row of little circles in a line indicated the number of days needed to reach the water. We later learnt that they live in small tribes, have no tribe chiefs, do not practice agriculture and do not keep animals.

They are a nomadic people with a deeply rooted division of responsibility between men and women. They survive through hunting and the local desert vegetation. They do not wear animal skin, as it is warm enough all year round, so they remain naked. Marriages are arranged within the small tribe group or between tribes, with a single rule – no crossing of blood relations between brothers and sisters, parents, and children, or first cousins. But in their community, the wives of my brothers are also my wives, and their children automatically become my children. Among them there are no widows, widowers, or orphans – even though death is frequent. Any boy who has turned seventeen and has mastered hunting can marry a twelve-year-old girl chosen by the mothers. These mothers are the only ones who can navigate this familial maze and decide who can marry whom. They live collectively in one place if there is sufficient food. When the food runs out, they burn the ground and move elsewhere.

"But the animals," I asked, "won't they perish in the fire?"

"The animals leave the area before the people do," came the answer.

Frosty led us onwards along the wooden path, at the edge of that unbelievably green and lively meadow. Everything here seemed fresh and protected from wind and heat. The mountain seemed to pull its belly inward, creating this meadow all the way to a hollow formed by the junction of two sides of the mountain meeting at a right angle. Up on the crest, tiny like dots, bound together by a rope, a group of climbers were trying to cross from one face to the other. At the junction of the two slopes, the rock had been polished by falling rainwater, and at the bottom, in the narrow V-shaped channel, a small pool of drinking water reflected the sky. Here both people and animals came to drink, and here, at dusk, hunters lay in wait for their prey. It was now clear why only in this spot we found the freshness of a meadow that seemed like paradise.

Back at the hotel, we received the key to our unit. An elegant building with wide spaces and an inviting restaurant in the entrance, with two majestic Chinese lions, gilded in gold, and in the middle a Siamese-style statue. Passing by it, we entered an interior courtyard with a huge swimming pool flanked by palm trees, and around it several long white buildings with terraces full of flowers. We found our room – spacious and very cool – with a minibar, paintings, mirrors and a splendid, covered terrace. Flowers in pots along the edge, chairs, table, and a lounge chair inviting you to lose yourself in it, even briefly. An unexpected oasis in the middle of the desert, inviting reflection. But our time was limited. At six o'clock Ella had planned for us to return to the bus to witness the sunset in front of Uluru and record the splendor of the changing colors of the mountain at dusk.

Refreshed after a shower and in clean clothes, the bus dropped us in front of Uluru, where dozens of other buses were parked. Ella, behind a long table laden with chips, sandwiches and bottles of champagne, played host for our group. Unfortunately, the sun was only partly visible and the effect of the color changes on the mountain was minimal.

27 March – Alice Springs. It was not yet seven in the morning when hotel staff knocked at our door to collect our bags and take them to the coach. Vali and I followed them in haste to the hotel café, but at that hour our appetite did not match the trays full of food, compotes, and fruits. As usual, I limited myself to two soft-boiled eggs, a toast, a glass of orange juice and, of course, a cup of coffee. The motor coach took us again to Uluru – but this time it stopped at the Aboriginal Cultural Centre, which is a reservation organized and largely run by the authorities. A park surrounded by a high fence of stakes driven into the ground, a huge metal tank for drinking water in the form of an enormous upright barrel standing on stilts inside the fence, a souvenir shop, and toilets – and that was all there was to see.

After a while a bushman appeared, accompanied by a white interpreter. The Aboriginal man, of medium height, dark-skinned, with thick, uncut hair, black beard and flat nose, was barefoot, dressed in light-colored trousers and a yellow shirt. After he was introduced, he asked – through the interpreter – not to be filmed, though he allowed photographs. Behind him the interpreter, a young blond man, carried a handful of sticks of different lengths and several other objects. The bushman walked ahead of us along a narrow path that forced us to advance behind him in single file and stopped under the shade of a strip of canvas stretched across poles over our heads. He sat down on the bare ground and signaled for us to take a seat on the logs around him. He began talking with the help of the translator – although the translator could not always keep pace with him, and the bushman sometimes translated himself into English.

He picked a leafy branch from a nearby tree and, using a wooden chopper, cleaned it of leaves. Then, while gently pounding it on a cloth, he extracted a small handful of seeds, removing the fragments of leaves. Meanwhile the interpreter gathered some dry grass and thin twigs for a fire and placed them in front of the bearded man. After snowing the seeds on the cloth, he lit the fire with a cigarette lighter and took from the pile of sticks a shorter one, about the length of a forearm, with a rounded tip, which he began to heat in the flame, continuously turning it. He then poured the hot tip over the seeds on the cloth. The seeds seemed to melt and blacken, turning to liquid like tar and sticking to the rounded end of the stick. One of the sample objects he had brought looked like a club made in exactly this way, with resin from these delicate seeds. He then spoke about women's and men's traditional tasks and how the elders instructed the children in handling weapons and hunting.

He spoke about the universality of their teachings and the collective experience passed on orally from tribe to tribe, eventually returning to the source from which it came. In his simplicity, this uneducated man drew a circle on the dry earth with a twig and showed how a legend born somewhere at a point on this circle travels around and becomes the common property of all. And in this way, they learn from each other, accumulate knowledge and hand it on to new generations. This story made me look at the man in front of me with different eyes; he no longer seemed a "savage" from whom one could learn nothing. The "savage" in front of me was a philosopher.

After the discussion and a few demonstrations in handling weapons – in one of which he even had me throw a spear (which was in fact just a straight stick) – we returned to the bus and set off for Alice Springs.

A long road lay ahead of us – almost three hundred miles – through the red desert, indifferent to our speed and endlessly repeating itself with only small variations. In his deep voice Frosty told us which family owned this land – that this property, crossed by the road, stretched about sixty miles in length and roughly the same in width. He also told us about the lives of those who look after the cattle – that unlike American cowboys they don't ride horses but use scooters or motorbikes to drive the cattle. Often helicopters are used to gather them from the plains.

Driving through the desert became monotonous. Many people tilted their heads and began to snore, while I continued matching numbers in my sudoku book. Halfway along, the bus stopped at the only building we had seen beside the road in almost three hours – a kind of roadhouse restaurant, with hot and cold food and a collection of Aboriginal art objects.

Aboriginal people are not accustomed to working – especially since the government gives them welfare payments.

Traditionally they have never needed money. After the colonization of Australia, European influence had a damaging effect on them – many became addicted to smoking and alcohol. Europeans also introduced venereal disease. Today the situation can be summed up like this:

Farmer: "John, here's your pay for today's work. If you work again tomorrow and the day after, I'll give you a permanent job."

John: "Why permanent?"

Farmer: "If you work permanently, you can go to the bank, open an account and save the money."

John: "And then?"

Farmer: "Every week you'll get more money and put it in your account."

John: "And?"

Farmer: "When you've saved a good sum, you'll be able to retire and rest, without a single worry."

John: "Ah! But that's what I'm doing now!"

In their language, the Aboriginal people have a word for us that translates as "ants." Ants – that's how they see us. Perhaps that's what they're trying to express through the dots in their paintings?

After more hours through the red emptiness, the horizon began to take on the shapes of hills and valleys. We crossed bridges under which there was not a drop of water, although Frosty continued to tell us that during rainstorms the water can rise above the bridges. The farms we passed had no fences and only occasionally could we see yards enclosed with barbed wire. Drinking water for the cattle is pumped up from deep wells and poured into basins. In this area, distances are so great that it is impossible to have a school and a teacher for the one or two children of a family living on a property of hundreds of hectares. That is why "The School of the Air" was created in Alice Springs through a personal initiative. It was later extended to almost all regions. This school started over radio and now works via the Internet: each registered child receives the necessary equipment – a computer, video camera, printer, books, and notebooks, etc. Through the Internet, the child is in direct contact with the teacher, who gives the lesson by video, questions each pupil, checks whether the lesson is done with or without help from parents and can monitor each child's progress. I liked the idea so much that I donated a book for one of the future pupils. Others in the group did the same.

On the way to Alice Springs, we stopped at a camel farm. Needless to say, Rose did not miss the chance to take a camel ride. For me, the heat was so great that I would have preferred not to stop at all. But with the engine turned off and the bus doors wide open, and with swarms of flies finding you no matter where you try to hide, it was actually better outside than inside.

I filmed a tour with my video camera and, after persuading a few camels to pose, I discovered an enclosure where several kangaroos were basking in the sun. In the center of the pen stood a kangaroo from whose pouch the hind legs of a joey were sticking out. Probably the joey had crawled into its mother's pouch for a dose of fresh milk. I liked the image and kept filming until the end. When the mother got tired, she pushed her head into the pouch and gently pulled the insatiable little one out, after which she carefully cleaned the inside of her belly.

At last – Alice Springs. A small, clean town in the center of the MacDonnell mountain chain, along the Todd River, whose waters reflect the spectacular grandeur of these rocks. But unfortunately, this river is dry, except during the rainy season – as happened that night, after which we were privileged to see it flowing the next day. Before going to the hotel, we had a chance to wander for an hour in the town center, on Todd Street Mall. Vali and I walked down the main street, full of shops on both sides. Many tourists, souvenir shops, clothing stores, bookshops, restaurants, etc. Vali wanted a cappuccino, and we entered a restaurant with a garden. On the walls were framed paintings of exceptional beauty. We took a table near the window facing the street. Interesting – here, as everywhere in New Zealand, most shops have wide awnings covering the pavement, supported by thick metal bars.

It started to drizzle, and passers-by walked under these awnings. But across the road, beyond the church, there was a small park without benches opening onto the street. Two older Aboriginal women were sitting on the grass – one with a baby in her arms – undisturbed by the rain. A barefoot little boy of about four, with curly hair, played around them, in front of passers-by.

After the cappuccino we continued along the street. There were more Aboriginal people. Some were sitting on the pavement, leaning against the buildings, with bottles hidden in bags from which they drank. Young women, in groups of two or three, children following them, moved back and forth along the pavement, talking, some barefoot, others in sandals, paying no attention to those passing by. We reached as far as the building housing the local bank, where groups of Aboriginal people occupied the street in both directions. It suddenly felt unwise to go any further and we turned back to the bus.

Sydney

March 28, Sydney. The night before, we went to bed late. The reason: we had gone to a nearby farm for a nighttime barbecue under the moonlight, just as it was meant to be, with demonstrations and stories about the lives and work of the farmers. The experience costs $125 per person.

Around six in the evening, several minibuses arrived and took us along the mountain road to the farm. Through the windows of the vehicle, we watched kangaroos avoiding the car headlights along the road, hiding among the trees and greenery at the roadside.

We arrived at a plateau where the rock had been blasted for stone, and now the excavation had stalled due to a legal dispute between the owners and the government. Long tables, like at a wedding, benches, and a network of electric lights above. Groups of visitors gathered around Danny, a tall young man who demonstrated boomerang throwing and how it circles through the air and returns to him. Then we were invited to sit on tree trunks arranged around a fire pit smoldering under ashes, in a hole in the ground. A man, approaching fifty, took a cauldron, filled it three-quarters with water, poured in flour until it was full, mixed with his hands for several minutes, covered it with a lid, and buried it in the embers. By the end of the night, each of us would eat a piece of this tender, warm bread, spread with kangaroo butter.

The feast was more than abundant, with enormous grills of meat that melted in the mouth, sausages and salads, wine, beer, and other drinks at will, but most importantly, the stories from the lives of the locals, anecdotes, and even music. What was missing, however, was the clear night sky, to which everyone's gaze was directed, because someone was supposed to speak to us about the stars of this hemisphere and show us the Southern Cross. Unfortunately, this part of the program could not take place. In fact, it rained heavily during the night, and in the morning, short bursts of rain accompanied us all the way to the airport.

On our farewell tour of Alice Springs in the morning, we crossed the Todd River, which had been dry the day before but had now dangerously swelled up to the level of the bridge. We then visited the Desert Park, which stretches over a large area at the foot of Stuart Mountain. This park explains the aridity of the land and the relationship between plants, animals, and humans. It is fascinating to see how hundreds of species have adapted to the conditions of the Australian desert, using the sparse local resources to survive for thousands of years.

In the park's immense projection hall, after a documentary film that ended with a stunning tableau-like image of a lush area with greenery, trees, and mountains as a backdrop, the screen rolled up to the ceiling, the wall behind the screen drew back like a curtain, and we were left seeing the real image, shining in daylight, just as it appeared at the end of the film.

On the way to the airport, we gathered the last pieces of information about Alice Springs, data that cannot be mentioned here due to space constraints. What is particularly interesting is that this town in the center of the continent originated as a telegraph repeater station around 1860. Since all populated centers formed along the coasts of the ocean, communication from one end of the continent to the other was done via telegraph. Due to the immense distance between diametrically opposite towns, messages were often lost. Therefore, they needed to be retransmitted from station to station until reaching their destination. This is how repeated stations came into being. These stations were supplied by camel caravans imported with their Afghan handlers, but after the apparition of automobiles, the camel were let unsupervised at large. Today, the number of camels has multiplied so much that, now they have spread throughout the center of the country, threatening the already rare desert trees by eating their leaves. In the local industry, camel meat has become an export product.

Before continuing our journey through the airport, we said goodbye to Frosty, our guide and driver through the desert, and above all, the first and most eloquent of all those who shared and showed us so many interesting things in this region.

Sydney. It is said to be one of the most beautiful cities in the world. I do not deny it. From the airport outside the city to downtown, during rush hour, through a network of underground tunnels, it takes 10–15 minutes. We traveled by bus along streets flanked by imposing buildings, wide storefronts, streets crowded with pedestrians, and the usual bustle of big cities. We were dropped off at the Four Seasons Hotel, and as soon as we received our room keys, Rose and I rushed to the reception, for our interests knew could not be delayed.

Even from Toronto, I had hoped to take advantage of being in Sydney for two days trying to attend a live performance at the Sydney Opera House. As soon as we arrived in Cairns, I called the opera to request tickets for Thursday, March 29, but the show was sold out.

Rose planned to climb the Sydney Harbor Bridge, which is done in small groups of people, linked together, walking along the outer curve of the bridge support. Below them, cars and trains pass at high speed. Even here, the demand exceeded availability, especially at sunset, so her chances of obtaining a ticket were as slim as mine.

At the reception, a friendly girl asked me to fill out a form with all the details. I would receive the result the next day in my room, but deep down, I already knew it what to expect. Taking the elevator with Vali and Rose to our rooms on the 14th floor, Rose insisted that we go together to a restaurant that evening, her treat. However, Vali asked Ella what we could do that evening, and she suggested a harbor cruise.

Around seven in the evening, after a refreshing shower and putting on fresh clothes from our suitcases left in the room after the boat ride, Rose came to take us into the city. The hotel was on George Street, one of the main north-south arteries, right at the start of Circular Quay (port of countless ferries and routes connecting various locations, islands, and even New Zealand). Above the quay, solid metal and concrete poles carry express trains, which come and go with tolerable noise. Across from the quay, a wide boulevard with spacious sidewalks and many modern art pieces rising two stories.

This boulevard bypasses the quay and leads to the Opera House. I wanted to go there first, but Vali, intrigued by Ella's words, wanted to ask for information at the port. At eight o'clock, there was a one-and-a-half-hour ferry trip around the harbor. We bought tickets and waited, though I was disappointed that we wouldn't see much in the dark, especially since the next day we would take the same cruise for lunch.

The ferry filled in less than two minutes. We found seats on the upper deck, at the stern. It was cool and windy. When the ferry started moving, the speakers began describing the sites we were passing, and a hush fell over the deck, so every word of the announcer was absorbed reverently. The city center buildings were beautifully lit, and the variety of neon signs dazzled the eyes. We passed the Opera House, its sail-shaped roof beautifully illuminated with different colors that seemed to emanate from within. A construction that cost two million dollars in 1970, designed by a young Danish architect who won the competition for the best project. The design had to be modified many times due to calculation errors, and finally, after 15 years, the building was inaugurated in 1971 by Queen Elizabeth II. Surrounded by water on three sides, it was built on reclaimed land near the port, bordered to the south by a hill crowned with a government building.

A little further on are the Royal Botanical Gardens. From the ferry deck, gliding in the dark over the harbor waters, we passed many other interesting sites, harder to distinguish in the dark, although the sky was clear with countless stars. Rose and I tried to spot The Southern Cross. Other ferries and yachts, their decks illuminated with sparkling lights and loud music, passed by in both directions, sometimes crossing the announcer's line of sight.

After a while, the ferry moved to the northern shore of the harbor, but here, being a residential area, there was less to note. Turning back towards the Harbor Bridge, passing beneath it, we were greeted by the colorful silhouettes of Luna Park buildings, whose entrance is guarded by a grand Arc de Triomphe decorated with thousands of lights. I regretted not having a video camera for this magical view.

Returning to the southern shore, we passed Darling Harbor, where the former warehouses of the old port were converted into upscale apartments owned by film and art celebrities like George Clooney.

By the time we returned to the quay, the streets and port had thinned, and we barely felt hungry. Vali had noticed Giovanni's Pizza the day before from our hotel window on George Street and wanted to go there. It was a restaurant encased in a glass tower with a splendid street view, serving not just pizza but any menu item. We left the place almost at midnight, after a dispute with Rose, who I would not let pay for the meal alone. Returning to the hotel, we learned that two ferries had collided in the harbor earlier, and some passengers had perished.

March 29. After a good breakfast at the hotel restaurant at 8 a.m., we met the whole group on the bus. In daylight, it was easier to get acquainted with this modern, lively, and well-maintained city. A suspended monorail, perched on concrete pillars, circles much of the center and Darling Harbor, next to the city casino, a colossal building with many steps at its entrance. Continuing its path, the monorail stops inside department stores, the stadium, and theaters.

The number of parks and recreational spaces in Sydney is impressive. Then our route passed through residential areas with beautiful houses perched on cliff edges, where the bay waters crash relentlessly, creating the impression of a futile battle against the mountain. We traveled along beaches and arrived at Bondi, with a wide sandy beach and several cafés and restaurants. Here, you could relax under umbrellas on a terrace at the edge of the beach, sipping a cappuccino, while others explored shops for souvenirs. Perhaps that was the point of stopping at Market How near Town Hall, where we were given an hour for last-minute shopping.

Returning to the bus, we took a shorter route to Darling Harbor, where we were to board a catamaran for lunch and a harbor tour. Unfortunately, the announcer's voice was drowned out by the general noise of travelers who were more attentive to the food served in heated and cold trays. News about the previous night's accident was still confusing; investigations were ongoing on both shore and water.

After lunch, when the catamaran stopped at Circular Quay, Vali and I dashed out—I asked her to wait at the hotel—and I ran to the Opera House to see if tickets had appeared for that evening. It started to rain, and I arrived nearly soaked. No tickets. I returned to the hotel wet. At the reception desk, the clerk pulled two unexpected tickets for that evening's show from a drawer. I thanked God that no tickets were available at the opera, which at a maximum price of

$230 per person would have added to my already costly evening. The hotel tickets, with exceptionally good seats in the box, cost only $130 per person.

Pleased with the result, I decided that after a good bath, I would do nothing until the evening when we were to attend the show. Rose called from her room to say she had also secured tickets for the bridge climb at 4:30 p.m. and wished us a good time at the opera. She also got a ticket for an Opera House tour the next morning at 5:00 a.m., meaning we would have no time for farewells, as we had to leave for the airport at 7:00 a.m. She wanted to meet for breakfast before five, but with all our luggage open for the formal opera preparation, we knew we would spend a good part of the night repacking each suitcase. Meeting was no longer possible.

Around six in the evening, we left the hotel for the opera. That night, *The Marriage of Figaro*, a three-and-a-half-hour performance, was scheduled to begin at 7:30. The opera was close to the hotel, but the rainy weather raised the question of whether to call a taxi. Leaving the hotel, the rain had stopped, so we walked, though Vali feared her high heels might disturb her. Arm in arm, we passed Circular Quay, amused as some women hurried ahead to see who was out at this hour in the harbor, dressed for opera.

The Opera House sits on a plateau reached by climbing many small steps, reminiscent of the ascent to great Roman Catholic cathedrals, intended as a penitential ordeal for those wishing to atone for sins. We arrived half an hour early. Around the building, there are many restaurants and bars in the basement, young people seated at tables overlooking the bay, and street vendors selling hot dogs from stainless steel carts. At seven sharp, we could enter the foyer, but not the auditorium. A small, narrow, rather dark space, unfinished concrete, stairs rising on both sides around the hall. A program seller boot charging $20 for a booklet, and another boot selling very expensive CDs. We went out upstairs to the terrace. The sail-shaped roof extended almost to the plateau. The roof was covered with white ceramic tiles, cemented together over the reinforced concrete floor. This gave the glow seen the day before when colored spotlights made the structure look surreal. The Opera House houses at least four institutions: Sydney Opera, Sydney Symphony, and two other theaters.

To enter the hall, we climbed several steps to Zone 24, where we were seated. The interior was matte black, with red velvet-covered chairs. The first half of the hall had a conical ceiling of intimidating height, which then abruptly dropped vertically, disappearing parallel to the ascending balcony seats. The black-dominated interior made me feel as though I were inside an Egyptian tomb inside a pyramid. Our seats were excellent, in the center box of the horseshoe-shaped balcony. The view was perfect, with no one in front of us and a fair distance to the stage. Behind us, the balcony continued at least thirty more rows, and I doubt those at the back could distinguish the faces of artists on the stage.

The performance was good, sparing in stage effects. The singers, especially Suzana, were admirable. The audience was rather indifferent, especially during the duet between Rosina and Suzana, perhaps one of the most beautiful duets ever written. I was glad not to miss the opportunity to see it. However, the hall's acoustics seemed off. Rarely have I attended a live opera, sat centrally, and been unable to discern the direction of sound. In this hall, the sound loses its stereophonic effect; in duets, trios, or quartets, voices blend indistinctly. By comparison, the new Toronto Opera, modest as it seems, has acoustics where every breath, note, and instrument can be heard.

March 30. This morning, Ella took us to the airport. We parted warmly, as you do with someone you feel attached to but know you will not see again soon. She had completed her mission and was returning home to New Zealand. We faced about 20 hours of travel, but the longing for home, children, and grandchildren was a strong magnet. "There is no place like home!"

This travel journal is interesting and important, primarily for Vali and me, as it will help us relive the places, events, and people we encountered on this trip. It was a beautiful life experience that enriched us emotionally and intellectually, helping us see and understand more about other places, people, and cultures. It was expensive and tiring, but fully worth the money and effort. For those reading this, I can only encourage anyone to take the first step toward discovering new horizons, which will reward the effort with unforgettable beauty and emotions.

April 14, 2007

The Pearls of the Indian Ocean

The cruise was exceptionally beautiful. In Bangkok, we rested at the hotel after the fatigue of 26-hour journey, as we couldn't find tickets for a direct flight from Toronto. The following morning, we took a city tour—although we had already seen the city in the past—with the specific aim of visiting the Royal Palace grounds again, which still fascinates me with its architectural style, mosaics, and exuberant colors as nowhere else in the world. That evening, we were taken to the ship, not before driving along new boulevards in areas filled with modern highways and buildings, suggesting that investments in this country, Thailand, are massive.

On board we found all our luggage already in the cabin and hurried to the dining room to meet those with whom we would be sharing our evenings for the next thirty days. As it happened, two very pleasant couples greeted us. The first, Gale and Larry from Florida, have been married for 50 years, are very wealthy (they told us they were once invited to an official reception in honor of George W. Bush and his wife), own a private plane and a farm of over eighty hectares in Idaho. They became attached to us, and we spent many pleasant moments together. The other couple, from England—rather difficult to understand because of their accent—quickly joined in with the conversations at the table, sharing jokes and stories that delighted us evening after evening.

The next day we arrived in Vietnam. We did not wish to visit Saigon again, as we had seen it two years earlier, so we limited ourselves to making a few small purchases in the port, especially two lacquer paintings with mother-of-pearl figures for our children, Marius, and Ancuța. My wife Vali didn't agree with the purchase, but the children were delighted when they received them.

Singapore and Kuala Lumpur are both cities of rare beauty and cleanliness; it is difficult to decide which side of the coach to look out from, even though we had seen these places before. As we passed through the labyrinth of well-aligned streets and boulevards edged with flowers and greenery, we marveled that, in temperatures above 40 °C, such gardens can be maintained. On the way to Kuala Lumpur, we also visited the Batu Caves, a series of enormous caverns reaching heights of one hundred meters which, because of their religious significance, contain a number of Hindu temples. But to reach these caves one must climb at least 272 steps, in the company of many monkeys which follow you, stare at you, or else completely ignore you.

Sailing south through the Strait of Malacca between Malaysia and Sumatra, we saw endless lines of ships waiting for authorization to enter the port of Singapore. I have never seen such queues of ships anywhere else. Although nobody doubts Singapore's economic prosperity, the sight we witnessed was a strong confirmation of it.

Our next stop was in Penang. To be honest, I think we chose the wrong tour—or perhaps the town simply lacks many interesting sights. We visited the historical part of the city, where, more than 150 years ago, a handful of Chinese settlers established their first furnaces and altars. I couldn't tell which part of the city was hardest hit by the tsunami, because our visit took place just days before that catastrophe; but I doubt that the modern part of the city near the port suffered as intensely as the poor historical quarter. There, in most houses, people live crammed into a single room on wooden platforms covered with a blanket, sometimes sixteen people in a family, separated only by mosquito nets at night. In the mornings, thin elderly women sit on the doorstep with the door behind them open, and when I looked inside, I could see both the living space and the altar with burning candles where they say their prayers.

In Phuket—also an island seriously affected by the tsunami—we heard for the first time the expression *"gypsy fishermen."* These people live all along the coastline in their long narrow boats covered with makeshift roofs and float inside a canal rich in fish. They didn't seem richer or poorer than most of the population who live in small huts scattered on both sides of the road. The island, of rare beauty, revealed to us a Buddhist temple almost rivaling those seen in Bangkok, where the *stupa* (a funerary monument) is shaped like a golden tower. Around the temple, sheets of 24-carat gold are sold in small squares, like gold leaf flat pieces of about two centimeters, which worshippers stick onto the statues of the deities they venerate. The ashes of Buddha are kept here, placed high in the top of the golden tower in a splendid miniature stupa set inside the main one. Around it lies a complex of buildings, prayer halls, and many monks whose devotion is deeply moving. We also saw the modern resorts recently built for tourists from around the world—and where, unfortunately, many experienced their last joys before the apocalypse stirred from the depths.

We were already on our way to India. In Cochin—a town built by the Portuguese around 1500—we took a tour through narrow streets smelling of damp, fish, and other odors, until we became bored. We left the group and took a "taxi" (a three-wheeled motorbike with a double seat in the back and a roof to protect from the sun) and made a rapid circuit of the town, in which we acquired three cashmere shawls and other souvenirs—not altogether inexpensive. Among other things, we visited the Synagogue and the Raja's Palace. The synagogue, entirely different from the ritual style of construction I know, was built as a consequence of the influx of Jewish refugees from the Holy Land when the Romans occupied the whole region. I was surprised to find paintings illustrating the arrival of the first Jews in Cochin in the 6th century B.C., and again in the 1st century A.D., when Roman persecution in Jerusalem had intensified.

The Raja's Palace, built by the Dutch in the 16th century, has mural paintings covering the walls of several rooms, representing legends from the *Ramayana*. Unfortunately, they are difficult to decipher, and in many places frequent repairs covered by new plaster have destroyed what remained. It is a pity that nobody could protect such artwork—important both artistically and historically—knowing that the paintings portrayed legends more easily read in pictures than through writing, known only by a very few.

Two days later we reached Bombay (now called Mumbai). It is difficult to form a definite opinion when you find yourself in a place where beauty alternates with misery—where the contrast is so striking that, shocked and bewildered, you reserve judgment for a later time after your feelings have sorted themselves out. Splendid buildings from the Victorian era blend with modern constructions. The Taj Mahal Hotel, built at the beginning of the 20th century facing the "Gateway of India," has a modern extension—a thirty-story tower—which integrates with the original style and does not clash with it. Schoolchildren in clean uniforms, boys and girls of all ages, walk along the streets in noisy but orderly groups. Large, tidy schools. Luxurious houses and shops line the boulevards, where traffic flows on the left, like in London, and is often interrupted by the leisurely crossing of a sacred cow. At the same time, we saw a multitude of beggars sitting on the ground with children in their arms, and numerous children blocking the way asking for money, pressing their hands to their mouths to show that they were hungry.

We visited Gandhi's house, now a museum, and were profoundly impressed by the depth of the quotations displayed, the multitude of photos, and the exhibits from the life of this great man who introduced to the world a principle of determined yet peaceful protest. We saw several temples, including a Jain temple—one of the earliest sects to prohibit the division of society into castes. Finally, we passed by the *Dhobi Ghat*, the place where the city's laundry is traditionally collected each day, washed, dried, ironed and returned to every doorstep. It is truly a sight worth seeing—just as one should not miss seeing one of the trains arriving and departing from the city, packed with people hanging on the steps and even on the roofs, like terrifying clusters of grapes.

Our most important visit in Bombay took place after lunch, to the *Elephanta Caves*. These lie on an island reached by boat from the Gateway of India and the trip takes about half an hour. The were discovered by the Portuguese in the 16th century and were named after the enormous elephant carved in stone guarding the island, supporting a smaller elephant on its back. The island is only slightly larger than the base of the mountain that rises in its center. You climb more than 150 steps—or, for a few dollars, are carried on the shoulders of four porters who carry you on a wooden throne up to the cave. At the top is a wide, level stone terrace. In the mountain in front of you is an entrance like a portal, supported by two stone columns about five meters high. The columns rise from square bases and become round above, ending in broad, round capitals reminiscent of the Ionic order.

Inside, a few steps lead to a vast hall guarded by similar columns placed at intervals of about five meters, aligned perfectly both lengthwise and crosswise, supporting the ceiling. In the dimness, one can see beyond these columns at the back of the hall, bas-reliefs of mythological scenes and enormous sculptures reminiscent of those guarding the tombs in the Valley of the Kings at Aswan in Egypt. All these mythological compositions are dedicated to Shiva, who in the Hindu religion is the deity of supernatural power, the third in the Hindu trinity, after Brahma (the Creator) and Vishnu (the Preserver). To give an idea: the hall is about forty meters long and equally wide. Each mythological panel is in relief, about five meters wide and up to the ceiling in height. In total there are nine such panels arranged symmetrically from the northern entrance. Each one is different in subject, and at the center of the hall, on the back wall of the cave, stands the triple figure of Shiva: in front view and in profile on either side—his left side showing wrath, while the right is serene and almost feminine. On either side of the central figure are two more compositions. The cave has three entrances, and on the walls flanking each entrance are further mythological scenes. And do not forget the twenty-seven columns, aligned both lengthwise and crosswise at equal distances.

Now imagine that this entire work of art was carved out of solid basalt rock with the tools available in the fourth–sixth centuries A.D.

After seeing this cave, the pyramids of Egypt no longer impress me in the way they once did—for they were constructed above ground, placing block upon block like a game of cubes—whereas here, the rock was chipped away, fragment by fragment, cut deep into the mountain's body, where the smallest mistake would have been irreparable. How many free people—not slaves (ancient coins were found inside, proving that the workers were paid)—labored in darkness, heat, and dust to create this work, whose author is unknown? Accordingly, one may ask, to whose plan was this work made—lasting centuries until its completion—resulting in such a unified masterpiece that even with modern technology and today's machinery would be difficult to accomplish?

The tragedy is that, after Vasco da Gama discovered the cave, the Portuguese, considering its sculpted figures to be pagan expressions contrary to Christian faith, fired their cannons at the sculptures, destroying much of their beauty – but the rock proved stronger. The damage is extensive, but the brilliance and skill of the artists remain visible across four or five centuries. And I ask myself: why, in any of the art history books I have consulted and still cherish, isn't anything mentioned or written about the **Elephanta Caves**?

The Seychelles did not impress me very much. The afternoon spent there seemed to remind me more of the idyllic life of a small provincial town from our own lands. Mauritius is a beautiful island, with an exotic sound, Creole faces, and an extinct volcano. It is renowned for a "lunar landscape" park, where the sterile soil displays zones of different colors – from light yellow to dark red and here and there even violet, like the colors of military camouflage.

Réunion Island is different – French culture, considered a distant province of France and subsidized by the French government; for that reason, I believe, it is richer and with a much higher standard of living than its neighbored islands. The volcano is still active; the crater is accessible to tourists, but a walk along the coast becomes as memorable as a stroll along the Riviera itself.

Skirting Madagascar on the western side, we reached South Africa, at Richards Bay. Here we met a Zulu tribe and took a safari into one of the reserves. From the ship we travelled by coach to a hotel near a Zulu village, preserved apparently as a museum for the benefit of tourists. It would seem that many still have not abandoned their original way of life inherited from their ancestors. Deep inside the African continent, traditions, clothing, lifestyle, and tools are still those of the past. Their weapons remain shields and spears; they speak their own language and emotional messages are communicated symbolically through beads of various colors and patterns. These beads, sewn into bands, can be worn as bracelets, necklaces, chest adornments or even around the hips. Unmarried women do not cover their breasts; a man may have countless wives, for whom he must pay the father with eleven cows and build each of them a separate house. A married woman is not allowed more than four lovers – which is why AIDS and HIV have reached such proportions in Africa. They are highly superstitious and still believe in shamans and witches who hold important positions in their communities.

The safari excursions took place over two days in lush jungle, using open 4×4 vehicles with seven people in each. We saw numerous animals, both on land and in the water – sights impossible to describe – and learned, firsthand, many of the laws of the jungle.

Cape Town is a dream city. Ahead rises a massif more than a thousand meters high, topped by a wide, flat plateau – this is the Table Mountain. To the left and right there are two peaks: Lion's Head and Diamond Head. The center of the city lies between the port and the mountain. Everything is new, beautiful, elegant, and clean. Going toward the mountain, the road leads among attractive villas in various architectural styles and an abundance of vegetation. You could ascend in a rotating cable car that turns 360 degrees, allowing you to admire the panorama in all directions.

If you rent a taxi, you can reach **Cape of Good Hope** in just five hours. There you can admire the place where the Atlantic and

Indian Oceans meet. Not far from that point lies **Cape Point** – marked by an ancient lighthouse established by Vasco da Gama, and on the summit, you'll find a stone marker showing the directions and distances to London, New York, Beijing, etc.

This strip of land is continuously crossed by countless cars and buses filled with visitors from all corners of the world, disturbing the peace of the true owners of this land – the **ostriches**. Half domesticated or simply enraged by the intrusion of strangers into their quiet realm, they run, alone or in groups, after every vehicle. Moreover, ostrich eggs, decorated by local artisans skilled in carving the smooth eggshells, are among the most sought-after souvenirs in this region.

On the way back to Cape Town we passed **Boulder's Beach**, where, in recent years, a colony of penguins have come to lay and hatch their eggs deep in the hot sand along the coast sheltered by rocky outcrops. A little farther north, along the coast toward Cape Town where the mountains plunge into the ocean, the sight of a cascade of apartment blocks rising like terraces of a gigantic staircase facing the water and the sun leaves visitors dreaming of a holiday in just such a place.

Leaving the city behind and heading toward the airport, barely five minutes after passing the last houses, for at least ten miles on both sides of the road you encounter another face of the city: the *shanty towns*. Entire districts of shacks improvised from anything – plywood, metal barrels, corrugated iron, many of them rust-colored – packed together, no bigger than the length of an adult and about as high, with roofs held down against the wind by stones and heavy objects, unfold like an open wound, leaving the bitter taste of helplessness. Such a beautiful and rich country, and still in this century, it must find a solution to the continuous flow of hungry people arriving from the interior of the continent, with no training whatsoever, just to swell the ranks of unemployment—which has already reached forty per cent.

The trip was rich not only in what we saw, but in all that we learned across those thirty days. The cruise director organized a number of speakers, who delighted us during the days at sea with lectures of a high academic level. Most of the daily talks covered our future port stops, local, regional, and global politics, deep history, and the present, as well as the history of navigation, recent discoveries in astronomy and even classes in graphology. These captivated most of the passengers on board. The theatre, with over six hundred seats, was filled to capacity – many people were content to sit on stairways – even though at the same time many other activities were available on the ship. Listening only to the level of questions and the comments during those lectures was enough to recognize that the audience was almost as knowledgeable and engaged as the speakers themselves. At the end of such a forum, other academic institutions would have issued diplomas of completion and credits to those present. I hope that other traveling companies has such well-balanced packages for their customers as I was lucky to attend on his trip.

21 August 2008

Unique Moments from an Unforgettable Journey

Who can teach me how to briefly tell the story of a journey where every moment demands a pause in order to reveal the reader the details so rich that cannot be left untold? A year ago, a newspaper page caught my eye: *24 days – Amsterdam to the Black Sea along the Rhine, Main and Danube Rivers*. It was the only time I had ever seen such a trip advertised. The idea of travelling through the heart of Europe along its flowing arteries, past the most important medieval castles, large and small cities, and the picturesque charm of so many regions across fourteen countries, including four capitals—convinced me to contact the company and reserve a cabin. I knew that riverboats are not the size of those that sail the seas; they have only three levels and a maximum capacity of 130 passengers. Our ship, the *Scenic Sapphire*, one of the most modern, was less than 12 meters wide to pass through the sixty-eight locks along the route, and 136 meters long. As the rivers are crossed by many bridges, the ship's height is limited as well: for this reason, the pilothouse on the upper deck must be lowered on hydraulic supports when passing under the lower bridges. Naturally, in those areas passengers are not allowed on the upper deck, which is normally fitted with sun loungers, armchairs under sunshades, and a running track.

We boarded on April 25 in Amsterdam, and our first reaction

was to the reduced size of the cabin—where the space between walls, furniture and bed barely made room for a person. Otherwise, everything could be considered quite comfortable. A good number of passengers had already had the chance to meet that morning at a luxury hotel in the city center, while waiting for the coaches that would transfer everyone to the ship. By six in the evening, we had unpacked and were getting ready for the first dinner on board. Before that, however, in the lounge/bar, we had our first briefing with Peter, the cruise director. These meetings would be repeated every evening. Little by little we began to grow familiar with Peter, whom we came to like, with the bar and dining room staff, with the three captains (all Romanians), and with the rest of the crew.

The following morning, those who had not yet visited Amsterdam took a tour by boat along the city's canals, while the rest of us visited a provincial farm where the level of the fields lies below that of the surrounding waters, protected by dikes. In the next place, Zaanse Schaans, a picturesque line of wooden windmills that have survived the technical progress of today, dominated the scenery. These windmills, in their time, won the battle against the waters in the lowlands by channeling away the excess water and drying the land.

Back on board at lunchtime, the engines were started, and our ship began its journey eastward. Gliding over the mirror of the Rhine, the scenery began to unfold on both sides of the ship at a slow pace that allowed us to take in the richness of feeling provoked by everything we were passing. Sitting in the comfortable armchairs of the lounge bar, coffee cup in front of us and cameras hanging ready from our necks, we delighted in this incredible display of shifting landscapes—something incomparable to travelling by train or car, because the river's speed rarely exceeds twelve kilometers per hour.

That next morning, we continued upstream toward Cologne, where we were scheduled to arrive after lunch. Cologne (Köln), the fourth largest city in Germany with a population of over ten million, is one of the oldest settlements in Europe, founded by the Romans in 38 BC. Its famous Gothic cathedral, covered in sculpted stone and lace-like arabesques, imposes itself on the visitor by its two massive towers, whose complicated structures could not be fully appreciated because of their height and the rain that day. It dates to the fourth century, but when the relics of the Three Magi were brought to Cologne in the 12th century, the old cathedral had to be enlarged; the present structure was only completed in 1880.

After a short tour of the city, the coaches took us to Marksburg Castle, dating from the 12th century, the only one along the Rhine to remain intact — the others having been destroyed in the numerous wars between France and Germany. Many have since been rebuilt over the past two centuries.

The Rhine, one of the longest rivers in Europe (1,320 km from the Swiss Alps to Rotterdam in the Netherlands), is connected via canals to the Main and the Danube, making it possible to travel from the Black Sea to the North Sea over 3,500 kilometers. Since Antiquity, the Rhine has been of great economic and strategic importance, used by the Romans both for transport of goods and as a natural frontier of the empire. Today it is the most heavily travelled river in Europe, used by massive barges carrying oil, ore, and timber, as well as by tourist vessels. The distance along the river is marked every kilometer and entering the narrow and most romantic part of the Rhine—between km 529 and 685, from Koblenz to Rüdesheim—we saw spectacular scenery dominated by low mountains almost entirely planted with vineyards. On the crests stood the ghostly silhouettes of medieval castles, which had to be brought closer to the eye with camera zooms.

After Koblenz, at the confluence with the Moselle, rises the 120-metre Lorelei rock, reminding us of Heinrich Heine's poem about the golden-haired beauty who combed her hair and sang a song that cast a spell on sailors, many of whom lost their lives attempting the dangerous passage beneath.

Absorbed in the beauty of the surroundings and trying to immortalize on film everything we passed, I did not notice a woman approaching me to ask, in Romanian, whether it was true I was Romanian. She told me she was from Canada, but that her great-grandmother—originally from Romania—had insisted that all her children speak Romanian. Four generations have passed and they all still speak their ancestor's language. Naturally, we became good friends from that moment. It was Vera and Cliff Fontaine from Halifax Street in Regina (Saskatchewan). After the fall of the dictator Nicolae Ceauşescu, the church they attend in Regina heard about the horrors in Romanian orphanages and decided to help. Vera, who could already communicate with the authorities in Romania, was the best person to represent the group. At one orphanage, she was asked to find someone in Canada willing to adopt a seven-year-old girl who had been promised to a German family that had backed out the adoption on the last moment, and the child had fallen into deep depression. Vera was not a young woman and already had four grown children, but still she called her husband Cliff in Canada and suggested they adopt the little girl.

Eighteen years have passed since then. The girl, Dalia, took over her mother's flower shop in Canada. She is married, and I had the joy of meeting her in Bucharest. Timing our arrival in Romania, she and her Canadian husband came to meet her parents and enjoyed a holiday in Romanian country. Seeing this young, beautiful, and intelligent woman, I cannot help but reflect upon the miracle wrought by those people for a child who would otherwise have had no chance in life.

That afternoon, April 28, we visited Rüdesheim and took a cable car up a hilltop park where the *Niederwalddenkmal* rises — an allegorical statue representing Germany, commemorating the unification of Germany in 1871 after the Franco-Prussian War. From Rüdesheim, at Mainz, we left the Rhine and continued along the Main toward Bamberg — 396 kilometers away — but first we stopped in Miltenberg, from where coaches took us to Wertheim, known for its high-quality glass making, wines, beers and delicious Bavarian sausages...

We found a romantic, medieval little town with houses half framed in heavy wooden beams, located at the confluence of the Main and Tauber rivers – an area also known as an excellent place for holidays and recreation. In the center of this picturesque town, the guide told us a story that happened 70 years ago. A group of Nazis decided to hold a demonstration in the town center, and the town council worried that the city would suffer because of the protest and that tourists would stay away. The mayor decided that only God could save the situation. On Sunday, the day scheduled for the demonstration, the Nazis arrived in uniform and gathered in the square in front of the cathedral, stirring restlessly at the microphones when, suddenly, the church bells covered the entire event, ringing long and endlessly until the demonstration dissolved. Unfortunately, this "miracle of the Lord" did not remain without punishment.

The Main River is 529 kilometers long and flows into the Rhine, passing through Bavaria, Baden-Württemberg, and Hesse. Since 1992 it has been connected to the Danube by the Rhine–Main–

Danube Canal, which includes thirty-four locks that allow ships to navigate. The highest point above sea level is at the Hilpolstein Lock, at an altitude of 406 meters. The most important city on the Main is Frankfurt, which was not included in our program.

30 April. Morning excursion by coach to Rothenburg, a medieval city in the center of Franconia, preserved with the authenticity characteristic of the Middle Ages and dating back to the 10th century. In 1274, Rothenburg received the privilege of being an "Imperial City" from King Rudolf of Habsburg. This exempted it from taxes and helped the town's trade and development. Thus, it became one of the top twenty fortified cities of the Holy Roman Empire. At the start of the 17th century, during the Thirty Years' War, mainly Protestant Rothenburg was besieged by Catholic troops and, after they left the town almost empty, in 1634, the bubonic plague devastated the population. During the Second World War the town was bombed by retreating Nazis, but the American troops, aware of its historic importance, refrained from using artillery in its liberation.

In the Middle Ages, river and well water was contaminated because there was no urban sewerage, and the favorite drinks of the population were wine and beer. This habit, rooted in ancient times, was kept to the present, as proved by the quality of the region's wines and beers.

Evenings on the ship hosted many encounters with locals – folk dancers, musicians, and craftsmen. A glass blower from Wertheim shaped various objects in front of us from Pyrex glass, which some of us hurried to buy as souvenirs. Around the bar, with a last glass of wine or dancing to the music played on the piano by Zoli, a talented musician from Hungary, we ended the day and went to bed. On the way to the cabin, we would stop at the small office near the entrance to take the information sheet for the following day and exchange a few words with the duty officer, who, on the night shift, was a Romanian woman, Irina Panov. Although very young, she had already worked for several years on ships and was married to one of the butlers of the ship, Wiech Krzysztof, from Poland, who spoke perfect Romanian.

Of the entire crew on board, thirteen were Romanians – including the three captains, seamen, stewards, and cooks. In the dining room, many waiters greeted us with "bună dimineaţa" (good morning), but only two of them were Romanians: Bodea Andra and Punei Ioan. I met Mihai Manolache, the chief captain, at the command desk while the ship passed through a lock so narrow that only the width of a hand separated the ship from the concrete walls of the canal.

"I never let go of the ship, sir," the captain told me, focused on the navigation line.

In Budapest he was to hand over command to the second captain, Din Ioan, because back home his newborn son – only two months old – was waiting to meet him for the first time.

Bamberg, one of the few Bavarians medieval towns not destroyed in WWII, is famous for its cathedral with four 81-metre towers, dating from 1004, containing the tomb of Emperor Henry II – and also for its smoked beer (*Rauchbier*).

Nuremberg, the city of the *Meistersingers* celebrated by Wagner, has a glorious historic past and a less glorious recent history, considering the importance Hitler and the Nazis gave to this place. At that time, they turned the city into a theatre of fascist propaganda, organizing demonstrations with hundreds of thousands of Nazis parading before the Führer. As the unofficial capital of the Holy Roman Empire, it gained importance in the 13th century because it lay at the crossroads of trade between Italy and northern Europe. Declared a free city by Emperor Frederick II, it became a center of the German cultural renaissance in the 15th and 16th centuries. It was besieged and occupied by Swedish troops during the Thirty Years' War, and declined afterwards, recovering only in the nineteenth century through industrialization. During WWII, Nuremberg was systematically bombed – more than 6,000 residents died, and hundreds of thousands were displaced, but in the following years it was rebuilt and restored to its former appearance. In 1945–46, the International Military Tribunal in Nuremberg tried and convicted the authors of the crimes committed by the Nazis during the war.

Before nightfall, we began sailing toward Regensburg on the waters of the Main–Danube Canal, through a hilly region with winding valleys of rivers and roads. Imitating Roman engineering, the builders of this canal created several aqueducts large enough to carry a ship of the size we were on; and so, we were amazed to see roads, cars, trucks, and even other ships passing *under* us. The engineers who made this possible surely deserve top honors.

Regensburg, the first stop on the Danube, is marked by a stone bridge still in use today, built in 1135–1146, which witnessed the passage of the armies of the Second and Third Crusades on their way to the Holy Land. The city has a remarkable history, going back to the second century. It was Christianized in the seventh century and became one of the most important cities in the Middle Ages, surpassing in building activity, in 1517, any other German city – something that can still be seen today in the number of buildings declared by UNESCO as world cultural heritage.

Sailing down the Danube, only ten kilometers after Regensburg on the left bank stands Valhalla – a structure that imitates the dimensions and appearance of the Parthenon in Athens, built by Ludwig I of Bavaria in 1841 as a national pantheon commemorating, through 121 statues and many plaques, the most important German artists, writers, and philosophers.

The Danube is the richest endowed river and the second-longest in Europe (after the Volga); 2,860 kilometers long, it passes through ten countries from the Black Forest to the Black Sea and flows by four capital cities (Vienna, Bratislava, Budapest, and Belgrade). It drops 680 meters in altitude before reaching the delta and has been a major economic and political artery. It also stood as the border of the Roman Empire for more than six hundred years, with Roman roads running along its banks.

At Passau: 160 people, four coaches to choose from, three different destinations. Two coaches took the road to Cesky Krumlov in the Czech Republic, one went to Salzburg in Austria, and the other remained in Passau – all to meet the ship again in Linz later in the afternoon. Since many, including ourselves, had already visited Salzburg in the past, we gathered information about Cesky Krumlov, about which we had never heard before. We did not regret the decision. A small town in Bohemia – a talisman of historical buildings surrounded by the river Vltava, which loops around like a noose – is dominated by a castle perched on two cliffs, connected by a three-level vaulted bridge of gargantuan dimensions. An extraordinary place that deserves far more than the few hours we had available. Unfortunately, we did not have the opportunity to visit the interior of the castle – the second largest in the Czech Republic – which has maintained a functional Baroque-style theatre (from 1766), staging only three opera performances a year, and keeps a renowned collection of arms and porcelain.

5 May 2011. Morning excursion to Melk Abbey in Austria, an opulent Benedictine establishment built in baroque style on the ruins of a Roman fortress overlooking the Danube. The site was offered to Benedictine monks in the 11th century and became an important center of schooling and culture. In 1750 the monastery was rebuilt and enlarged to its vast present size, housing treasures of art, painting and literature in buildings that illustrate the finest example of Austrian baroque. The church of the abbey inspires awe with its ornamentation, frescoes, sculptures and overall ensemble, added to by the painted ceiling and above all the altar representing God, Christ, and the Holy Fathers of the church. Our veneration was rewarded with a wonderful organ concert that made every fiber of feeling within us vibrate that day.

Back on the ship during lunch, we resumed the smooth gliding over the Danube, meandering through the Wachau Valley, surrounded by forested hills dotted with medieval castles, vineyards, and gardens on our way to Dürnstein. Here comes the legend that Richard the Lionheart, returning in 1192 from the Third Crusade, was captured by his enemy Leopold V of Austria and imprisoned in a Dürnstein castle. Eventually he was released after paying a ransom amounting to one-third of the wealth of England. More recently, the hotel overlooking the Danube in the town served as one of the last hideaways for Princess Diana and Dodi Al-Fayed shortly before their tragic death.

During the night we arrived in Vienna. Coaches awaited us at nine in the morning for a tour of the Ringstrasse, the Parliament building, St Stephen's Cathedral, the Imperial Hofburg Palace, and a passage in front of the Spanish Riding School just as the famous Lipizzaner horses were returning from exercise. Rarely has the history of a city had so many occasions for triumph and decline as Vienna. Originally settled in primitive times (fifth century B.C.), by the fifth century A.D. it had become a Roman frontier outpost against Germanic tribes. Attacked in the 12th century by Mongol tribes and then ruled by the Babenberg's, it later became, from the 15th century, the residence of the Habsburg dynasty, which transformed the city into the capital of the Holy Roman Empire and a center of arts, science, and music in Europe. In 1804 it became the capital of the Austrian Empire and, from 1867, the capital of the Austro-Hungarian Empire. In the 20th century, after the First World War and following Hitler's rise to power, from 1938 until the end of the Second World War, Austria's capital was shifted to Berlin. In 1945, Vienna was divided among the four powers and remained under occupation for ten years. Today its international prestige is ensured by hosting many important world forums, a thriving cultural atmosphere, music, art, and a constant pilgrimage of tourists. In the evening, a special concert at the Liechtenstein Palace by the Wiener

Imperial Orchestra, with opera and ballet soloists, was offered.

The next day the ship remained in Vienna, but three options were offered: a day trip to Bratislava, a tour of the Habsburg summer residence of Schönbrunn, or a tour of the Vienna State Opera followed by a visit to a famous Viennese café for coffee and cakes. We chose Bratislava, where we had never been before. The city itself reflects the suffering it has endured throughout its turbulent history. For a millennium it was a strategic location on the Danube, disputed between Austria and Hungary, which had its capital here from 1536 to 1784. Today it is the capital of Slovakia, with a population of almost half a million inhabitants, many universities, museums, theatres and art galleries and – although many modern buildings are notable – the old town is dominated by medieval buildings in baroque and rococo style and a famous fortress-castle from 1430 that towers 85 meters above the Danube.

8 May 2011. The capital of Hungary, Budapest, presents a remarkable diversity of styles between the two settlements on either side of the Danube, Buda, and Pest. On the western bank, Buda is guarded by the famous Matthias Corvinus Cathedral, 700 years old – a jewel decorated inside with remarkable mosaics that cover the walls – the equestrian statue of the holy king Stephen, founder of Hungary, numerous palaces and museums, and the Fishermen's Bastion, a stone platform offering an unequalled view of Pest across the river. In Pest, the most important building is the Parliament, a construction that emulates the Westminster Parliament in London, without the Big Ben clock tower. Wide avenues lined with imposing buildings retain their original appearance and are joined by modern street-level shops. The Eastern Railway Station, Heroes' Square with the Millennium Monument and the Tomb of the Unknown Soldier, flanked by the Museum of Art and the Palace of Art; the Opera House and the Philharmonic are monuments that must be seen. Remarkable too are the Chain Bridge over the Danube, guarded by lions at each end, and the first European underground railway line. In our free time we wandered the central streets and entered St. Stephen's Basilica, dedicated to the founder of Hungary and exhibiting, behind the altar, the mummified hand of the saint and a plaque translated into ten languages containing the following inscription in Romanian: **"To the HOLY RIGHT HAND. The history of the *Holy Right*. The relics of Saint Stephen, founder of the State. 15 August 1038 Saint Stephen died. 15 August 1083, at Szekesfehervar, he was canonized. His right hand was found intact and has since been venerated by the people. The fate of the Holy Right was troubled: it was kept in Bihor (Transylvania), Ragusa (Dalmatia, today Dubrovnik). In 1771 it reached Vienna and later Buda. In 1944 it reached the West, and on 19 August 1945 it was returned to Hungary."**

Back on the ship, it was the last night for some travelers who ended their journey here and, after 15 days together, we shared impressions, jokes, and personal stories. The farewell left a deep feeling of regret. For those who continued the journey, an excursion to Szentendre was organized – a kind of open-air village museum where farmhouses from various localities and historical periods of Hungary have been transplanted. On the return, the old familiar faces were replaced with new ones and, starting with the shared lunch, new relationships were formed. Before going to bed, we left Budapest with the thought that very soon we would be at home again, in Romania.

10 May 2011. The last day in Hungarian and EU territory, but we would have the opportunity to visit Kalocsa, the home of *paprikash*, followed by a visit to an animal farm in the Hungarian *pusta*, where we were greeted with *palinka*, *debrecziner* sausages and a spectacular riding demonstration, like in cowboy movies in the Hungarian version. After a short stop in Mohacs, a modern town at the border, we headed for the Croatian frontier. Throughout the journey we moved from one country to another without difficulty, and – except in Hungary – used a single currency (the euro) without needing to show passports. Entering the territories of Croatia and Serbia, which are not part of the EU, border officers came onto the ship to collect passports, check them, and approve our entry. Depending on their mood, this procedure can sometimes take hours.

Vukovar, Croatia. For someone who witnessed

bombardments as a child, the spectacle seen in Vukovar brought back the horror caused by bombs and the terror of facing death. After half a century under Tito's authoritarian rule, people – Serbs and Croats alike – formed friendships, shared joys, and sorrows, and let their children marry without considering whether they were Catholic or Orthodox. After Tito's death, Yugoslavia fractured into nationalist interests, and the Serbs under Milosevic tried to prevent the state from splitting. The results were catastrophic: thousands of deaths, material destruction, hatred, and terrible memories. Vukovar reminded me of the Grant neighborhood in Bucharest after the bombings of 1944. The ruins speak for themselves.

After another border stop, later the same day we arrived in Novi Sad, Serbia. A refined city that I had long heard about – especially because "Novi Sad" was written on the medium-wave dial of old radio sets. It has a rich historical past: as early as the 16th century, a fortress was built on the riverbank to oppose the Ottoman armies. In the city center there is a pedestrian street – closed to car traffic – lined with attractive shops and outdoor cafés all the way from the main square to the town hall. Even though it was a Wednesday (a working day), the cafés were full, the streets crowded and the atmosphere relaxed. In the church behind the town hall, we admired the beautifully sculpted tower with its elaborate decoration; the altar, rich in Byzantine icons, is a genuine work of art, and many devout women prayed in silence, bowing to the ground.

Belgrade. The morning began with a visit to the Kalemegdan Fortress, perched on a promontory at the confluence of the Danube and Sava rivers, evoking the trauma of the battles with the Turks who gained control of it in 1527. The history of the city goes back to the fifth century when Celtic tribes founded it. It was first mentioned in documents in 989, but it was captured forty times by foreign armies and has risen from its own ashes each time. Today, with two million inhabitants, it is an important economic center in Europe, with technical, artistic, and cultural achievements worthy of mention. The city tour also included a visit to the Cathedral of St. Sava (still under construction) and the memorial house, park, and grave of the former president Tito.

After an evening on the ship with a performance by a folk-dance group, our floating hotel resumed its calm gliding over the moonlit Danube, heading towards Iron Gates.

13 May. A day on the ship, with a barbecue and ice cream on the upper deck. Anxious not to miss anything, we woke up very early, grabbed a quick cup of coffee and settled down, cameras ready, in a chair that offered panoramic views outside. As we advanced, the Danube became narrower between the steep rock walls that rose to block its way. Here and there a house appeared along one bank or the other, a train entered a tunnel on the hillside, or a car drove along a road.

At one point, on a hill to the left, a little church with whitewashed walls appeared, forcing the river to turn around it, with behind it the view of a valley running between two cliffs, with a stream flowing towards the Danube and a bridge carrying the road across. Above the bridge, carved into a tall white rock, the mighty head of Decebalus appeared – a magnificent colossal symbol of our nation, at least twenty meters high, depicting his serene face with a convincing expression of determination that resisted the Romans for years and years. On the opposite side, a little further down near Dobreta, we saw the Tabula Traiana – the only remaining witness of the famous Roman bridge over the Danube, built by Trajan in the year 103, before it was submerged by the construction of the two hydroelectric stations in 1971 at the Iron Gates. Here the waters had been raised ten meters, creating a large basin bordered on the left bank by the harbor of Orşova.

At that moment, our ship reached one of the locks of the Iron Gates hydroelectric station, and on the upper deck the cooks were already preparing sizzling steaks and all kinds of food on the grills while the waiters hurried among the tables with drinks: white and red wine or beer. While guiding the ship through the lock, Captain Din Ion and his assistant, Crăciun Constantin, spoke to me about the difficulties of living far from their families and the problems this causes. "My daughter grew up at home only with my wife. I wasn't there to see her grow up, to protect her or to contribute to her education. My wife did all that alone," said Captain Din. "After the return voyage this summer, I will move onto my own ship – it's being built now – and bring my family on board. My daughter will study with us on the ship and later, who knows, maybe I'll build a house somewhere closer, in Germany. It will be different, you'll see," he added. Meanwhile, under a contract with a company, the bank has granted him the necessary funds to acquire a riverboat, and, with God's help, Captain Din will soon be able to fulfil his plan. I truly wish him every success.

The next morning, we reached the Bulgarian border at Svishtov and re-entered the EU. This time the customs formalities went faster and, as the coaches were already waiting outside, we drove to Veliko Tarnovo, a town nestled in a mountain depression. In the 12th–14th centuries it was the capital of the Second Bulgarian Empire and was declared the Orthodox Rome, but centuries of Ottoman occupation interrupted its development. From the 12th century remain the ruins of the Tsarevets fortress – the former royal palace and the old Patriarchate. The prosperity that followed the expulsion of the Turks in the 19th century led to the construction of imposing houses, churches, and universities.

On the way to Ruse, where our ship would wait for us in the evening, we stopped in the village of Arbanassi, Bulgaria. Here, because the Sultan abolished taxes in the 16th century, prosperity helped the creation of beautiful estates surrounded by fortified walls, many of which have recently been transformed into hotels or guesthouses. But the highlight of this locality was visiting the Church of the Archangels Michael and Gabriel from the 17th century, whose interior is completely covered with wall paintings representing icons, saints and biblical scenes relating to the birth, passion, and crucifixion of Christ – in vivid color and, without exaggeration, breathtaking. Among its founders was the Cantacuzino family, and inside is a tomb marked "Constantin Brâncoveanu," which initially confused me as I knew that the earthly remains of the great Wallachian ruler are buried in the Church of St George in Bucharest, rebuilt by him in 1705–1707. In the village another church from the same period, slightly larger than this one – the Church of the Nativity – is equally beautifully painted inside, and though I do not know who created these works of art, I feel it would take me months to explore and decipher the stories and symbols conveyed through the paintings – such as "The Wheel of Life", a symbolic image of the rise and fall of the human spirit.

Under the Saligny Bridge at Cernavodă lies the port of the city, which is the final point of our cruise – even though the ship would host us for one more night. But that morning the coaches would take us along the Danube–Black Sea Canal, past the Candu nuclear plant (designed by Canada), and along the Murfatlar wine estate to Constanţa and Mamaia. The visit in Constanţa began with a tour of the Archaeological Museum, which reveals exhibits left by our

Roman ancestors – valued even today as part of the treasure of the family from which we descend. The statue of the eternally young old poet Ovid stands in front of the museum, bearing this inscription on the plinth: **"Beneath this stone lies Ovid, the poet of gentle loves, vanquished by his own talent. O you who pass by, if ever you have loved, pray for him – may his sleep be peaceful!"**

Our guide led us down a side street to the Cathedral of St Peter and Paul, and as it was Sunday morning, it was full of people. We could barely squeeze inside for a few moments so as not to disturb the liturgy. On the way to the cathedral, the street lined with sumptuous buildings – once distinguished symbols of civilization and prosperity – hurt our eyes and feelings by their neglect: crumbling stucco, balconies near collapse and windowpanes missing. Continuing our walk along the seafront in front of the port towards the Casino building, the sight of this art nouveau monument – its windows broken and plaster peeling – exceeding any nightmare or imagination, made me regret not having stayed on board the ship.

After a short stop in Mamaia, a few steps on the golden sand of the beach and touching the emerald crystal of the sea, we headed back to Murfatlar, where a hearty meal awaited us at the winery: stuffed vine and cabbage rolls, steaming *mămăliga*, and plenty of ruby-red wine, accompanied by a traditional band that made many of us jump up and join a multinational *hora* dance.

Back on the ship, with much regret we started packing again – the suitcases had to be placed outside the cabin doors early in the morning. That evening, Captain Din drank a glass of champagne with us to wish us a safe journey, and we bid farewell to our dear friends in the ship's crew, wishing them good luck in their travels and the days ahead.

16 May 2011. On board the coaches, we headed towards Bucharest, passing fields of greenery stretching beyond the horizon, on a sunny day that warmed not only the weather but also our hearts. For more than two hours I gazed outside with a little disbelief, because it looked too beautiful to be true – I did not see a single piece of uncultivated land, nothing ugly, nothing to offend the eye. Until the coach entered the streets of the capital – and I suddenly saw those terrible Ceausescu-era apartment buildings, meant for the working people to live in, now even uglier, with the concrete stripped of plaster, cars parked on the pavements rust-eaten and obstructing passers-by, and grotesque graffiti deepening one's heavy mood.

On the way to the Palace of the Parliament – Ceausescu's culminating work – the view improved somewhat and the fountains along the main boulevard softened the harsh impression left from a few minutes earlier. As much as I dislike admitting this, I am convinced that Ceauşescu has inscribed himself forever in our history, through the one thing that will endure for centuries – this building with which his name will remain associated. That colossal structure of marble and granite, with all its miscalculations, design errors and shortcomings, is still grand, opulent and remarkable for showcasing – unlike any other creation – the craftsmanship, skill and talent of those who contributed to it, considering that all the workmanship and materials, from the crystal chandeliers and hand-carved furniture to the woven carpets, were entirely created in Romania – and of this we can be proud.

The tour of the capital continued with a stop at the Cotroceni Commercial Centre, where we were surprised to discover an ultra-modern mall – spacious, air conditioned, with luxury shops like those in the Eaton Centre in Toronto, spotlessly clean (even in the restrooms), attractive and well designed. We then travelled along Bucharest's old boulevards, where too many buildings are now masked over their entire height by enormous advertising panels.

After passing Victory Square, on Jianu Road, the guide stopped the coach in front of an imposing building with a huge, gilded crucifix rising above the wrought iron fence next to the gate, telling us that this was the house of the owner of Steaua Football Club, Gigi Becali. At that moment, the gate happened to open and Mr. Becali himself, at the wheel of a black Mercedes, stopped and motioned the guide to enter. The young woman, incredulous, stepped down from the coach and asked him if she had understood correctly. Becali confirmed the invitation, and, with hesitant steps, we approached the side door. Mr. Becali stopped us, stepped out of his car, and gestured for us to go through the **main** entrance, where his staff, informed by phone, were already waiting at the top of the stairs with the doors open.

We entered a salon of elegant spatial harmony, balance, and good taste, displaying a marble staircase with wrought iron balustrade decorated with gilded laurel leaves leading to the upper floor, a white fireplace supporting a Venetian mirror reaching to the ceiling, several paintings with religious themes adorning the walls and two large, gilded icons near the entrance. We, forty foreigners who filled a bus, seemed to invade the tranquility of this palace which, in the past, belonged to the great industrialist Max Auschnitt. It was confiscated by the communists and, after Ceauşescu's death, claimed by his heirs and sold to Gigi Becali on the condition that he restore it to its former grandeur based on the original plans. Careful not to disturb anything, we passed from room to room, photographing the rooms in general and in detail – his personal office (with a family portrait of his wife and children and a statuette of Saint George slaying the dragon standing on the desk), a small adjoining room equipped as a computer room, and on the opposite side, the conference room, dominated by a long table surrounded by many velvet-covered armchairs. On the large side terrace, the garden – marked by a fountain – was surrounded by paved walkways, a carpet of grass bordered with small red flowers and, in the background, a stand of majestic trees blocking the view into the distance.

While each of us was happy at the opportunity, our guide still trembled, unable to believe such an event possible – something that no one would ever have believed plausible, especially if you were Romanian. I do not know what prompted Mr. Becali to invite us into his house, but certainly this event revealed another side of his personality.

While we visited the Palace of Parliament, our luggage had been transferred to the Radisson Blu Hotel on Calea Victoriei and was now waiting in our rooms. After dinner at the hotel restaurant, we used our free time to meet a few old friends.

The next morning, we visited Bran Castle, much appreciated for its historical value as well as for the writings of Queen Marie, who was deeply attached to this medieval castle (so different in structure from those she had known) and who discovered in it many specifically national elements. But what impressed me even more was to see on the roads the changes in the country's appearance – the impressive number of new, tall, spacious, modern buildings, wider and freshly asphalted highways, and many pedestrian overpasses especially in the villages along the route – and even the appearance of the villages themselves, which seemed to have dressed in more festive clothes.

After touring the cities of Western Europe, I feared that foreigners would see embarrassing things in my own country. But that didn't happen. Our country is more beautiful than ever, and I am proud of it. And, despite all complaints and political scandals, I conclude that Romania has made a glorious historic step forward.

21 June 2011

Album Pages

The last stop of the voyage was in Venice – the eternal Venice. Over the course of twelve days, we travelled successively through places of unique beauty, different in appearance and rich in cultural and historical traditions that breathe in every finely carved beam, in the chiseled stone, in the woven carpets and the delicacy of multicolored handkerchiefs. It was a cruise on a smaller vessel, the *Royal Princess*, which departed from Athens in Greece, toured the Black Sea and the Sea of Azov, and ended in Italy, at Venice.

At Meteora, in Greece, where clusters of rocks rise from the flat, palm-like plain to heights of several hundred meters, like gigantic stone horns pointing into the sky, the emotion literally takes your breath away. On the tops of these rocks, monks built, from brick, wood and stone, prayer sanctuaries of unique beauty and grandeur. But none of the guides or historians have ever been able to answer the question of how it was possible to transport the construction materials up there, more than seven hundred years ago, when even today professional climbers face unimaginable dangers of reaching the summit. Nowadays, a paved road connects the six operating monasteries, which are visited daily by tourists and pilgrims. It was no small surprise to meet there three young nuns who had come from Romania. The monks of Meteora are masters in painting icons, both mural and beautifully framed ones that can be bought in the small village shop – whose sellers are Romanians.

In Yalta, the road winds along the strip of land between the sea and the granite height of the Iaila Mountains until we reach Alupka Castle, built by Prince Vorontsov in 1828. Churchill and the British delegation were hosted here during the conference between the USA, Britain, and Russia. The conference between Roosevelt, Churchill and Stalin – the one that was to decide the fate of our country and all of Europe in 1945 – took place at Livadia, the Romanov summer residence, a palace with more than 100 rooms furnished in various styles and considered, by the members of the family of the last Tsar of Russia, Nicholas II, to be the place where each member of that unhappy family enjoyed the most beautiful days of their lives. Our access to the Swallow's Nest, a castle perched on a rock rising from the foam of the Black Sea, was not possible. A great pity! Nevertheless, we managed to admire its superb silhouette from a short distance, from where the grace of this unique structure could be photographed.

The visit to Odessa was no less impressive, offering the chance to admire sumptuous aristocratic palaces of pre-revolutionary Russia, such as the palace of Count Tolstoy (a cousin of the great writer), of Gagarin, of Novikov and others. Wide streets, alleys lined with century-old trees, the Potemkin Steps – made famous when the sailors of the ship of the same name revolted against their officers in 1905 – the Opera House and a gallery of statues in the city center seem to recount a period of abundant prosperity in the past of this city, which was destroyed and rebuilt after the Second World War and about which so little is known.

Istanbul reveals itself as a gigantic anthill in full activity, day, and night, hurrying incessantly along the Golden Horn and the Sea of Marmara, over which two suspension bridges – groaning under the traffic – connect the European to the Asian continent. Enormous in every sense, the city stretches beyond the horizon on both shores, home to over thirteen million people, many of whom press themselves aggressively in front of you, trying to sell you a book, a scarf, or a bundle of postcards. The most important building – Hagia Sophia – dating from 537 AD, still survives after a millennium and a half, although it required many restorations. The size, proportion, elegance, and color beauty of this classical monument of Christianity remain hard to equal even today. Facing Hagia Sophia stands the Blue Mosque, built a thousand years later, in the 16th century, which seems more like a copy of the former – despite the opulence of its marble, stained glass and tiles covering the interior. Without equal, however, are the constructions from the time of the emperor Constantine (303–337 AD), such as the Cistern of the 337 Columns – more than eight meters high and supporting a vaulted brick ceiling – remaining as evidence of the mastery of Roman civilization.

Topkapi Palace welcomes its visitors through the Ceremonial

Gate, guarded by two stone towers and crenellated walls. Inside, multiple buildings – containing the throne room, dormitories, harem, eunuchs' quarters, treasury, and annexes – began to be erected in 1472–1478, with successive additions continuing until the 19th century; yet stylistically, they are like those of earlier periods. The richness of the patterns and the coloring of the tiles that cover both the interior and exterior walls represents the most relevant testimony to the tradition and architecture of those buildings. The Covered Bazaar, as well as the Spice Bazaar, is undoubtedly one of the tourist sights that cannot be overlooked on a visit to Istanbul.

Venice, however, remains – incomparably – one of the most distinctive monuments of medieval civilization. The barbarian invasions on their way to Rome in the fifth century forced many inhabitants of the territories of Venetia, Padua, and Treviso to flee from the destructive hordes to the islands of the lagoon, in the north of the Adriatic Sea. There, the refugees built flat-bottomed boats, houses erected on piles, and floors made of stones carried from the old mainland, and lived together with their cattle, adhering to their inherited customs and traditions.

Over the years, the Lombards and the Franks tried repeatedly to subjugate the lagoon dwellers – which led to the union of the islanders and, in 829, they succeeded in stealing from Alexandria, Egypt, the body of Saint Mark the Evangelist and bringing it home as the patron of their city. In the following centuries, the Venetians continued to maintain a policy of freedom and independence, making an alliance with Byzantium against the pirates of the Adriatic and the Normans. During the Crusades, the Venetians realized the advantages of transporting the expeditions to the Holy Land, paid in gold and silver. The Fourth Crusade ended the centuries-long competition between the Venetians and the Genoese for supremacy in the Mediterranean, resulting in the victory of Venice, whose ships returned home loaded with priceless riches – merchandise, gold, spices, silk and works of art.

However, after the fall of Constantinople in 1453 and after Vasco da Gama discovered India, the islanders' supremacy at sea began to decline. In exchange, a great revival took place in the fields of construction and the arts. It was in this period that the Venice we know today took shape: St. Mark's Square was enlarged, the Doge's Palace was built, the stone Rialto Bridge – which replaced the old wooden bridge – was erected, and no fewer than 150 church belltowers were raised above the roofs of the new buildings. Centuries of decline followed, but Venice continues to inspire with its unique beauty, with the constant yearning of its people to live in freedom, and – for those who love history – with the four gilded horses adorning the terrace of St. Mark's Basilica, the symbol of the city.

8 December 2012

Lost in the World

I close my eyes, hoping to probe undisturbed into the unfathomable depth of my thoughts, which seem to jump around in a chaotic dance, making it hard for me to catch a loose thread in that tangled ball of ideas that refuses to stay still for even a moment. I see myself arriving in an unknown station, in an unknown world, without knowing where, how, or why I got here, for I don't remember ever choosing this place. I look around, knowing I cannot stay long in a station, but I have no idea where I want to go. I step aside from the path of other lost travelers and sit on a bench at the edge to analyze my situation.

I was a provincial who came from a marginal neighborhood on the outskirts of Bucharest. What did I know back then? Seen from Grant Bridge, the world looked like a distant universe, whose paths ran under that bridge and ended at one of the ten platforms of the North Railway Station. How many times did I stop, looking with a touch of envy at the happy people behind the windows of those elegant coaches, with golden inscriptions, who could travel into the wide world. How far away they seemed from me then! The passing thought that I might one day escape into the great wide world was as remote as a flight to the moon seems today.

From the Grant Bridge, the outside world seemed different: the image was grandiose and full of mystery – happy people populating cities whose buildings vanished into swirling clouds and basements lit like daylight, swarming with human bustle beneath the earth. Riches and peace draped these places in magical, heaven-like hues, and in those moments of dreaming, waking up to reality took effort to resume the walk to the butcher's shop, where one had heard that meat was being sold there. I didn't know then that fate would let for me a narrow opening to escape to West.

The provincial in me entered the Western world like Chaplin's vagabond – without a penny in my pocket, unable to speak the language of my fellow men, with no one to show me the way – a wanderer without purpose among people with stable lives, that's what I was. I knocked on doors that too often were slammed in my face – not for help, but for a job. Any job. I wanted to show them I could work, that I was capable and not afraid of hardship. And finally, I succeeded. I was hired as a maintenance worker at a luxury hotel. The manager asked me to organize the workshop with solid work benches and multiple inventory shelves—and I did so. The manager was so pleased that he called the directors to see what I had done. The directors were so pleased that they asked him to do the same in the other departments. In the end, everyone was satisfied – except my own boss. Many people came directly to me for any kind of problem, and he started to pick on me. In the end, I was dismissed. It hurt, but I gained a bit of "Canadian experience."

Other jobs followed, other lessons, and finally, after three years, I found work in my profession. The sun began to show its face again. The nest we had left "back home" transplanted itself here. Our children grew up comfortably and grew wings to fly on their own. Everything around us began to shine brightly. With new sense of purpose, we became confident and optimistic. The pride of being who we were – of being able to adapt, to learn and to respond to issues we had never faced before – made us realize our own value, which we had never appreciated before. We were happy for every new day, for every new thing we acquired, for our little home that was coming together, for everything around us and for being able to call ourselves Canadians. The dreams of our youth took on their true form here, coming to fruition beyond even our most optimistic expectations – and this feeling of fulfilment lived undisturbed in us for a long time, until we crossed the threshold of the new millennium. From then on everything began to change – even more so in the last years.

The sun still rises every morning; the days unfold as they did in the past – sometimes warm, sometimes cold – in the rhythm dictated by seasons. But in our souls, something had changed. Gloom, doubt and despair have settled. Our values are no longer the same ones we praised throughout our lives. Our children's families are built on shifting sands, without consideration to tradition, faith, and stability. Our grandchildren have their minds stuffed in schools with invented histories, worse than those planted in our heads by the communist regimes, and they are incited to destroy the world built by us and those who came before us. Today's world no longer tends to build; it buys everything from outside. Our young people, with university diplomas in their pockets, are serving McDonald's clients and find relaxation in their free time in front of dubious programs full of debauchery, rape, and violence, abundantly viewed on all TV channels. The Church lines up in political fights with social activists and pushes into the same ranks as its defamers – the atheists. And above all, the scythe of death stalks us at every street corner. Terrorists, anarchists, thieves – by profession or by inclination – madmen and vagrants raised in the sewage of ghettos where no law exists – lurk in the shadows for the opportunity to launch a deadly, indiscriminate attack, merely for self-affirmation or gain. And I am afraid. I am afraid of the inheritance I leave to our children and grandchildren; I am terrified by the world in which they will have to survive – a world that is not the one we planned and for which I toiled my entire life. I fear the imminent repetition of the biblical punishments that eradicated Sodom and Gomorrah. This time the eradication will be apocalyptic.

That is why I now see myself arriving in an unknown station, in an unknown world, without knowing where, how, or why I got here, for I do not remember having consciously chosen this place.

I sought a path to a more peaceful life and, without noticing, the road made a sudden turn, from which I no longer see how we might return to the dreamed-of world – the one I glimpsed from the Grant Bridge.

I was a provincial who came from a marginal neighborhood on the outskirts of Bucharest. I reached the summit of my dreams that uncovered the beauty of the world and Lord, please give me back the world I once dreamed!

1 September 2013

From Russia, With Love

When general confusion reaches its zenith, when reading the morning newspaper has become a tiring habit, causing more headaches than interest, and the television, too, is left somewhere muted in a corner of the room, you almost feel like forgetting everything and going somewhere far away — far from all worries, doubts and daily boredom. So, I went to the other side of the world, to Russia. There couldn't have been a better time than now, when the whole world follows with bated breath the unfolding events in Ukraine; nothing could be more interesting than finding out what the ordinary man on the street thinks about all this.

Indeed, the fourteen days spent in Russia enriched my knowledge with emotions, enjoyment, and a bag full of interesting observations.

Moscow greeted us with a dark sky, rain, and cold days. Only toward the end of our five-day stay there did the sun show itself for a short while so that we could witness, at dusk, an impressive cavalcade of war machines on their way to Red Square for a final rehearsal in front of the Kremlin, in preparation for the military parade the next day — May 9th, Victory Day over fascist Germany.

But before that, Moscow treated us to multiple tours in and around the city, a ride on the various metro lines, which allowed us to admire metro stations built during Stalin's time, and a visit to the

Kremlin, where we saw the National Armory Museum, which offers visitors, besides medieval weaponry, a rich collection of crowns, caftans, dresses, carriages and jewelry dating back as far as a thousand years.

There was also a visit to the National Museum of Cosmonautics, and many others. On the second day of the trip, we were taken to a concert of the Zlatous ensemble, held at the Ilia Glazunov Art Gallery, where one painting drew my attention: an old man with a face furrowed with deep wrinkles, whose kind smile brought light into the composition, dressed in a worn-out padded jacket on whose chest shone the Star of Socialist Labor. The jacket looked like it was blackened by work in a mine, and tufts of cotton protruded here and there through the rips.

His right hand held a raised glass of vodka, and on the wall behind him hung numerous posters and slogans featuring Gagarin, Lenin, and various fiery figures of socialist competition. The title of the painting was "To Your Health." I could not make out the painter's name, but I know the painting was on loan from the Tretyakov Gallery. The painting did not suggest the cheerfulness of a celebration, but rather the tragedy of this old man who had wasted his entire life driven by slogans – from which he was left with nothing.

His tragedy, the tragedy of a life wasted in vain, is like the tragedy of the old people in our own country – including my own generation – and this should open the eyes of those who still advocate an order sustained by slogans and lies.

Russia has remained Russia, and nothing can change it. The general mentality is that they started no war; not they, but others attacked first. They defended their country and in the end they won. It is as if a general amnesia has gripped the entire population, and I wonder how they managed to forget the invasion of Hungary on 4 November 1956, when the Soviet troops drowned the anti-communist revolution in blood. And how have they forgotten the Prague Spring, likewise crushed in the blood of the 72 Czechs and Slovaks killed by the armies of the Warsaw Pact (Romania excepted) which invaded Czechoslovakia on the night of 20–21 August 1968? And still more recently, only five years ago, between 8 and 13 August 2008, Georgia had to cede the region of South Ossetia after the brutal intervention of Russian troops, who bombed numerous towns and urban centers of the country.

Just as now in Ukraine, the main justification appears to have been the security of Russian citizens displeased with the policy of those governments. As there is no real security of borders between the former Soviet states, it is easy to infiltrate hostile elements from one side to another, and thus any referendum may be decided by a dubious majority brought in from outside.

After having visited the White House, the Pentagon, and the Kennedy Space Center, it is difficult to draw parallel with what we saw visiting the Kremlin and the National Museum of Cosmonautics. As a general rule, once inside the Kremlin, during the nearly one-kilometer walks from the entrance to the Armory Museum, the guide was strictly forbidden to give any explanations about what we were passing. We had to proceed in silence, without stopping, and photography was forbidden. Only on the return route, along a different path, was the guide allowed to explain the names of the churches inside and photographs were allowed.

The Cosmonautics Museum is surrounded by a grandiose park with numerous statues and an impressive obelisk symbolizing the launch of a Space Shuttle aircraft (American model). The museum itself, modest in size, spreads over two floors, with most exhibits in miniature models. In the lower hall there is one of the modules of the Mir Space Station, which was the largest artificial satellite of Earth – today surpassed by the International Space Station, of which it is now a part. I asked where the Canadian Arm was. The guide knew nothing of the existence of this Canadian contribution, used in every assembly maneuver of the station.

The tour ended with the appearance of a Russian cosmonaut, in the style of a press conference, who had stayed in space for six months. Someone asked whether the Americans had really been the first to reach the moon. His answer was a categorical YES – but, he added, the Americans made the mistake of broadcasting to the public a stage production filmed in a television studio with Neil Armstrong proclaiming that it was "one small step for a man, one giant leap for mankind." (No comment.)

During the fourteen days of our visit to Russia, we stayed on board a tourist vessel traveling between Moscow and St. Petersburg on various canals, including the Volga and the Onega and Ladoga lakes, and finally the Neva River. Russia possesses infinite wealth in art, culture, and folklore. Their hospitality is proverbial and offered with warmth. In the two major cities, Moscow and St. Petersburg, life pulses with untamed energy day and night. The streets are flooded with endless lines of modern cars, and the pace of new construction is visible everywhere. Almost everyone has a cottage (dacha) outside the city where they grow their own vegetables and fruit. As I said, Russia has remained Russia, only slightly different from before — where Stalin, Brezhnev and now Putin are regarded with esteem, respect, and a great deal of trust in their words and their policies.

31 May 2014

Pagoda

I had no intention of describing what I saw—or did not see—in the land of the Japanese, because, within the space limitations of a newspaper, I would only create more confusion than clarity. But after the disheartening performance of the Conservative Party candidate during the first debate for the presidency of the United States, sadness made me choose this subject after all. A similar sadness made me speak up in front of a group of Americans who were visiting the "ground zero" site of the second nuclear bomb explosion over the city of Nagasaki, which definitively ended the horrors of the Second World War.

It was a day in mid-September, in which the heat and humidity competed to push the mercury up the thermometer. Inside the nearby Atomic Bomb Museum, hundreds of schoolchildren in blue and white uniforms followed the spiral route that descends, accompanied by documents and photographs, toward the place where horror can no longer be described in words. Films, models, and remnants from that day in 1945 revealed atrocities that shook visitors to the core, no matter their age or gender.

I read placards, statements and watched the films; I followed all the documents and suffered along with all the others — but nowhere did I see any indication that the militarist Japanese government was repeatedly warned to stop its aggressive actions in the region and to renounce war. Even after the explosion of the first atomic bomb over Hiroshima, Japan continued to fight America with all the arsenal at its disposal, causing new victims and taking prisoners. I was stunned to read one panel stating that: *"President Truman wanted to evaluate the destructive power of the atomic bomb created as a result of investments in the Manhattan Project."* That, and nothing more — not one word about the Japanese attack on Pearl Harbor, nor about the horrifying war crimes in China and Korea — yet the visitors and generations of children leave this museum overwhelmed by the idea of cruelties committed by the Americans against a supposedly "peaceful" people like the Japanese. This kind of propaganda is inflammatory and disgusting.

Last year, in August, seventy years passed since Japan's capitulation after the two atomic bombs. At ground zero, the park is surrounded by monuments from many countries, most of them from the former communist bloc, to which have been added Cuba, Brazil, Portugal, and others.

But I was stunned to find, recently, a monument erected by the United States. (Apparently President Obama, after visiting Nagasaki, wanted to leave behind an apologetic memorial.) Many years ago, when I visited Hiroshima, the United States, England, France, and other Western countries had no monument at ground zero.

When I commented on this in my group of visitors, a mature person reproached me for daring to offer such an offence to the Americans. People tend to forget who the aggressors were and who the real victims are. The museums and the media continue to misinform the public — and this is surprising, coming from those considered to be allies.

I respect Japan and envy the ingenuity, seriousness and energy with which the Japanese transformed a country that, seven decades ago, had been completely shattered and deprived of economic and material resources, yet in just a few years managed to contribute to global progress with high-quality products, placing itself in the front line of scientific and technological development. Three decades ago, I saw cohorts of Japanese technicians in the great international machinery fairs; with notebooks in their hands, measuring tools and cameras, they were climbing all over the exhibited machines — American, German, English, etc. — and then, two years later, I was shocked to see the exhibition halls already filled with Japanese products.

In the mid-1980s, I was involved in the purchase of a 1000-ton Aida transfer press with six stations and two movable beds, which allowed the change of production programs in only seven minutes. For almost fifteen years, that press was the pivot of our company's survival in the competitive world of first-class production at a reduced price.

During my recent visit throughout Japan, I found that this nation deserves admiration for what it has achieved — for its roads, its tunnels, its imposing buildings in all regions of the country and its achievements in all fields. From shipbuilding to high-speed trains, cybernetics and electronics, the Japanese can pride themselves on major accomplishments and on a peaceful, spiritual, and civilized way of life.

Passing through Tokyo, I noticed in passing many enterprises — such as Toshiba — occupying imposing multi-story buildings with not a single window. I knew that many of these are fully automated and therefore operate in complete darkness. I recall an old joke: it is said that such a factory had only two employees — a man and a dog. The man's duty was to check that all the machinery functioned properly, and the dog's duty was to make sure the man didn't touch anything.

In their religion, Buddhism is respected more as a principle of life and coexistence with all other beings than as a strict religion. Shintoism brings them closer to nature, through the veneration of nature's divinities, the cult of heroes and ancestors — in a sense similar to that of Canadian aboriginals. By interweaving these two concepts, they achieve a spiritual balance that animates them to cope with daily reality. The pagoda is a pyramidal building with several tiers, patterned on the South-Asian stupa. These levels represent earth, water, fire, air, and the sun, which is an element of space. On this highest level of the pagoda are housed the sacred remains of Buddha, to be worshipped forever. Here are gathered the aspirations of the Far-Eastern world, waiting for a sign of association from the rest of the surrounding world, to live together in peace and understanding.

The pagoda could become a universal symbol. The world is hungry to find solutions to problems that today trouble every person who is concerned about the future and the fate of those who follow us. Trump's blunders do not encourage any optimism regarding the resolution of the present Gordian Knot — rather, they deepen our pessimism. But neither would the election of Hillary Clinton as president of the world's greatest power bring much reason for hope.

Above every pagoda, our destinies remain in the hands of the One on High.

27 September 2016

A Holiday Like No Other

Age, blame it! Insurance for a trip abroad is another pain that adds as a few others on the usual list that couldn't be neglected. But this year, since I was on the same list of medications as last year, the cost of insurance was more lenient, I went to Arizona for two weeks, where the atmosphere is dry, which helps rheumatism.

That's how we ended up in Phoenix, after a flight with Air Canada on a packed airplane, where we barely managed to get the last two seats, on the very last row next to the toilets, for luck of reservation in advance. Now seat reservations require an extra fee. After a night in a hotel, we found on Trivago—advertised as the cheapest at $165 without breakfast—I was glad to be able to explore the city center on foot the next morning, on a splendid March day, just right for celebrating St. Patrick's Day.

Our walk was rewarded with the sight of modern constructions around the intersection of Centre Street and Buckeye Road. From there we could appreciate the perfectly parallel and perpendicular street grid, shining with cleanliness, and the magnificent shop windows of this elegant commercial center—small enough to be covered on foot in one morning, with necessary stops for a coffee at a café table placed in the shade on the sidewalk. That's how we came to admire the opera building, surrounded by life-sized bronze statues, the cathedral, and—no less important—the Rosson House in Heritage Square, built between 1895 and 1915 in the Victorian style, around which the Phoenix University complex was later established.

With a rented car we made our way to our final destination, a tourist resort in the White Mountains, on a huge plateau more than two thousand meters above sea level, in the locality of Pinetop. What surprised us was that, despite the altitude, vegetation was as rich as in the lowlands, and the resort buildings were positioned so that each cabin had its living room and balconies facing an immense pine forest with trees over thirty meters high. In this cozy living room, equipped with a gas fireplace and a large window almost spanning the whole width of the wall, I was amazed to see, right in front of these glorious trees, a gently descending slope with a quiet stream, and then, rising again, the forest stretching as far as the eye could see. Every evening, I waited eagerly for the appearance of Labiş's doe from his poem *The Death of the Deer*, coming to drink a mouthful of water—but she never showed.

Instead, old friends from home whom we hadn't seen in almost twenty years came from California to spend a few days with us, and the joy of reuniting poured into every fiber of our being, along with memories of our youth, of adventures and excursions taken together in days when it felt like the whole world belonged to us.

Fort Apache is in the heart of an Indian reservation bearing the same name, an hour away from us. In a meticulously chosen strategic location, the fort played an important role around 1870 in protecting American settlers in the Far West from the Indian warriors who were continuously forced to cede their lands to the whites. Inside, many original buildings remain—the headquarters and wooden annexes—but the most important part is the presentation at the visitor center, where a member of the local tribe speaks about the culture and beliefs of his people.

Two hours to the north, near Holbrook, lies the Petrified Forest—a monumental treasure of evidence spanning from prehistoric times to the present, a tapestry of colors and layers exposed in strata over millions of years, from the Triassic period, enriching our knowledge with fossil traces from bygone eras. This National Park, covering 52,000 acres, is crossed by a road over fifty miles long, with numerous viewing stops allowing tourists to admire the vestiges of past epochs.

Some 255 million years ago, this region was a tropical plain with lush vegetation, dinosaurs, fish, giant reptiles, and tall trees up to sixty meters. But over the next two hundred million years, the continents shifted, new regions rose up, the climate changed along with the river systems, burying plants and animals in sediment layers that, over time, absorbed various minerals, became fossilized, and petrified. Scattered across the park, parts of these prehistoric trees—now transformed into marble-like formations in unimaginable colors—can be admired and even purchased at the Rainbow Forest Museum or the Agate House near the entrance.

At the end of the route, we reach the *Painted Desert*, where the color layers cut by dried canyons look like a sliced layer cake, allowing us to admire the stratifications—from white, orange, and red, to blue.

To reach Montezuma Castle, you must head north on Highway 17, near Camp Verde. In a hollow in the mountainside, thirty meters above the valley floor, the natives built, some 8–nine hundred years ago, a structure of stone and mortar with five levels and twenty rooms. The first Americans who discovered it believed it to have been built by the Aztecs and therefore named it Montezuma. In fact, it was built by farmers who, during the torrential rains that filled the fertile basin of the region, sought refuge there in safety.

A little further north lies the modern town of Sedona—an exquisite spa resort surrounded by ruby-colored mountains in breathtaking shapes and formations that cannot be described, but which constitute one of the key sights on the list of every lover of nature and urban planning.

And, bearing in mind that Arizona is also home to the famous Grand Canyon—with the picturesque Colorado River winding along its bottom—and the mountain formations of Monument Valley in Navajo Park, made famous by the western films, I don't think I'm wrong to recommend to readers *a vacation like no other* in this region. As for insurance costs, medical bills and flight new-invented charges, let forget them all, for we came richer than expected in our souls.

3 May 2017

Jerusalem

President Trump, fulfilling one of his campaign promises, has recognized Jerusalem as the capital of the State of Israel and has decided to move the United States embassy to the city. In addition to the international storm caused by this decision and despite it, many other states such as Czechoslovakia, Guatemala and Romania, are willing to recognize Jerusalem as the capital of the Israeli nation. What is it that drives these countries to respond so promptly to this highly controversial statement? Nothing more than the desire for justice.

For far too long, humanity seems to have ignored the legitimate right of the Jews to reclaim the land of their ancestors, after a sinister fate and the expansionist ambitions of rival great powers drove them into exile to the furthest horizons. They were scattered like leaves blown by the storm to all latitudes of the world, forced over two thousand years to endure antisemitic hatred, the fury of repeated pogroms encouraged by the authorities and, ultimately, to face death in concentration camps. Now, seventy years after the proclamation of the State of Israel, the United Nations still refuses to acknowledge the legitimate right of this people to return to their ancestral homeland, just as it refuses them the right to establish their capital in the city of David—Jerusalem.

The fate of this city, one of the oldest in the world, has

endured—like the Jewish people themselves—over the course of four millennia, periods of brilliance, arousing the envy of many powers, as well as times of misery, cruelty, and ruin. Throughout its long history, Jerusalem was destroyed twice, besieged twenty-three times, attacked fifty-two times, and captured and recaptured forty-four times. It retains the testimony of the struggle to preserve faith in the one God—faith which, in many cases, was desecrated by the worship of idols created by man, and was severely punished, as the Bible tells us, by disease, plague, war and disaster.

The golden age during the reigns of King David and Solomon—glorified for the transfer of the capital of the united Israelite kingdom to Jerusalem in 1006 BC by David, and the building of the First Temple by Solomon—was the reward for their loyalty to God and for their contribution to the strengthening of the state and of the faith. The palace of King David and the First Temple—both now documented by recent excavations—illustrate the level of culture and refinement reached in those times.

After the death of King Solomon in 926 BC, tensions between the northern and southern tribes led to the separation of the state into two kingdoms. In the north, the Kingdom of Israel, conquered by the Assyrians in 722 BC; and in the south, the Kingdom of Judah, with its capital in Jerusalem, which remained independent until 586 BC, when it fell to the Babylonians under Nebuchadnezzar. He destroyed Jerusalem and the Temple and ordered the deportation and dispersal of tens of thousands of inhabitants to Babylon.

The word of the Lord and His messages have always been brought to the faithful by the prophets of the time, who were considered true leaders of the church and guides of the people. After the destruction of the First Temple and the death of Isaiah, the disoriented crowd—without guidance and under pressure from the idolaters of Babylon—fell into bondage. Having lost their connection to God, they paid dearly for losing their faith. It was only seventy years after the death of Nebuchadnezzar and the fall of Babylon to the Persians that forty–two thousand exiles returned from captivity and driven by a strong religious impulse, attempted to rebuild the Temple. But it could not be completed until Darius I became King of Persia, in 522 BC.

The Second Temple was consecrated in 516 BC by the prophets Haggai and Zechariah, who prophesied that "the glory of this Temple will be greater than that of the first," even though Israel was under foreign occupation.

When Persia was defeated by Alexander the Great in 332 BC, Judaism came under Hellenistic philosophical influences, which caused deterioration in the relations between Hellenized Jews and orthodox Jews. The orthodox group revolted and, under the leadership of the Maccabees, created in Judea the Hasmonean dynasty, which lasted from 165 to 37 BC, when the Romans, under

Pompey, occupied Judea.

Under Roman rule, Herod was one of the great kings of Judea, extending his domination as far as Arabia, initiating many construction projects and renovating the Second Temple. After his death, in 4 BC, taxes, the interruption of construction and the discontent of an impoverished population led to the first revolt against Rome.

It was against this background that Christianity emerged. Christ became, for many, a guide, a prophet, and the Son of God. The Christian disciples brought the word of the Lord with fervor throughout the world, spreading Christianity everywhere among peoples hungry for hope in a better and more just world.

After the Romans, during the Byzantine era, the Church of the Holy Sepulcher was built. Later, Jerusalem was captured by the Arabs in 638 and Palestine was transformed into a caliphate. The Arabs built the Dome of the Rock—with its golden roof—on the foundation of the Second Temple destroyed by the Romans, thereby creating the indestructible physical unity of the three great religions in an inseparable embrace. During the first crusade, the Jewish and Muslim defenders of the city were massacred, and the population fell below 2,000.

The city, crowded with pilgrims from all over the world and under the protection of the Knights Templar and Hospitallers, was transformed into the Kingdom of Jerusalem. But in 1187 the Muslim rush under Saladin drenched Christendom in blood. Other crusades followed, then Ottoman rule, followed by British rule and, finally, the struggle for the independence of Israel.

The biblical prophecies of the Old and New Testaments foresee the return of the chosen people to the city of David as a sign of the time of the Savior's return to dispense justice on earth. The permanent attachment of the Jews to the Holy City of Jerusalem has been a dominant desire passed down from generation to generation because there lies the source of this people's survival.

4 January 2018

Canada, a Paradise Under the Northern Star

You don't know where I am right now? I'm in southern Alberta, in a resort called Paradise Canyon, located at the bottom of a canyon about thirty meters deep, where the waters of a river called The Old Man River give life to the prairie along nearly four hundred kilometers. What am I doing here? I'm on vacation. I got behind the wheel in Toronto and in four days I arrived here. But that's not what I want to tell: the real story is to be able to put into words the emotion of the beauty of the places crossed over the 3400 kilometers, following the sinuous route of Highway 17, the "Trans Canada Highway," on which I had never driven before.

The picturesque lakes carefully skirted by the road, the endless forests and the bare rocks often split by human hand where the highway had to push through the vast distances, brought delight to our souls hungry for natural beauty and that divine tranquility that only the silence of nature can offer. In the northern part of Ontario province, towards Thunder Bay, circling Lake Superior, there are so many places where, instinctively, you want to stop, even just for a few minutes, to absorb— with your eyes, with your breath and with your heart — the unique landscape unexpectedly encountered along the way. In the old European continent, places like these would have been carefully exploited, and millions of tourists from all over the world would endlessly swarm through, appreciating their beauty.

Here, however, only a few people bring their little boats to these places and, except for a few inns, lodges, and some sparsely spread campgrounds along the road, you see nothing.

After an overnight stay, the winding road carries us west, for three hundred kilometers, to Dryden, through a lonely wilderness where, aside from the beauty of the landscape peppered with lakes and forests, there isn't a single house, settlement, gas station, or rest stop for a glass of water or other necessities. After Kenora, we enter Manitoba, a land of different character, where the plain is vast and smooth like a sheet of paper, with an azure, circular sky arching over the green fields. The Trans Canada Highway widens to two lanes in each direction, with a maximum speed of 110 km/h, and stretches out in a straight line like a laser beam.

At the gas station, we can hardly believe our eyes in surprise: the cost of gasoline is thirty cents per liter lower than in Ontario. Across the sea of fields as far as the eye can see, the domes shining in the sun like church spires turn out to be grain silos, often seen along the road. Passing Regina, in Saskatchewan, the flat field begins to roll with gentle hills and valleys, and the road climbs a steady slope, announcing from hundreds of kilometers away the approach of the Alberta mountains.

Lethbridge is the third-largest city in Alberta, after Edmonton and Calgary. It is in the southern part of the province, has a population of 93,000 and lies only 130 kilometers from the Canadian Rocky Mountain range. This is the resort where I now find myself. Naturally, the attraction of the mountains cannot be ignored, so we chose the shortest route to them: Waterton Glacier National Park.

The unimaginable beauty of the glacier-fed chain of lakes, in which endless mountain ranges exceeding three thousand meters in height are reflected and extend beyond the borders of Alberta into British Columbia and, to the south, into Montana, which hosts Glacier National Park.

As a landmark, I chose the Prince of Wales Lodge, built in 1926–1927 by the Canada Pacific Railway, on a hill overlooking upper Waterton Lake. It was named Prince of Wales in honor of the man who would become King Edward VIII of England, who later abdicated in favor of his brother, King George VI, father of Queen Elizabeth II. Built of timber in Alpine style, with four stories, it looks more like a Bavarian castle transplanted to Canada.

A true paradise of countless species of plants and animals that enliven this inexhaustible treasure of unique beauty, which at every turn reveals new facets of grandeur — waterfalls and eternal ice on the peaks. The park is at the same time the birthplace of the great rivers that cross the continent to the west, east and south. The Colorado River empties into the Pacific, the Saskatchewan flows across the prairie to Hudson Bay, and the Missouri reaches the Gulf of Mexico, joining the Mississippi.

More than anything, here we see traces of human presence going back thousands of years, extending into southern Alberta, where natives — the Nappi tribes, known as the Blackfoot — once ruled these rich lands with inexhaustible natural resources, plants, and animals. The bison provided clothing, food, and shelter because the hides were used for the famous circular tents. Just like their forerunners, the mammoths, the bison disappeared when the white man, building the railroad, discovered a new form of amusement: buffalo hunting not for sustenance but merely for sport.

Rich in resources and history, the region of the Crowsnest Pass was and remains an important coal basin that supplied both the continent and Europe during the period of industrialization at the start of the 20th century. Numerous mines opened in the region became places of work for many immigrants; many, tempted by better wages than in other occupations, built houses, families, and villages here and there. One of them, the village of Frank, founded at the foot of Turtle Mountain, was instantly buried at sunrise — as people were still asleep — on April 29, 1903, under the rocks that broke loose when an entire mountain slope collapsed onto the village. The catastrophe resulted in at least ninety deaths and many injuries.

Visitors to the region will be occupied discovering many other places of great historical and cultural importance, such as Head–Smashed–In Buffalo Jump, a prehistoric site illustrating the collective buffalo hunting of the First Nations, forcing them — terrified by Indians wearing wolf heads — to jump over a deep cliff. But, above all else, the Trans Canada Highway has grown like the string of a necklace, linking— from one edge to the other — indescribable gems, villages, cities, and natural monuments between the two oceans, Atlantic and Pacific.

25 June 2018

The Persistence of the Yellow Flowers

On the small patch of land behind the house, the plush carpet of mown grass felt pleasant to the bare feet of the children as they chased the ball in the height of summer. Back then, our pride—and that of the neighbors who had given up fencing off their properties as a sign of good neighborliness, was that soft and even lawn on which their children and ours could play freely. In time, the children grew up, we got older, the city council decreed a ban on the use of poisonous herbicides, and the grass behind the house became speckled with yellow flowers that resist every attempt to get rid of them. I was reminded of those flowers now, upon returning from my second trip to China, sixteen years after the first.

I first visited China with a group of American tourists in 2002, shortly after September 11th. It was a gala reception, with high-ranking officials and an official banquet held in a building near Tiananmen Square, as a sign of hospitality and encouragement of tourism from Uncle Sam's country.

We visited Shanghai and the surrounding areas, Xian—where the entire city seemed transformed into a giant construction site, but where we were surprised with the encounter of the famous terracotta warriors, their history commented in a cautious tone—and then, back in Beijing, we went to the Great Wall, the Forbidden City, and the gardens of the Summer Palace.

Once given free time in Tiananmen Square—which at that time was practically deserted—a group of Chinese visitors from the eastern provinces surrounded us and asked to have their picture taken with us, both in groups and individually, leaving us with the impression that photos with us were more important than the Forbidden City in front of which we were standing.

During our recent tour we found a completely changed China, as if a miraculous metamorphosis had taken place, equivalent to the rebirth of Italy in the Middle Ages. A modern, dynamic world, in full motion, with new kinds of vehicles of European and American production rolling along wide and well-maintained boulevards and roads lined with flowers. Pedestrians were well dressed, fashionable, stylish women, and civilized-looking young people—no tattoos, no ragged clothing, and no rings in noses, ears, or eyebrows—surrounded by streets flanked by imposing buildings of dozens of stories, of various architectural styles radiating balance, imagination, and enviable beauty.

In Shanghai, the skyline has grown with new constructions breaking the 500-meter barrier, including one that exceeds six hundred meters. Public transport is provided by subways, buses and, in certain cities, monorails gliding along a single concrete beam at high elevation, connecting directly to department stores and other points of interest.

The route between central Shanghai and the airport is serviced by the magnetic levitation train, without friction, which covers the 60-kilometer distance at 431 km/h in just 7 minutes, coming every 10 minutes. The bullet train, which took us from Shanghai to Yichang for a five-day cruise on the Yangtze River, runs at over 250 km/h.

The ship, *The Goddess Cruise*, with many spacious and clean cabins, hosted, in addition to our group, many Chinese tourists who seemed to hold responsible positions, but here, as in other hotels, they were noisy and elbowed their way ahead of others at the food counter.

The construction of the six dams on the Yangtze River covers only partially the ever-growing need for electricity, but it is a significant accomplishment for China, especially considering that numerous settlements along the river have been flooded and tens of thousands of families had to be relocated to new apartments in the newly built towns along the mountain slopes. People seem animated by China's economic momentum and eagerly await the creation of new industries, roads, canals and links with remote regions, although they openly admit that they are forced to steal technology and know-how from Western researchers, because they have neither the resources nor the time to perfect their own research.

The foreign visitor is overwhelmed by the splendor of the

landscapes among the mountain gorges, where the river and its tributaries glide peacefully around us. Once, these tributaries were only little strips of water meandering among rocks, but now, after the dam, with the water level raised by more than three meters and filling the valleys, they have become navigable rivers. China's history and cultural heritage are everywhere, especially in the quiet places along the lakes and rivers, in the picturesque form of pagodas, numerous prayer houses, old tea houses and the many statues— some of them celebrating communist ideology.

We attended two sold-out productions, in the style of Cirque du Soleil, one of which in Beijing was unforgettable, featuring, live on the open stage, a waterfall with an impressive water flow, cascading right to the feet of the spectators.

Achievements of this kind, I believe, can only be created in a system where there is no opposition, where any order coming from "above" is an undeniable law for everyone and executed at all costs. This is visible on every street corner through the presence of police cars, the taking of photographs and digital fingerprints in airports, and the many black uniforms everywhere—and especially in Beijing, the city that houses the Party leadership. Pedestrian movement in certain areas is restricted by cords, even though Tiananmen Square, the Forbidden City and the Summer Palace are now packed with tourists and nationals from everywhere.

China's political and economic influence is present in every corner of the globe, becoming truly the second power of the world. The policy of the American administration to demand that NATO member states pay their contributions to the alliance has caused discontent in Europe and a kind of vacuum— which China is quick to fill. Just like the yellow flowers in the garden behind my house, it will be difficult to uproot once they have taken hold.

January 27, 2019

About People

Alchemy

I don't know how easy it is for some people, but whenever I must write an article, I spend days searching for an argument that might lead the reader into the labyrinth of my ideas. This time, I was luckier; the argument burst forth miraculously when I least expected it. Alchemy – the science of transforming lead into gold. Why? Well, isn't that exactly what we need today? Ask our honorable Prime Minister, who has burdened us with taxes even worse than the Turks did back a century in Europe. Because of him people sit in the dark in their houses, afraid of the smart electricity meters with double-rate pricing exactly at the hours when one most needs electricity. Or the Minister of Finance, who wonders why the costs of identical goods are higher here than in the United States now that our dollar is equal with theirs? Has he forgotten what taxes he imposed on the border? Or what can our politicians say about the price of Canadian gasoline, which is sold in the United States well below the price we pay here? And let's not even mention Mr. Obama, who sees himself as a new Robin Hood, plucking the wealthy through taxes so he can help the poor.

Yes, **Alchemy** is the subject I need. Science or myth, if it could produce gold in our days, alchemy might pull us out of the troubles that abound around us. Who isn't worried about the steep path down which all the world's economies are sliding? Who isn't scared today of the terrifying predictions of darkness suggested in the near future, out of which rotten miasmas of poverty, corruption, and wasted lives in senseless struggles appear like ghosts, disturbing our days? If faith in God will not help us out of this situation, then maybe the solution must be found elsewhere: *Alchemy*.

In fact, the alchemy we learned in school was viewed as a parody of science, some kind of tool in the hands of charlatans to fool the naive into believing they could transform ordinary metals into gold and silver. That was largely true. But very few people know that alchemy was not only a science, but also the source from which true science developed – chemistry, medicine and, more than that, a philosophy.

Alchemy was born in Egypt, due to their belief in life after death and the practice of mummification, which helped them discover new preserving substances. Almost nineteen hundred years before our era, *Hermes Trismegistus*, a pharaoh renowned for his wisdom and knowledge of nature, wrote numerous books, only a few of which have survived – among them the *Emerald Tablet* (*Tabula Smaragdina*). The Tablet claims that matter is unique and that all forms of manifestation derive from a single root, a single thing, a single ether. Unfortunately, most of his writings (and those of others) were destroyed during the burning of the Library of Alexandria in the fourth century AD.

At the same time, in China, research with positive results was being conducted, aimed at lengthening life through natural remedies and physical exercises. Isolated from the world by their famous wall, this science developed only locally. In India as well, research led to significant discoveries, such as inventing steel and identifying metals by the color of the flame they produced. The next name, recognized as the most important after Hermes, is that of *Jabir* (Geber), who lived around 750 AD, born in Mesopotamia, author of over five hundred works, of which only three remain. He was the first to describe components of corrosive sublimates, red mercury oxide, and silver nitrate.

In the same period, another Arab alchemist, *Rhasis*, became famous for his technique of transmuting a base metal into gold. *Al-Farabi* was the most learned man of his time, as was *Avicenna* (Abu Sina), born in Bukhara in 980 AD, who concludes the list of great Arab alchemists. After occupying Spain, the Moors introduced the first alchemical knowledge in Europe.

In 12th-century Europe, *Artephius* wrote *The Art of Extending Human Life* and is said to have lived one thousand years, learning the craft from the books of Hermes. The 13th century brought numerous authors in the hermetic science: *Adolph of Castile*, *William of Loris*, *Jean de Meung*, and *Arnold of Villanova*, who studied medicine in Paris but was also a prestigious theologian and alchemist. The experiments of alchemists suffered under the

Inquisition, being accused of witchcraft. Many were tortured and burned at the stake.

Albertus Magnus (1234–1314) retired to a cell and devoted himself to studies. When he died, his disciple *Aquinas* wrote in *The Treasury of Alchemy* about Albert's and his own successes in the art of transmutation of metals into gold.

Ramon Llull, with a volume of 486 writings covering topics ranging from grammar to rhetoric, medicine, theology – and the first important author of Catalan literature – was born in Mallorca in 1232. In 1263, Llull had a revelation which led him to monastic life and a mission to convert the Muslims to Christianity. He learned Arabic from his own slave and went to Africa to accomplish it. He later met Arnold of Villanova who found Llull's book, *The Great Art*. He is said to have discovered the *Philosopher's Stone*, which made him become a zealous Christian. *Lapis Philosophorum*, in Latin, is a substance capable of turning base metals into gold or silver but can also be used as an elixir of life, creating rejuvenation or even immortality. It is a symbol of everything that can be perfect and radiant. Llull died in 1315 aboard a ship on his way to Mallorca.

Examples continue throughout the years, and many people succeeded in obtaining this *Philosopher's Stone*, either through personal experiments or after being entrusted with it by someone whose confidence they had won. Many seekers were condemned, endured terrible torment, perished in flames and derision.

Between the Inquisition on one side and greedy kings on the other, this was the price paid by those zealous researchers to whom we owe not only our esteem, but also numerous discoveries from which we benefit today. After them, right up into the last century, the list of those who delved into hermetic science continues, with many attempts at transmutation and equally many medical wonders.

The common denominator of these lives, without exception, leads to the conclusion that they were driven along this path by spiritual motives, not material ones. They were inspired by the vision of a perfect human being, freed from disease, freed from limitations of physical or mental faculties, and endowed with a high degree of conscientiousness.

Perhaps today, even among us, anonymous and modest, there are descendants or disciples of hermetic philosophy. If you know someone who meets the qualities above, please let me know.

September 26, 2011

What Canada Gave Us

Thirty-seven years ago, in the refugee camp at Lavrion, Greece, among us, those waiting for an immigration visa to Canada, a joke was circulating: "As the bible tells, after Moses managed to lead the Jews out of slavery from Egypt, God asked him where he wanted to take them. Moses, who was a little lisping, began to stutter: Ca… can… ca-na… The Lord, losing patience, took the word out of his mouth and said: I understand, Moses. You want Canaan. Canaan shall be yours! Unfortunately, Moses had in mind to ask for Canada, but it was too late."

Arriving in Toronto, in May 1975, we were lodged first at the Victoria Hotel on Yonge Street, across from the O'Keefe Centre. The days were warm, the streets swarming with cars, we had received some money from the immigration office, but not knowing the language and not knowing anyone in this city, we did not know where to go to buy something to eat. Saturdays and Sundays were even worse, because all the shops around us were closed, and the windows covered with curtains, behind which nothing could be seen. And somehow, I also came down with galloping pneumonia, with fever and chills, which kept me in bed for more than a week. Luckily, an acquaintance from the camp gave me the number of Dr. Dinu Dumitriu, who immediately came to see me at the hotel and got me back on my feet.

Thanks to the immigration office, which allocated us our first money in Canada, we were directed to go to Welcome House and enrolled at George Brown College for English language courses, we were able to settle in our first Canadian home and, shortly thereafter, obtain our first jobs. I, at a hotel, in maintenance, and my wife, at a jewelry factory, as a polisher of tiny gold objects. We were, however, happy, and the few household items we had, bought in installments from Sears, represented all that could be most refined in our home and, when we met with our friends from the camp, our only acquaintances, we marveled that we could be so lucky to live in such conditions, only a few months after our arrival here. For who could have imagined that, after the experience back home, where the shortage of housing was a chronic problem, upon arriving in Canada we would be able to live in an elegant building with many floors, in a bright apartment, equipped with all necessities, whose rent could be paid from our minimum wages, without the fear of not having food. No, in our generation, of those who went through the camp, I know no one who was dissatisfied with the Canadian welcome, with any lack of interest from the authorities, or with the lack of opportunities, although no one managed, at the beginning, to work in their field of experience. That came years and years later.

Today, as veterans, we look back with pride at the success of our lives, incomparable with the other lives of those who remained in the country, limited by ever-growing needs, because of shortages, the most important of which was the lack of possibilities for growth and a better life. We look with pride at the successes of our children, raised here, educated here, and who have become honored members of the communities in which they live and work. And, with the same pride, I raise my eyes toward the third generation, the children of our children, who grow under the shining sun of Canada, true Canadians, who will carry with them, further on, our banner—of honest work, of fulfilled duty, and of faith in God.

1 July 2012

A Man

Next to me, a young woman with an infant in her arms, who I don't think was more than two months old. Her husband, in the crowd of the airplane, was trying to settle her with the luggage and everything needed, because his seat was all the way on the opposite side of the plane. The stewardess was begging passengers, without success, to exchange seats with them, so they could be placed next to each other, after my wife and I had given up our aisle seats, where there was more space around. The flight from Amsterdam to Toronto was going to be long, the fatigue exhausting for anyone, but for the newborn the noise, the bustle around, and the cramped place in economy class would be intolerable. Being together with her husband would have been easier both for the child and for them. In the end, an elderly gentleman gave up his seat and sat next to me, in the woman's place. I commented with my wife on the generosity of this humane man, in contrast to the others around, who, although traveling alone, did not want to give up the lukewarm comfort of the seat into which they had settled.

The gentleman next to me asked what language we were speaking. I told him we were Romanians. He wanted to know if we were coming from the country. I told him that we were returning from the end of the world. Indeed, we were returning from a cruise through the Norwegian fjords, which had taken us all the way to the

North Cape, the northernmost point of the European continent, far beyond the Arctic Circle.

That is how we met the gentleman next to us, the physicist Walter Hardy, from Vancouver, who was returning home after an absence of six months in Geneva, where he had collaborated on some experiments at CERN (European Council for Nuclear Research). Thanks to Dan Brown's book *Angels and Demons*, I had enough information to launch into a volley of questions on the subject: "What do you think of Dan Brown's book? Can his scenario about antimatter be real?" I asked. "Oh, but that's not the only book written about CERN. There must already be more than half a dozen, but they are in the realm of fantasy. There are many things that are not yet known; concrete answers do not come easily." "But very recently I read that at CERN they succeeded in obtaining atoms of anti-helium and anti-hydrogen. Isn't that true?" (While I was in the plane with Mr. Walter N. Hardy, from the University of British Columbia, I did not know that he was one of the 40 members of the international ALPHA group, which announced for the first time, in Geneva, on April 26, 2011, that they had managed to trap 309 atoms of anti-hydrogen for a period of 1000 seconds or 17 minutes – see the article *'Antimatter atoms trapped for 16 minutes'* by Emily Chung – CBC News.)

Our discussion continued to advance with questions and answers interrupted by the pause for serving the usual meal or drinks, but each time, without suspecting the identity of this gentleman, modest, shy as a teenager, whose answers left no doubt, although they were spoken without the superiority of a know-it-all. He told me about the research carried out at CERN on the Large Hadron Collider (LHC), which has the shape of a tunnel with a circumference of twenty-seven kilometers and is buried underground, at a depth of one hundred meters, between the border of France and Switzerland. A true technological wonder, which mobilized unique engineering and financial efforts, considering that for lowering one of the numerous parts of an important detector, each weighing over two thousand tons, a special construction crane had to be rented from Belgium.

Since 1954, the date when CERN was founded, and today, the scientific collaboration of the twenty member countries has brought humanity numerous discoveries, whose merits cannot be overlooked. One of the most important achievements is the creation of the World Wide Web (www.com), at Meyrin, Switzerland, the most powerful data-processing equipment, which makes experimental results available to all humanity and has become the most important communication network on the entire planet.

Returning to antimatter, already in medicine and in many other disciplines practical applications have been introduced. In medical imaging Positron Emission Tomography (PET), Gamma Rays, and Positive Beta Decay are used. Experiments with antiprotons promise the cure of certain cancers in a method like that currently used in Proton Therapy. Groups formed of experts from all corners of the world continue to work at this huge international laboratory, trying to find answers to each problem that arises, a solution in the face of each obstacle, and although the road is difficult, each new day brings a fragment of hope that the time, effort, and fatigue have not been spent in vain. Potentially, antimatter could be the energy source of the future, much more powerful than any energy source known today, and could constitute the fuel of interplanetary flights in a reduced volume, but with excess energy. At the same time, antimatters can be used as one of the deadliest weapons of mass destruction.

We parted in Toronto from Professor Dr. Hardy, we are going home, he in transit to Vancouver. We promised to continue the discussion on the web and wished each other success and health. Coming home, I looked up his name on the Internet: Walter N. Hardy, Professor in the Department of Physics and Astronomy at UBC, author of 513 publications, collaborator, and co-author of 762 publications and cited by other authors 1389 times.

I remember, ashamed, that I asked him why he doesn't write a book, to which he replied that he had helped others to write. But I cannot help asking myself why a man of such value, representing all of Canada, with his has most glorious results in science research and technology, was not granted an honest seat in business class of the flight by our government? If he had been a Hollywood star, a celebrity, or a soccer player, there would have been no problem finding funds for his best accommodation. Instead, Professor Dr. Hardy had to pay from his pocket for the transportation cost after such an important mission from which all of us will profit.

1 July 2013

Tristan

I don't think you know Tristan, the first of my grandsons, who is about to finish high school this year. He is an intelligent young man, taller than me by a head (who isn't?), with whom I take pleasure in talking whenever I have the chance, because he and his family are in Ottawa, while I am in Toronto. It is a great pity that he cannot read in Romanian, just as most of our children, schooled on this continent. On other side, I cannot bring myself to write correctly in English, with which I already have great difficulties being understood by anyone, because of my accent.

So, I was trying to tell Tristan what articles I had written lately and how difficult it is these days to find a subject to treat objectively, without falling into the sin of political confrontations, with which the newspapers are full, although no one bather to asks what is true and what is not. For Tristan, life is a kind of flow of successive days, without differing too much between them, but I, used to sort events by degrees and categories, see it a little differently. Between past and present, I see a clear line of demarcation, which could be delineated with mathematical precision. I have the impression that, somewhere, at a not very distant date, a serious rupture occurred, like the crack that split in two the city of Ronda, in Spain, or the Grand Canyon, in Arizona. A deep split, axe like, that broke the past from present, at the turn of century that produced this cataclysm named Y2K (the year 2000).

Why Y2K? Because every computer in the entire world had to be, willingly or not, replaced with a new system capable of reading the year 2000 date, and through this, the technical capabilities of the new installations were raised to an exponential level. The new computers were able to process infinitely more commands simultaneously and much faster than the old ones. They could create three-dimensional images, whose resolution was impeccable. Without this qualitative leap at the global level, the technical progress of recent years would not have been possible.

Turning my gaze into a 360-degree tour, without Y2K I don't think we would have reached today the computerized creation of Oscar-winning animated films, iPads and iPhones, Skype, or Facebook. What do all these have to do with Y2K? It enabled generations of young people, who now had at their disposal much more sophisticated communication systems, to push cybernetic technology into a true information explosion, unknown in the past and adapted to all sectors of daily life. It was a small and insignificant step made by each of us, which marked a gigantic leap in the technology of the future and artificial intelligence. And that was only the first step that fundamentally changed the appearance of the world as we knew it in the past.

The second step that changed the world was a simple

calendar page with the inscription September 11, 2001. It was the date, the day that shook the world and inscribed it in a new, irreversible historical stage, because never before had history known a more tragic moment than this, in which the products of human civilization, meant to bring people and continents closer together, could be turned into weapons of mass killing by a handful of fanatics who hate progress.

Since then, all efforts, both diplomatic and military, of the United States, under the banner of the UN, have not managed to stop and eradicate the suicidal doctrine of some terrorists located at the periphery of some Muslim countries, who want to impose on the whole world their religion, their way of thinking, their dress, and their lifestyle dictated by Islamic laws. Even more, the part of the Arab world that had practiced a liberal neutrality policy with the West, after the "Arab Spring" revolution, chose, like Egypt, the path to fundamentalism, a return to religious fanaticism hostile to any democratic ideas.

At this point, Tristan suggested that I write on this subject. As if torn from a dream, I looked at him, meeting his eyes that followed me with interest. In those eyes, I read the question of a child seized by unease: What is to be done? Few are those who think they know the answer to this question. And even fewer of those who think such an answer exists.

In the winters, even if the day continue to be warm and the sky is still clear, the householder prepares, knowing that hard times will come with terrible frost and blizzards. Perhaps many of these efforts will prove useless, but good preparation helps to get through the hard times more easily. The same must be done now.

Tristan is just as young and innocent as the year we are stepping into. He will actively contribute to the next qualitative leap, which will be made by technology, and there is no doubt that humanity will benefit from these changes that will make life easier for everyone. Unfortunately, these leaps in science and technology, however miraculous they may be, have not managed to make man better, more understanding, more adaptable to the needs of others. With all these modernizations, which have transformed the world from one day to the next, and which involve unlimited knowledge, virulent intelligence and much talent, our spirit does not manage to rise to the same level as the material progress of industry.

In each of us there is creative energy, with unlimited possibilities to transform the world around us, but, despite this potential wealth, we are spiritually poor and unable to change ourselves. We have lost the meaning of the word altruism and, along with it, faith. We have gained instead a false confidence that we are powerful, capable of mastering the world and the universe, we ourselves have become our own gods. And in the arrogance of these thoughts, we overlook the fact that we distance ourselves from our fellow men, who cannot rise to the same heights, creating cracks and chasms with those who were like brothers to us in days of suffering. For this reason, on the other side, before the abyssal split of Y2K was created, man was more trusting in life, more optimistic and more confident in his destiny than he is now. Tristan's generation will find the solution to solve these dilemmas.

31 December 2012

From One Thing to Another

When outside the frost is so bitter that it cracks the stones and there is talk it will get even worse, nothing seems more comfortable than sitting inside with a hot cup of coffee before you, flipping through the television channels in search of a more interesting program. This time (Friday, February 20), luck brought before me Dr. Oz, who began his program talking about "Past Life Regression."

With him was a young woman who had suffered from a certain phobia since childhood. Subjected to hypnotic treatment, she revealed, in trance, memories from a past life, with truthful details dating back a century.

That made me recall a similar situation, from the mid-1960s, when I came across an article in the Romanian newspaper *Scânteia* (or România *Liberă*), a full-page spread describing an incident that had occurred in Italy, with details and some photographs. At the time I was working in the team of engineers at an agricultural machine plant, and during a break we gathered around, reading and commenting on the article, which related that at a party, a group of young people decided at one point to demonstrate hypnotism. A girl offered herself as a medium and, once induced into a hypnotic state, to everyone's astonishment, she began to speak in an unknown language. Someone brought a tape recorder and recorded her entire monologue. The tape was played back for the girl herself, but she could not explain what it was about. Later, linguists from different departments listened to the tape, which eventually reached a professor specialized in ancient languages. He declared that the language was Sanskrit, and that the girl had related she had been a princess in Antiquity.

Nowadays, much is said about reincarnation, and many have come to believe in this process. What is surprising is that evidence from scientific experiments seems to confirm the existence of reincarnation. For instance, psychiatrist Ian Stevenson of the University of Virginia investigated reports from more than 2,500 children who claimed to remember their past lives. In one of his books, *Twenty Cases of Reincarnation*, Stevenson compared the words of children with those of deceased people whose life stories matched those recounted by the children. Even more: many birth defects, birthmarks, or scars verified in medical records, autopsies, or photographs of the deceased were identical to what the children remembered from their past lives. Of course, many scientists vigorously reject these theories, trying to bring proof and arguments to dismiss as implausible any attempt that invokes the theory of reincarnation.

Among those defamed by specialists is Dr. Daniel Amen, a psychiatrist and expert in brain disorders, and even Dr. Oz himself, because in his television programs he popularizes opinions and information not approved by medical authorities. Dr. Amen introduced a new tool in diagnosing nervous disorders, called "Single Photon Emission Computed Tomography" (SPECT), used for now only in his clinics. This psychiatrist, Amen, was also invited by Dr. Oz to analyze the case of the young woman mentioned above. In the SPECT carried out before hypnosis, the image was static, showing a single bright point. In the one during trance, the image reflected a constellation of moving bright points, which Dr. Amen identified as whirlpools of brain activity. Dr. Oz called them signs of "suffering."

In one of his experiments, Dr. Amen subjected a group of mice to a drastic treatment with cherry blossoms. The mice reacted with rejection, as though terrified. Generation after generation of mice inherited the same rejection in the presence of cherry blossoms, manifesting fear. The convulsions, the phobia, the inherited fear transmitted from generation to generation may have been the effect of an unpleasant experience of distant predecessors, which time could not erase or eradicate.

This experiment, revealed in a portion of Dr. Oz's program, made me reflect on the implications it could have on human society if we were subjected to a similar process. Our dread of darkness, our fear of the unknown, the anxiety caused by insecurity, these could all be effects of negative experiences genetically transmitted from our ancestors.

We are born into a family environment, surrounded by parents, relatives, neighbors, and friends, with whom we share our existence, our successes and disappointments, joys, and sorrows, and above all, the good and bad notions of each one of us. In our little surrounding world, I learned that some were Gypsies, other Jews, Boangheni, Turks, Greeks, Russians, and so on. We were taught to beware of some, not to trust others, and, as we matured, we began to realize that not everything we had learned at home matched reality.

Here, in Canadian society, it is remarkable that differences of nation, religion, and color have become insignificant, almost invisible, especially among younger generations, our children, and grandchildren. But the same is not true elsewhere.

Generations of children in Africa and the Middle East have been educated, since the founding of the state of Israel, to hate and to take revenge on the Jews and on all who infiltrated their space, culture, religion, and way of life.

As we saw in Dr. Amen's experiment, phobia is transmittable from generation to generation, a fact that today explains the worrying adherence of some young people to the terrorism propagated by ISIS through television, the Internet, and YouTube. Taking advantage of the decline of American prestige in the world and the unwillingness of the American president to respond decisively to international events, the reactionary forces of those who want to bring back red dictatorship, the Cold War, and international terrorism have been reborn like a plague that seems to have spread throughout the world.

Even more worrying is the fact that, among us too, many apologists and pacifists have appeared, increasing the general confusion. The wolves lurk in the shadows, and the shepherd less flock is scattered in disorder. Amid the preparations for elections, it is hard to identify in the crowd a solid figure, with vision and determination to clear the clouds, unite us, and show us the way.

We have remarkable minds, doctors, scientists, engineers, ingenious machines, and discoveries; we master the depths of the sky and the oceans, yet despite all these riches, we are poor in our quietness of following our days in peace. Still, despite all the threats, we know that in the end Reason, the Desire for Freedom, and Peace will prevail.

uary 23, 2015

On Christmas Eve

Santa Claus, dear old man, fills his sack with gifts for little girls and boys, to bring them as a long-awaited surprise on Christmas Eve. With the precision of a clock, every year Santa wanders snowy paths with the sack on his back, tireless in bringing a moment of joy to each child. At midnight, tiptoeing past their little beds, making no difference whether they are in a hut corner or under the canopy of a palace, he is always there. On such a night, miracles are possible.

Many years ago, it must have been soon after the Revolution, I spent a Christmas holiday in California. Many of our friends from Grant were already settled in that wonderful corner of paradise, with its mild climate, generous sun, and abundant harvests. Settled in a resort in Carlsbad, each day I drove, in a rented car, to Los Angeles and even farther, to visit friends scattered in the surroundings. Great preparations were underway, because it was announced that Mircea Diaconescu, "the Doctor," with his wife, would come from Germany to spend Christmas with us here.

The Doctor, raised with us in Grant, was a well-known dentist, teaching at the Institute of Dentistry on Calea Plevnei, and a great lover of music, conducting the renowned choir of doctors in the Capital. For this occasion, it was decided that we would greet him at the airport with the Romanian carol *Bună dimineaţa la Moş*

Ajun, in the version composed by Mircea. We gathered in a church hall in Loma Linda for rehearsals.

Among us, withdrawn, a man, a member of the church but not of the Grant group, was present. During rehearsals, I noticed that he watched, timidly, from his corner, my wife Vali and me, who had come from Canada. After rehearsals, our old friends, Tili and Mihai Manea, took us aside and asked us to do this man an act of kindness, if we could. That is how we met Valeriu Ciovică.

He was from Constanța. He had come about a year earlier with his eldest daughter, a medical student who received a scholarship at Loma Linda Hospital and had not returned. He had no green card. From being a teacher and high school principal in Constanța, he was now working as a laborer in construction and did not know how to bring over his wife and younger daughter, left at home. In America it was not possible. Canada, however, was closer. Could we invite them to come to us?

The meeting at the airport with Mircea was festive. When they appeared at the automatic doors, at Mihai's signal, nearly thirty of us began to sing, drawing everyone's eyes: "Bună dimineaţa la Moş Ajun..." Embraces, kisses, tears of joy, and finally we went to the Burnea family in Glendale. Food, memories, stories, and a sleepless night.

Back home, after a short New Year's cruise from San Diego

to Mexico, we made the official invitation, at the consulate, for Camelia and Antonia Ciovică. By May we received notice that they would arrive in Toronto. We did not know them. We prepared placards on cardboard. They came!

Camelia, a French teacher, spoke not a word of English, timid, communicating more with her eyes and a constant smile. Antonia, a thirteen-year-old girl with ebony hair and reserved in speech, knew English better than we did.

At home, we gave them our daughter Ancuța's room, she having just married and at her own house. In the basement, we had a ping-pong table where we played with the children. Antonia soon became my partner. Vali and Camelia could be considered sisters, one older, one younger. They were everywhere together. Time passed quickly.

Among our Toronto friends, Mrs. Doiu was also a French teacher, and her advice seemed the most suitable. From a professional point of view, Camelia, with her teaching experience, could easily find a post as a teacher in Canada. Antonia would have to start school in September. The Ciovică family's case in California was being handled by a lawyer who kept dragging out the process. The only practical solution was their settlement in Canada.

So, we took them to the immigration center to apply for permanent residency. But every document had to be submitted from outside the borders. The U.S. Consulate in Toronto received the public only on certain days, and applicants were numerous. From experience, I knew people lined up as early as 5 a.m. I went with the girls to request visas on their passports for one day in Buffalo, where they could file the application for Landed Immigrant status for Canada. They received the U.S. visa in December.

On the phone, this time, the Ciovică family's joy was boundless. Whatever the situation, after so much waiting, uncertainty, and stress, they would reunite in Buffalo, even if only for a single day. There they would decide what to do, and, with God's help, soon they would be together again. I took two days off before Christmas; Vali and the girls prepared sandwiches and fruit for the road, and we left for Buffalo.

Ciovică, with his elder daughter, was waiting for us outside, at the gate of the Canadian Consulate. They waited outside until we finished filing the paperwork and then led us to the motel where they had spent the night.

The next morning, at breakfast, Valeriu told us they had decided to take the bus together to California. They were already reunited here and no longer wanted to wait apart, for who knew how long. Vali and I returned home saddened, because we had lost the girls we had grown so attached to, but joyful for their joy. It was Christmas Eve.

Today we consider ourselves family. This summer we met again in Arizona with Camelia, Valeriu, and the Manea family. And we relived the moments of that Christmas Eve in Buffalo, embodied in our souls as a true miracle.

November 20, 2017

Mama Floarea

At the foot of Crângaşi Road, born as a continuation of the descending slope of the Grant Bridge, memory widens the image of this now-defunct neighborhood, which today has taken on another appearance, with other people, other problems, and a different life. The small houses of the street, toward Grant Market, which rarely rose higher than a single story—and even then, only in exceptional cases—have today become a flowing thoroughfare, hemmed in by the dams of concrete giants that house multitudes of swarming people from dawn until late at night. Instead of the wagons pulled by a scrawny horse toward the market, or sometimes even by a pair of gray beasts with necks locked into a wooden yoke, or of the carriages waiting at the street's edge, with coachmen wrapped in caftans and wide leather belts at waist and shaggy hats, today the road is crossed by cars and trucks like a merciless torrent running in both directions, from which it's best to step aside if you value your life.

The irreversible image of what once was still lingers in memory, and against its background appear beloved faces who animated those times with their soul's warmth, still alive in our hearts. For me, the face of Mama Floarea emerges, wrapped in a radiant halo.

When my sister and I reached puberty and could no longer

live in a single room alongside our parents, with a little kitchen where a table with four chairs barely fit, we were allotted a larger house. It was an indescribable stroke of luck to receive an apartment on the street, with two rooms, kitchen, and bathroom, in a paved courtyard, with wrought-iron gates and two rows of houses facing each other.

The owner was Mr. Diaconescu, a lawyer, past middle age, divorced from his wife who lived with Florica, the maid of the house, in the apartment across from us. Two other families occupied the other two apartments.

Mrs. Diaconescu was a reserved woman, still young, tall, beautiful, sewing fashionable dresses for elite ladies and women of the theater. Florica, or Mama Floarea, as we called her, was small in stature, from the countryside, with hair already graying, braided into a plait that reached below her waist, a stubby nose above a pair of thick lips on a ruddy face, keen black eyes, honest as a puppy's, drawing you into their glow like into the depth of a well.

Mama Floarea was lively and present everywhere. She shopped, bargained with vendors, could not read, or write but did her arithmetic in her head and no one could trick her. She cooked and cleaned, was up to date with everything happening in the neighborhood and always found time to share the latest news with my mother. In her, the secrets of our youth, the troubles we could not confess to our parents, our love, and disappointments, along with the constant lack of money, found a confidante, advisor, and often even the bank from which we borrowed small sums for a date with a girl.

Mama Floarea had no husband, children, or other family. Like our landlords, her past was kept hidden. Her family was Mrs. Diaconescu, whom she had served for many years, and us. She cherished us and adopted us without words or promises, with simplicity and pure selflessness. She shared in all our troubles, good or bad; when she cooked something good, she shared it with us; on holidays or at parties she stood beside us, and from her little, prepared small gifts for our birthdays.

Thanks to her, we had access to her mistress's telephone, who in time began to thaw her icy isolation from the neighbors, especially in those years of terror, when communism extended its reach even into this courtyard, sending the men of the other families to prison, accused of hiding undeclared gold coins. Searches were carried out at their homes and even ours; we were all interrogated, asked for written statements, and without knowing it, were caught in a long-running affair of which we had no idea.

When I discovered the literary circle at the Grivița Roșie Club and became a member, Mama Floarea lent me Mr. Diaconescu's typewriter and often appeared at the open kitchen window at night, when all was quiet, to ask me how my writing was going.

Once, on my sister's birthday, with the house full of guests, boys, and girls, I was stopped on Giulești Street by a police officer, on the grounds that I was talking too loudly at night while escorting two sister's home. He let the girls go off alone but forced me to accompany him to the police station. At the butcher's shop in Crângași, people were already lining up expecting a new transport of meat next morning, witnessed being accused by the militia officer. Someone who knew me ran home to announce that I was arrested. My father and a few friends came into the police station while the officer was interrogating me for the pretense of hooliganism. Mama Floarea called Mr. Diaconescu, who appeared after a while, completing the group of witnesses and defenders, before whom the officer, surprised by the unexpected appearance of so many people, insisted that I had disturbed the peace of the neighborhood and that it was his duty to bring charges. Faced with protests, he gave up and we all went home. I thanked the unknow person who came to tell my parents and the providence for his act, otherwise, I could have a jail sentence.

When Mama Floarea met us, I was still wearing short pants and my sister had braids down her back. We grew up under her tender gaze; she stood beside us at our weddings and later, when we had our own household, and our children who too were treated with her caresses, gentleness, and love. We lost contact with her when we left the country, and later, when the new Grant Bridge expanded over our house, we could no longer reconnect with Mama Floarea.

March 21, 2018

The Interview

Enough! I am sick of news about infections and deaths. I want something new, something normal, something in which I can find myself whole, undisturbed, and trusting in life. Something I long for, after the voluntary detention imposed by the authorities for more than two months. I need fresh air, the healthy green of just-our days of voluntary confinement. I want to surround the memories of these two months with something more cheerful, something I do not yet find in any tomorrow, and so I dig into the satchel of memories.

Oh, in this satchel I keep all the wealth of a lifetime; on it I lay my head at night to catch beautiful dreams, and in it I often find answers to doubts and fears. Here lies the resource of all past trials, the treasure of good and bad experiences, and the ark of faith that all will end well. So it happened, years ago, when I had just arrived in Canada, searching for a job closer to my training, after countless failures.

By 1978, it had been almost three years since my arrival and several months without work, after I gave up laboring in fields in which I was not qualified. Every morning, I scanned the job ads in the newspapers, and when I reached for the phone to apply, I could not overcome the fear and horror of another rejection. I was on the brink of despair, for I no longer had money to pay my mortgage or other necessities, when one January morning, the person on the other end of the line introduced himself as Mr. Marinescu.

Kindly, he granted me an interview that same day. He was a designer at a car parts factory and needed an assistant for details. After the meeting, he told me that the hiring decision depended on the deputy director of the factory, with whom I would have another interview at a date to be announced. This happened on a Saturday, at the end of the week.

The deputy, Berdh Mevinson, one of the first associates of that company, Magna International—which had quickly become a pillar of Canada's auto parts industry—was a man in midlife, with solid experience in metallurgy and factory management. He received me in his office, more preoccupied with problems in the workshop than with our conversation. He asked me a question, then went off to the shop floor for ten minutes, returning to hear my answer and ask another.

Almost an hour passed, our discussion constantly interrupted, dragging on uselessly, making me realize I had come in vain. My chances were clearly zero. I was angry, upset with myself for being dragged into this back-and-forth game, and decided I had to do something.

When he came back into the office, I stood up, closed the door behind him, and, standing by it as if to say no one leaves, I told him: "You asked me what guarantee I can give that, once you hire me, I won't leave for a better salary elsewhere? Look at this notarized paper confirming that I worked eighteen years in the same place. Do you think all those years, all those days were sunny, without problems or troubles? No! There were problems, failures, technical issues, gossip, but I didn't leave. There were offers from other companies, but I couldn't abandon the responsibility of projects I had started. I stayed, I corrected mistakes—many not even mine—and I did my job. You also wanted to know what guarantee you have that I'll be able to learn the specifics of the auto industry? Before you stand a full-scale assembly drawing of a steam turbine, made by me from the component blueprints. (Indeed, I had a temporary assignment at an agency doing drawings for Westinghouse Canada in Hamilton and was given this task.) As you know, my experience in design was limited to agricultural machinery. Still, I managed to complete this turbine, whose copy you have before you. Beyond that, I don't know what more I can say."

At the end, he shook my hand and told me he would decide in a few days who would be hired. More than a week passed without an answer. Later I learned that there were many candidates, and I was the first. Curiously, most of the time, those interviewed earliest are forgotten, and the position goes to one of the last. Yet it seems the impression I made on the deputy was so strong that he could not forget me.

That is how I was hired at Magna International, where I worked for the next twenty years. Years later, Berdh Mevinson confessed to me that Marinescu, under whom I was to work that first year, had strongly insisted on hiring an acquaintance of his. "Hiring someone is a lottery—it's hard to know who you're talking to," he told me, "But in your case I was lucky."

The luck, in truth, was mine. The beginning of the 1980s was full of problems—the economic crisis created by the rising value of the Canadian dollar forced many industries to move to the U.S. or elsewhere, Magna's stock fell below two dollars, and unemployment reached record highs. Our factory worked with a skeleton crew, we did not know if it would shut down, and we trembled in uncertainty. But we came through. After darkness and storm, the sun always rises. After all, "what is a wave, like a wave passes"

April 30, 2020

The Flyer with Wax Wings

We talk often. It seems normal at our age, because, as things stand today, life is fragile. Especially when you have no one closer. And they don't. We've known each other, for about a year. I had heard of them, of him in particular, from the pages of *Observatorul*, where he has a permanent column, *Panopticum*. His articles, an anthology of current topics—some historical, some literary, and portraits of remarkable people. We came to know each other better last year, when they stayed with us for a few days, at the invitation of myself and the Popescu family, the magazine's editor, during the launch of our books at the Nică Petre literary circle. Since then, we've stayed connected—an online note, a phone call, a moment on Skype.

The hours spent together revealed a meeting of minds, on most issues, and an understanding of day-to-day struggles. Like a new book, as you read it, you discover new things about the heroes inside it—so too did we discover the unsuspected stories from the lives of our guests, Dorina and Gavril Morariu. They met in their student years, in Timişoara, in 1957, but their friendship grew later, as members of the same sports club. That was when she discovered in Gavril his consuming passion for exploring the world beneath the waters, which set him apart from the other students. Studious, energetic, surrounded by friends who, in most cases, stood by him during his foray into the silent depths and even later, he formed the foundation of a union that has withstood all of life's ravages through more than 60 years of marriage.

Even in his school years, Gavril had acquired a passion for a heroic life, of adventure and discovery of something new, still unknown. With precocious maturity, he realized that in a country transformed into a prison, under permanent surveillance, the only possible area of escape was the impenetrable world of the deep. His closest friends shared similar passions: amateur radio, photographic art, film development, electrical engineering. He involved himself in each of these with eager curiosity, reading and studying how such devices worked. From articles, books, and various sources, he learned how one could dive deeper under water while holding one's breath longer, and how underwater photography could be done. From the magazine *The Hunter and Sports Fisherman*, he learned how underwater hunting could be done with a speargun. He designed and built one himself. To be able to see more clearly through the water, he made himself a snorkeling mask.

That was only the beginning. He gathered knowledge from old and new sources about how to reach greater depths with autonomous breathing apparatus and drafted a project of his own using compressed air. At his own expense, through searching, contacts, and often a dose of luck, he succeeded in building his own apparatus, which worked without problems. When he learned that diving could be done at the AVSAP club in Timișoara, he became a member. The club leadership refused to let him use his device but instead brought from East Germany a few devices that used pure oxygen—which resulted in the death of a young man in a lake, during the very first public demonstration. The accident, caused by ignoring the instructions for use, led to the complete suspension of diving activities within the club.

In 1959, Gavril passed his state exams, became an electrotechnical engineer, and was assigned to the "9 Mai" Workshops in the capital. The following year, he decided to cede his authorship rights to the Navy, as the only way to patent his autonomous underwater breathing apparatus with compressed air. With difficulty, he obtained a few successful demonstrations in the pool and at sea, then, in 1961, he was subjected to a humiliating staged competition with a protégé of the nomenklatura, equipped with a suit made in France.

A friend pulled him out of his depression, introducing him to a group of mountaineers and speleologists. Exploration of certain caves was blocked by completely flooded galleries, forming natural siphons that prevented access to the rest of the chambers. The autonomous breathing suit partly solved the problem, but the water inside, being very cold, could be lethal. Gavril designed a watertight protective suit and, with the help of a friend at a rubber factory, managed to build the first prototype. Again, failure. The director of the Speleological Institute categorically refused to give his approval.

Years passed, disappointments continued. New attempts, new hopes, more disappointments. Friends and collaborators infused him, each time, with the energy for new searches, and thus was born the idea of creating a permanent habitat for research of the seabed. For the first time in our country, three young friends—engineers Constantin Ignătescu and Gavril Morariu, and biologist Teodor Nalbant—joined efforts and built, on their own, an underwater habitat called the Submers Laboratory L.S.1. The habitat was launched on September 29, 1967, into the Izvorul Muntelui reservoir of the Bicaz hydroelectric plant, as a first stage of a long-term exploration program, based on the direct entry of man beneath the sea.

What happened afterward is to be read in the pages of the forthcoming book by Gavril Morariu, whose literary pseudonym is Gabriel Watermiller. Together with the two volumes of his English trilogy, *Soft Tales From a Refugee Camp* and *The Four Seasons of a Slave*, the new book will form a historical-literary document of a "lost generation," as he likes to call it.

Many times, the gods are unjust with men. Without reason, they create obstacles, strike the road with thunderbolts, bring from the depths of the earth dragons and beasts, and do not grant the hero a single breath of respite. Nothing illustrates more precisely the life of these people, worthy of praise and honor. They fought continuously, they tried tirelessly to create, to bring a modest contribution to humanity, but they found only closed doors, refusals, and lack of understanding. Perhaps, in other lands or in different times, they would have succeeded in all their endeavors. Only one single fortune served them as shield and gave them some light in their lives: the love that always reigned and united them, always helping them to overcome each new obstacle.

July 4, 2020

About the Culture

192

The New Dalí Museum in St. Petersburg

On January 11, 2011, the new Salvador Dalí Museum opened in St. Petersburg, Florida, and, being in the region, I had the privilege of visiting it a few days later. I admit that, over the years, I have often made the trip to St. Petersburg to admire once more the work of this controversial and eccentric artist, who revealed himself as a vanguard figure of 20th-century culture alongside Pablo Picasso and Constantin Brâncuși. My repeated visits were due less to admiration than to the need to better understand, to decipher the labyrinth of ideas, to interpret the world of symbols repeatedly used, like leitmotifs, in most of Dalí's paintings, which together create a sort of mythological world, where flies, crickets, solid objects transformed into flowing liquid, his own flattened image dripping across different planes, seem to say more than what is painted on the canvas. The colors, the brushstrokes left on the surface, and the technique he has used since his youth confirm, without hesitation, that we are in the presence of a true master of the brush.

The first Dalí Museum in St. Petersburg was inaugurated in 1982, thanks to the collection of ninety-six oil paintings and more than 2,000 other works of art acquired over four decades by Reynolds and Eleanor Morse. This is considered the most important Dalí collection outside of Spain, revealing his artistic evolution over the years.

Dalí was born in 1904, in Figueres, Catalonia, Spain, into a family where his father was a notary and a declared atheist, while his mother was deeply Catholic. From childhood, he was drawn to the beauty of the surrounding places, and at the age of thirteen, in 1917, he painted a landscape, *View of Cadaqués*, representing the town on the Mediterranean coast where the family spent their summers. At 18, in 1922, his paintings were accepted into exhibitions in Barcelona. From this period, we have his *Self-Portrait* (1921), in which we see his face in profile, with long hair, a pipe, and a wide-brimmed hat. "I let my hair grow long, like a girl's… as soon as possible, I wanted to look unusual," Dalí wrote. Later, this eccentricity would manifest in his famous twisted mustaches, like antennae. In 1925, in Barcelona, he opened his first solo exhibition. A year later, he met Pablo Picasso in Paris. At the age of twenty-two, in 1926, while at the School of Arts in Madrid, Dalí created *The Basket of Bread* as a personal test, demonstrating his ability to produce in painting profoundly realistic objects. In the style of Jan Vermeer, this work illustrates, with unmatched artistic force, the realism and simplicity of sliced bread in a woven basket. It could be said that this canvas represents the diploma any talented painter aspires to.

Other visits to Paris followed, where he encountered the Surrealist group founded by André Breton, to which he adhered, and where he met Gala Éluard, the wife of poet Paul Éluard, who soon would become Dalí's wife. Over the years, Gala would become not only his main model in almost all his paintings, but also the muse who inspired his most important works, toward whom the painter felt great love and lasting devotion.

In 1936, when the Spanish Civil War broke out, Dalí and Gala moved to Paris, and his fame expanded worldwide, his photograph appearing on the cover of *Time Magazine*. In 1938, Dalí met Sigmund Freud in London. Like many surrealists, Dalí was interested in Freud's theory of psychoanalysis, of the motives that drive human behavior, and the interpretation of dreams. As a result, Dalí would create irrational images, as in a hallucinatory dream.

Many of his Surrealist works can be seen in the museum: oils such as *Apparatus and Hand* (1927), *The First Days of Spring* (1929), or *Eggs on the Plate Without the Plate* (1932), among others. In film, among various projects, in 1945 he created the dream sequences for Alfred Hitchcock's *Spellbound*, starring Gregory Peck and Ingrid Bergman.

Between 1940 and 1948, Dalí and Gala took refuge in the United States, thus escaping the German occupation of France. A year later, he held his first retrospective at the Museum of Modern Art in New York. In 1942, he published his autobiographical work *The Secret Life of Salvador Dalí*. In 1943, he met Eleanor and Reynolds Morse, who would become his major collectors.

After the war and the use of the atomic bomb in Japan, Dalí became increasingly interested in nuclear science and declared that his art was "Nuclear Mysticism." Indeed, Dalí was fascinated by new scientific discoveries, which became major subjects in his works. He was interested in physics, mathematics, quantum mechanics, and no less in genetics and the structure of DNA. This was the period when, gradually, he moved from atheism to faith, leaving Surrealism behind, feeling that the art of his contemporaries was devoid of spirituality. He was convinced that theories in physics and molecular biology could reveal the mysteries of religion.

In 1956, he created the painting *Living Still Life*, in which Dalí reinterprets the traditional still life, using familiar kitchen utensils, in the realist manner of *The Basket of Bread*—a knife, plates, vegetables, a glass of wine, etc.—suspended in space and time in various positions illustrating movement. In this painting, Dalí introduced the importance of the spiral, which he considered the most perfect form of nature, using it as a cosmic symbol. While working on this painting, Dalí learned that DNA, only recently discovered, had the shape of a double helix.

Between 1949 and 1970, he created his great works, "The Master Paintings": *The Madonna of Port Lligat* (1949), *The Discovery of America by Christopher Columbus* (1958), *The Ecumenical Council* (1960), and *The Hallucinogenic Toreador* (1970). In 1971, Eleanor and Reynolds Morse displayed their Dalí collection in their home in Beachwood, Ohio. Later, they decided to donate the collection to the state. No museum was able to meet the conditions of this fabulous offer, and finally St. Petersburg offered to build a structure to house the entire collection. Thus, the Dalí Museum in St. Petersburg was born in 1982.

In 1974, Dalí inaugurated his own museum in Figueres, Spain. After being awarded the Grand Cross of the Order of Isabella in 1964, in 1982 King Juan Carlos granted him the title Marquis of Púbol, in recognition of his exceptional contribution to Spanish culture. Gala died in Púbol Castle, Spain, on June 10, 1982. Dalí, left alone, died at age 85 from a heart attack on January 23, 1989, in Figueres, Spain.

The new Dalí Museum building is adorned with fascinating architectural details that transport you, even from the outside, into the artist's virtual world. The building, a white concrete monolith rising three levels, is decorated with a fantastic transparent bubble called "the Glass Enigma," which curls around the sides of the building and ends on the roof. The Enigma consists of 1,062 triangular glass panels of different sizes and offers visitors the possibility to admire, from inside, the beauty of the Tampa Bay landscape. The center of the building is dominated by a spiral staircase connecting the ground floor to the third level, ending freely, like human aspiration toward the light filtered through the glass dome.

Visitors enter at the first level, where there are book and reproduction stands, a projection room showing a documentary about the painter, and a Spanish café. The second level houses administration and a research library for scholars, while the upper level, divided into two sections, hosts the collection of paintings on one side and selections of works in various media—drawings, book illustrations, sculpture, and also screenings of Dalí's films—on the other. Finally, one gallery is dedicated to works inspired by Dalí, where visitors can admire schoolchildren's works of impressive talent.

The construction, designed by architect Yann Weymouth, has walls almost half a meter thick and can withstand hurricanes with wind speeds up to 265 kilometers per hour, ensuring the protection of the collection in this region where hurricanes are not rare. In the old museum, when a cyclone was announced, the collection had to be moved to safer shelter. Here, the works are on the third floor, and metal doors can automatically or manually seal off the priceless treasure.

In the end, with each visit to the museum, without declaring myself a passionate admirer of Dalí's works, I believe I draw a little closer to the complicated genius of this great artist.

February 2, 2011

Commentary of a non-initiate

I have no intention of claiming that I know music, let alone opera, but ever since childhood I have felt a special attraction to this genre, which has the gift of blending the conflicts of the stage with music. My first contact with opera took place around 1947, when, after the opening of the Giuleşti Theatre near Grant Bridge, the Romanian Opera staged performances of *The Barber of Seville* there. The sets, the period costumes, the singers' interpretation, and the music lifted me out of the reality of a curious child sneaking clandestinely into the theatre hall through a side door left unlocked and transported me into a magical world that was to influence me for the rest of my life.

Then came the tickets distributed by cultural activists at school or at the workplace, paid for by our scholarships or wages, which were perfect for a matinee, bringing along the girl you were courting. It was a time when young people had the opportunity to be "culturalized" with the help of good performances of theatre and opera. The Romanian theatre, with very limited means, succeeded in offering the public high-quality performances, presented attractively and interpreted at the highest artistic level. In our memories never forgotten even after the passing of so many decades, performances like *The Civil Death*, with Ovidiu Brădescu,

Othello with Emil Botta, or *Romeo and Juliet* with Mihai Popescu are part of our conscience and artistic sensitivity. Same distinctions are doe to opera company and unforgettable operetta spectacles sung and directed by the famous tenor Ion Dacian.

Amused by the comic couplets of operettas like *Die Fledermaus, The Merry Widow*, or *Countess Maritza* with all those critical accents against the upper class, we used to ask ourselves whether the texts were original or adapted in such a way as to reflect at any cost the class struggle so much emphasized by the communist regime. I had to arrive in Canada and see the same shows performed here, in English, to realize that in fact the Romanian texts were "unaltered."

Regrettably, none of the world-renowned producers succeed, in many of the Canadian Opera productions, in matching the artistic level of the Romanian stage. Although these productions swim in money and boast singers of international value, the shows are poor, lacking in imagination, and fail to inspire spectators the enthusiasm of a truly special experience. I still remember today *Faust* by Gounod in Bucharest, with the fluidity of dances in *Walpurgis Night* that lasted more than 20 minutes, cut out from the program in recent performances. Likewise, the parade of Radamès' victory over the Nubians in *Aida,* or the matadors' parade in *Carmen.* All these crossed the ocean in our memories and watching surprised their purge, is not hard to understand why people are not interested on these shows after the producers eliminate the most exiting parts of the spectacle. Today's producers, directors, and creators tend toward cheap tricks, gestures, and clowning devoid of humor, which diminish the show message.

Why is theatre so different here? Style, language, the stage movement, and gesticulation often exceed our ability to understand the play, or what the authors wished to demonstrate. Many stage designers compete in inventing new versions that do not fit the setting or the action, complicate comprehension, and create confusion for the spectator. Many dramas and comedies, some classical, others more recent, are deliberately reinvented by producers. Classical works in which the heroes are unjustifiably distorted like *Michaela* in *Carmen*, whom director Lucian Pintilie turned into a blind woman; *Radamès* in *Aida*, equipped with a machine gun to hunt Nubians on stage; or more recently, at the Bayreuth Festival, Verdi's *La Forza del Destino* staged amid ruins of the Second World War, conflicted the historical events, location and the peoples' mentality of that time.

I was shocked to see, this autumn in Toronto, *Die Fledermaus*, in a production that led many spectators to leave the hall after the first act, outraged by the distortion not only of the set but of the very subject itself, with characters twisted, incompatible with the story line and authors' intent. To succeed, sometimes a table and three chairs on an empty stage are enough to transport the audience into special situations in which they participate with their whole being. Strauss's *Die Fledermaus* needed nothing more. The comedy of mistaken identities is so well outlined that all it requires for complete success is to let the actors play it as it was scripted. But no—the Canadian Opera Company (COC) had to change everything into an amalgam where neither the set, not the action, nor the characters could be recognized. With whose permission was the libretto of this operetta changed? Where was the humor of the prison guard Frosch in the final act, who here was turned into a grotesque precursor Nazi soldier? What excuse can the authors of this production have for transforming one of the most beloved operettas into a parade of depraved, caricatured heroes with grotesque appearances that banish the most precious element of this work: good taste.

In contrast, just a few streets down on Yonge Street, Opera Atelier staged a superb production of Carl Maria von Weber's *Der Freischütz*, which left a remarkable impression on every spectator. After the performance, upon leaving the theatre, I heard around me the most enthusiastic comments, which made me feel as if I had just attended a show in Romania.

November 4, 2012

Alexandra Nechita

"This is the piece through which I hope to achieve and to provoke the desire in each of us to leap beyond the tree of uniformity. It is important to understand the qualities that bring us together as one, and we must continue steadfastly, permanently, the divorce from life's banalities, in order to create our own identity. This is the strong conviction that exists in each of us, which must never be ignored and must remain in constant motion." (*Alexandra Nechita "Tunes Inside All of Us"*)

For years I have followed, not without obvious satisfaction and pride, the works of Alexandra Nechita, exhibited in the press, on television, and especially in the floating galleries of *Princess Cruises*, which carried me across all the world's meridians.

Alexandra was born in Vaslui, on August 27, 1985, three months after her father, Niki, had managed to flee the country to the United States. He settled in Los Angeles, finding work as a laboratory technician. Two years later, Alexandra and her mother, Viorica, were allowed to leave the country for America, where they reunited the family. Soon, the mother also succeeded in finding work as an office manager.

From an early age, Alexandra showed abilities different from other children; she was not drawn to playing with dolls, nor did she try to imitate others in play, but preferred instead to color in children's books with outline drawings. Her parents, going through the material hardships of their beginnings and worried about Alexandra's reserved attitude toward other children, stopped buying her coloring books—but the child, without protest, began creating her own drawings in pencil and ink, which she then colored herself.

Seeing Alexandra's attraction to drawing, her father bought her watercolors and other water-soluble paints before she was even three years old. At the age of seven, Alexandra began working with oil and acrylic paints, even though for her parents the expenses were not always easy to bear, though they hunted for stores offering the lowest prices for their child's supplies.

On April 1, 1994, when Alexandra was eight, she had her first solo exhibition, with about sixty paintings, at the Whittier Public Library in Los Angeles, something many do not achieve after a lifetime of work. Her talent was immediately recognized as one of the rarest child prodigies, akin to Mozart, whose abstract works, in the cubist style of Picasso, attracted large audiences and the attention of professional critics, who dubbed her "The Little Picasso."

Soon after, in spring 1995, the prestigious non-profit Mary Paxon Art Gallery offered Alexandra the chance to exhibit, an event that culminated in the spreading of her fame through media, the public, and critics, as an artist who mastered drawing and color, creating her own visual language in an abstract, cubist style with lyrical accents—capable of revealing a theme at only nine years of age. That same year, the Picasso Exhibition opened at the Los Angeles Museum of Art, which Alexandra visited with her parents. This was her first contact with the great painter's work.

At the age of ten, Alexandra was already producing canvases that not only had a central theme, but also a message: many of her paintings spread messages of world peace, such as *Peace is in Our Hands* and *Release the Peace.*

In November 1999, Alexandra Nechita was chosen by the World Federation of United Nations to lead the Global Arts Initiative, which included one hundred nations worldwide, thus becoming an Ambassador of Peace. In 2005, Alexandra unveiled her *United Nations Peace Monument for Asia,* in Singapore. She was also commissioned to create a series of paintings titled *Winning Together* for the Special Olympics.

Alexandra Nechita is no longer a child prodigy—she has become a young artist with a highly developed artistic personality, clairvoyance, and refinement. Abstract style is an intuitive gift that can only spring from the heart and soul of an artist; it cannot be learned in any school. "My studio is my palace. Every unpainted canvas is a door I open to step into my universe, letting my imagination breathe," the artist said at 14. "I want you to look at my paintings, but not only to look. I don't want to show an office or a table as a table: I want you to know how I feel about these things." This is how Alexandra wishes to communicate—transforming ordinary objects into forms frozen forever in her vision, leaving us both stunned and amused by what we see and what we begin to become through the understanding of that vision.

Critics continue to compare her to the great artists of the 20th century—Klee, Kandinsky, Dalí, and above all, Picasso. "I don't want to wear any other artist's shoes... All I want is to be known as Nechita."

Today, Alexandra Nechita's art has risen to a level reserved only for the great masters of painting. She is now the most famous female painter in the world, and her exhibitions attract crowds of visitors everywhere. Collectors, including major international corporations, have acquired Nechita's paintings and continue to pay exorbitant sums to obtain an original signed by her.

The honors and international awards justify Nechita's talent, recognized as the most important influence in 21st-century painting.

July 28, 2013

Communicating with the Future?

In George Orwell's book *1984*, the protagonist asks: "How can we communicate with the future?" A simple question that sparks the search for an answer. How can we communicate with the future? The answer seems easier to grasp if we ask: How has the past communicated with us? What would we know about the distant past if the Bible had not guided our steps through the earliest beginnings of humanity? What would we know about the Egyptians if not for the testimonies of the pyramids or the fabulous palaces of Luxor and Karnak, providing proof of the abundance brought by the Nile?

What would we know about the achievements of the Hellenistic geniuses, carried forward into our era by the Romans, perfecting art, urbanism, and military skill? What would we know about the Renaissance if not for creators like Dante, da Vinci, and Michelangelo Buonarroti?

What would we know about the existence of our predecessors if, throughout all ages, there had not been chroniclers and preservers who, with meticulous care and devotion, guided only by the desire not to let the creations of ordinary people fall into ruin, collected and protected them with love across generations, transmitting them to us so that we could recreate history? The past has been generous to us. From this past, we extract the sap of our present knowledge, ideas, and thinking, stimulating within us the desire to leave equally important evidence of our generation for the world to come.

But is that really the case?

My knowledge of art, in general, is modest. My cultural and artistic taste probably stemmed from the "speaker box" installed by the authorities in the 1950s in every home of our poor neighborhood. Until then, we did not have a radio, and few in the neighborhood could boast of one. From morning until midnight, the "speaker box" worked nonstop, informing us about the weather, news, politics, and music. Thanks to it, our lives were enriched with the music of folklore, modern hits in fashion, romances, and the afternoon of humor on Sundays. There were symphonic concerts transmitted from the Ateneum or the radio orchestra every week on Sunday morning, opera and operetta arias and theatre play. There were moments when we pressed our ears to the radio to hear socker game transmissions, or memorable Eminescu's poems recitals by famous actors. And there, I first heard *Cavalleria Rusticana*, broadcast from the Opera.

All these wonders came from a modest box operating 18 hours a day, broadcasting a single radio station.

Today, we have modern televisions with screens as large as a house, transmitting hundreds of channels simultaneously, yet none—except PBS—offer classical music, opera, ballet, or theater. Bookstores are going bankrupt and closing.

We also have newspapers, often published for the sake of commercial advertisements, read only in part by very few, except for those checking lottery numbers, the stock market, or obituaries. Very few sims are interested in learning what is happening around us, in the country or in the world. And we have mobile phones full of poor-quality films, loud music and reality shows that have nothing in common with reality. Our works of art no longer reflect life. The heroes in them have become grotesque figures, which, in their distortion, represent none of us. Noble human feelings are no longer an interesting subject, and as a result, our souls dry like un-watered flowers.

In our early years in Canada, toward the end of the seventh decade of last century, the Canadian Broadcasting Corporation (CBC) generously presented symphonic concerts, oratorios, and opera performances. The broadcasts by Norman Campbell of *Giselle, Sleeping Beauty*, and Handel's oratorio *Messiah* from Ottawa's Notre Dame Cathedral, were legendary. At the same time, TVO held us captive every Saturday evening in front of our screens with *Saturday Night at the Movies*, which not only presented classic films uninterrupted but also offered interviews with major actors and commentary about their films.

All these artistic and cultural manifestations of good taste have disappeared today, eradicated mercilessly from the nourishing substance of our consciousness and emotional needs, leaving us with a weakened immune system in the face of the avalanche of artistic trash to which we are exposed day and night by the media.

No one asks why the new generations—our children and grandchildren—so absorbed by new technological discoveries and electronic games, have never heard or learned anything about biblical stories, the works of great classical writers, composers, Master of Arts, and science or the first protagonists of early cinema like Charlie Chaplin, Buster Keaton, and Greta Garbo.

Moving from one house to another, it has always been customary to take the most precious possessions with us: icons, photo albums, paintings, books, and music you hold dear. Shouldn't we do the same when transitioning from one era to another? How can we forget to take with us the faith our parents instilled in us, memories of their past, and all that had warmed our souls throughout our lives, like the ancestral customs, and traditions? Yet appearances suggest we have left them behind like old empty boxes.

A walk through Scarborough invites you to enter Guild Park. There, a "guardian" with a heart, collected all the works of art that once adorned many old buildings in downtown Toronto and brought them to this small park to beautify it. Expensive marble columns supporting classical frontispieces in Parthenon style, white marble portals with chiseled flower in relief, leaves and vines hanging grapes, sparks in the sun along the pathways, and not far, behind the trees, the waters of Lake Ontario glisten. This stunningly beautiful park is, in fact, a cemetery of the city's richest buildings of the past, demolished mercilessly to make way for more profitable tall constructions. We assist with delight and curiosity, accustomed to admiring the art of specialists in imploding outdated buildings which shared a glorious time just half a century ago. Amid the frenzy of these new attitudes, I cannot help but ask myself again: how will we communicate with the future?

April 17, 2014

The Endowment of the Spirit

I recall from reading a biography of J.F. Kennedy that he was an avid reader. In his bedroom, on the nightstand beside his bed, there were always stacks of books waiting to be read. Even during his presidency at the White House, he always was available for reading. He was passionate especially about works of history and biography. Already in high school, he used to recommend that his classmates read the speeches of great orators of the time and of Antiquity. He had read, in their entirety, all the works of Winston Churchill, and in later years he often surprised occasional writers by making references, in conversation, to some of their more obscure writings, little known to the public. It is said that, of the entire Kennedy family, Jack was endowed with the most developed intellect.

Not long ago, an acquaintance from our community invited us to his home. I didn't know much about him—our wives knew each other better, having attended some classes together. In their home, I was surprised to find a splendid library covering an entire wall of a salon, filled with works of history, literature, and general culture, most of them printed in Romanian, which quite simply took my breath away. Many times, I asked myself how they had managed to bring here such a treasure of books, among them titles like the Romanian Encyclopedia, re-edited in different years.

This family, about whom I had known so little, modest in appearance, always present at our community's cultural events, gradually revealed themselves as people of fascinating culture, deeply knowledgeable in various fields, which surfaced in the context of recalling the experiences through which they had been forced to pass. Events of the past and present, some stirring shivers of pain, had not managed to extinguish the gentle warmth of their storytelling. The delight of that day, when we were welcomed with the sincerity of remarkable people who gave us the opportunity to know them better, will not soon fade from our memory.

From a physical point of view, all people are alike: two hands, two legs, two eyes, a mouth, a nose, a body, etc. True, some are shorter, others taller, some blond, others dark-haired, some with brown eyes, others with blue—but one cannot say that such features are what truly set us apart. If you cut off a man's hand, he will be a man without a hand, but he will remain the same as before. What truly differentiates us is our spirit. Our physical appearance does not define who we are, because it changes from day to day. By contrast, the value of the spirit is constant; it cannot be chopped away by surgery, and even after death, it continues to remain among us.

A good proof of this truth is the example of the great scientist Stephen Hawking, who, at the age of twenty-one, began progressively to lose the use of his legs, his hands, and in general any motor function of his body, due to a rare disease, Amyotrophic Lateral Sclerosis (ALS). Later he also lost his voice, but none of these impediments stopped him from affirming himself as one of the greatest geniuses of the 20th–21st centuries, being at the forefront of new research in physics, nuclear energy, and cosmology.

In a way, physical appearance is nothing more than the packaging of each one of us, whose essence is the spirit. The value of the human spirit has created everything that surrounds us today— it is the architect of the civilized world we live in.

Like any other value, the spirit too can be enriched. It is not enough to be endowed by nature with exceptional qualities—vigor, physical beauty, intelligence, talent, or the inheritance of a title of nobility or material wealth that places one ahead of others—because if the spirit is shapeless, all these qualities vanish. Without the guidance of our first steps in life from our parents, of teachers who gave us our first notions in deciphering the written word and numbers, without our own observations and experiences, the spirit would remain dry, like the kernel of an empty walnut. Gradually, however, all these forces, adding their contribution in layers that clothe the spirit like the skins of an onion, begin to outline our own identity, always hungry for new knowledge. And the more we feed this thirst for new knowledge, the richer the value of our spirit becomes.

The spirit is a hungry mouth, crying unceasingly to be fed. In the absence of nourishment, the spirit goes into hibernation, sucking its paws like bears in winter, it weakens, and in the end, it dies. Being always hungry, the spirit is capable of devouring with greed anything—either nourishing food or garbage. Technical progress has facilitated the promotion of new sources of daily information that no longer require the individual physical effort of reading to learn what is happening around us. Radio and television offer an easy alternative of information and, at the same time, fill every hour of day and night with programs of all kinds, which are not always assimilated by the spirit as an increase in its value.

The difference between a book read and one adapted to the screen is that, in reading, the reader visualizes the action described in the book, memorizes important dialogues, registers the images that move him, and all these together enrich his spirit. A film on the same subject may succeed in stirring emotion, but the spectator does not have the necessary time to assimilate, to the same degree, the complexity of situations, the thoughts of the characters, their eloquence, and the beauty of poetic images—thus he loses. But not all television programs adapt good-quality works. Most have no spiritual value whatsoever; they compete in shocking displays, gutter language, and explicit sex. Unfortunately, our children are exposed to such harmful programs, and many will try to imitate what they see, taking as models the characters and situations shown on screen.

Parents, it is necessary that we begin a campaign to promote good taste, true values, and the precepts inherited from our parents—and this campaign must begin in our own homes. If we want a future for our children of which we can be proud, it is necessary to monitor their contact with the outside world, encouraging them to read more than when they watch television. Let us talk with them more, have them with us at dinner, maintain activities with the entire family, and create an atmosphere of harmony in their lives and in ours. The spirit cannot be endowed in any other way.

June 8, 2015

The Hunt for Furs

For many millennia, nothing was known about these lands. But then, a bold adventurer, Columbus, seeking a new route to India in 1492 — when Italians were taxing the silks and spices of the Orient — stumbled upon the lands of the distant West, believing he had reached his intended destination. Other explorers followed his path and, in short order, began to carve new waterways toward the West, financed by the royal crowns of Spain, Portugal, and the Netherlands.

In 1497, another bold seafarer, John Cabot, set sail from Bristol, England, toward the West and discovered Newfoundland, for which Henry VII rewarded him generously with ten sterling pounds. Nearby, he came across a school of fish so dense that they could be caught by hand. Western European fishermen rushed in to seize this new wealth. Since the journey back was long, they began preserving the fish by drying it on the Atlantic coast, while the Indigenous peoples watched the newcomers from behind the trees — envying their metal tools, traps, knives, guns, and even clothing. The natives still lived in the Stone Age. In exchange for these goods, all they could offer were the hides and furs that clothed them. When Europeans saw the furs, they instantly recognized another treasure. Thus began the trading posts.

England's interest in the riches of the New World was awakened by these fishermen at the dawn of the 16th century. But while they explored the warmer southern coasts, the French chose the northern shores of the Maritimes. Jacques Cartier explored, in the name of France in 1535, the entrance to the Gulf of St. Lawrence, sailing inland along the great river as far as the turbulent waters allowed.

From a hilltop, he saw the endless river stretching westward, imagining it could lead to India. He named the place *Mont Royal*. Forced to winter in the frozen St. Lawrence among an Iroquois tribe, he called the land *Canada*, likely borrowing the word from them.

The authority of England, under Queen Elizabeth I, grew immensely after the destruction of the Spanish fleet in the English Channel and at Cadiz in 1588. With the Atlantic turned into a British lake, English explorers penetrated sub-Arctic regions between America and Greenland. In 1610, Henry Hudson discovered a new passage to Asia through a strait that opened into a vast bay later bearing his name. By then, England had already founded a colony in Virginia — named in honor of the Virgin Queen — and the first settlers brought by the London Company in 1607 faced countless dangers: Indian attacks, wild forests to clear, and, most cruel of all, the exploitative conditions forced upon them by those who transported them.

In England, religious conflicts between Catholics and Protestants after the death of Henry VIII had given rise to a group of Bible zealots known as Puritans. Persecuted and even expelled to Holland, in 1621 they received permission from King James I to cross the ocean aboard the *Mayflower* to the New World. A storm drove them further north, where they anchored at Plymouth, not far from Boston. There they founded colonies shaped by their strict religious beliefs — later immortalized in the story of the Salem witches.

Thus began the age of mercantile trade with the New World. Ships carried emigrants (instead of ballast) to America and returned laden with fish. Newcomers who could not afford the voyage had to work seven years for those who had brought them over. Soon, trading posts multiplied, fishing became a thriving business, shipbuilding and timber exports to England proved profitable, and waves of Puritans and other settlers continued to populate the New World.

By 1630, the population around Massachusetts Bay had reached 16,000. Although many nobles — granted vast lands in the New World — tried to enforce feudal laws of landlord and tenant, both in Virginia and New England, such laws could not take root. Land was abundant, Indian raids had to be faced without royal protection, and clearing and cultivating virgin soil was hard enough without also paying rent. This failure of the aristocracy to impose rents had lasting significance: it laid the foundation for the democratic spirit of America.

But things unfolded differently in Canada.

Here, fur trading with the Indigenous peoples grew rapidly, and King Henry IV of France granted monopolies and lands to nobles and merchants, on the condition that they establish a French colony in Canada — under the name *New France.*

The success of this vision belonged to Samuel de Champlain, a former soldier, sailor, and above all, skilled geographer. On his first voyage in 1603 along the St. Lawrence, he saw the possibility of planting French settlements along the river to control the fur trade. The following year, he returned with 120 settlers. Their first stop, St. Croix Island in the Bay of Fundy, was soon abandoned due to lack of fresh water and timber. In 1605 they moved to Port Royal in present-day Nova Scotia (then called Acadia). By 1608, Champlain established a trading post at the natural fortress site of Quebec, thus founding the oldest permanent settlement in Canada.

As he pushed westward, Champlain, like Cartier before him, imagined the St. Lawrence as a possible route across the continent. He allied with the Algonquin against the Iroquois and, in 1609, discovered the lake that still bears his name. With Indigenous guides, he explored Lake Huron, the Ottawa River, and later Lake Ontario, setting up forts and trading posts.

Appointed governor of New France, Champlain tried to increase the number of settlers. But the monopoly companies opposed farming or settlement — they wanted only furs. A devout Catholic, he also sought to Christianize the natives. Jesuit missionaries and nuns soon arrived, founding Ville-Marie (Montreal) in 1642 with a church and hospital.

The turning point came in 1661, when Louis XIV, the "Sun King," and his finance minister Colbert took direct control of New France. They sent troops, funds, and settlers, creating a royal administration of governor, bishop, and intendant. The first intendant, Talon, boosted colonization by granting free land, encouraging farming and crafts, and even importing young women (the "King's Daughters") to marry and build families. Large families received subsidies — a tradition that continues in Quebec even today.

By the early 1700s, New France stretched far beyond the Great Lakes, down the Mississippi to the Gulf of Mexico. Meanwhile, English colonies grew only along the eastern seaboard. Competition for furs sparked alliances with different native tribes, fueling wars between France and England, mirrored by Indigenous rivalries — Iroquois siding with the English, Algonquins with the French.

The rivalry erupted into repeated wars. While victories shifted back and forth, the final blow came during the Seven Years' War (1756–1763). In 1759, General Wolfe scaled the cliffs of Quebec in a daring night maneuver onto the Plains of Abraham. The French under Montcalm were defeated. Both commanders died in battle. By 1760, Montreal surrendered, and New France ceased to exist. Canada became British.

But Britain treated Quebec differently than the rebellious southern colonies. By the Quebec Act of 1774, the French Canadians were guaranteed their language, religion, and civil law. Thus, while the Thirteen Colonies declared independence in 1776, French Quebec remained loyal to Britain. Waves of Loyalists fleeing the Revolution resettled in Nova Scotia, New Brunswick, and Ontario (then called Upper Canada). Toronto began as a Loyalist settlement named York.

And so, on this North American continent, two sibling peoples took root side by side — outwardly similar, yet with distinct characters. Together, through hardship and blessing alike, and with the grace of God, they have managed to live in peace and prosperity to this very day.

February 19, 2017

The Wedding of Zamfira

An evening gathering with friends, around a barbecue in the garden, is always a relaxing occasion for joy and, in most cases, an opportunity for the exchange of ideas that awaken the spirit numbed by daily routine. I recently took part in such a gathering, responding to an invitation from friends, and I must confess that the few hours spent together were memorable, both for the delicacies offered by our hosts and for the quality and variety of the discussions around the table. Most of the guests, people with life experience, who had already seen their children grown up, some even with grandchildren, shared their memories, many with humor and various stories they had lived or only heard about.

I didn't know, for example, that in the village of poet Coșbuc, formerly named Hordou, in Bistrița-Năsăud, in 1966, on the 100th anniversary of the great poet's birth, it was decided, as a sign of homage to recreate *The Wedding of Zamfira* exactly as he described it in his verses. On this occasion, a whole festival was staged, invitations were sent throughout the country and abroad, an artistic director was brought from Cluj to set up the event, and villagers were assigned to the various roles.

During rehearsals, a 16-year-old girl, Ana Cifor, who lived at the edge of the village, with a minor role among the callers who were supposed to lead the bride and groom to church, was noticed by the director, who immediately decided that only she could play the role of Zamfira. The girl refused, saying she had no time for rehearsals, but with the support of the village mayor, she took the role, and since then everyone called her Zamfira. Even today.

Charmed by the beauty of this simple country girl, people from everywhere — a university professor from Cluj, even an American producer staying at a hotel in Bistrița — came with marriage proposals and Hollywood contracts. But Ana simply refused:

"How could I leave my darling here and abandon my village?"

Indeed, beside Ana's house, at the edge of the village, Vasile, her childhood friend, was waiting. He couldn't see Ana in the role of Zamfira since he was doing his military service. Their love blossomed when he returned on leave, for the funeral of his brother, who had died in an accident. Two years after the festival, Ana and Vasile married quietly at the Cultural Centre.

"Our wedding wasn't with horsemen, it wasn't with alpine horns, we only had fiddlers," said Ana.

Since then, 47 years have passed, they have one child, and they live happily in the village, without a car, electronic novelties, washing machines, or other comforts:

"We wash our clothes in the yard as always, and that's where we go to the toilet, too."

The one who might have become a great star of the silver screen chose a simple rural life, without ever regretting her choice.

But the story doesn't end there: the newspaper *Mesagerul* (The Messager) from Bistrița-Năsăud recounts the full story of the International Folklore Festival *The Wedding of Zamfira*, which this year held its 23rd edition. More than 5,000 artists participated, from at least two hundred countries, and specialists and spectators came from all corners of the world. The idea belongs to Professor Dorel Cosma, who recounts the beginnings of the festival.

After graduating from university, he was assigned to a rural school in Șieuț, Bistrița, which gave him his first contact with village life — with the wonderful people there, the women carefully sewing national costumes or dowries for their daughters, with the music and dances at village gatherings, thus discovering their beauty. Over time, together with students and their parents, he organized folk art exhibitions, had the chance to work with choreographer Tiberiu Danciu, and consolidated a troupe that, in 1985, managed to win the Grand Prize in Dijon (France), the "Golden Necklace" — a performance unmatched in Romania.

After many international meetings, he began to dream of creating an international folklore festival in Bistrița, but this wasn't possible before 1989. Only in 1991, overcoming many obstacles and a lack of resources, did he manage to organize the first festival with international participation. Asked why he named it *The Wedding of Zamfira*, Dorel Cosma replied:

"What other moment in a person's life could bring together all these elements? Of course, only a wedding. And so, we began to entice Zamfira at an international level. The festival has nothing to do with Hordou, the birthplace of Coşbuc in our county. I only borrowed the title of the great poet's masterpiece and the theme of the wedding."

At the first edition, with all preparations complete, they waited nervously to see who would come from the invited countries. Many predicted total disasters. Late in the afternoon, the first bus appeared. It was the Bulgarians. A little later came the group *Palace* from Greece. Soon after, Turkey and France arrived. The festival could begin.

This year, from July 25 to 31, the 23rd edition of the festival took place, on the stage in front of the Palace of Culture, with participants from eight countries. *"There could have been more editions, we would have liked a rounder number, but there were years when politics rudely interfered in this story, stomping on this festival with heavy boots, so we intervened with the World Folklore Union and stopped the event from being held."* On YouTube, many aspects of this remarkable festival can be seen by searching *"Nunta Zamfirei 2018."* It's an opportunity to brighten our faces, to rejoice that in our homeland such beautiful things still take place.

Of course, there were other subjects discussed that evening in the garden, otherwise we wouldn't have stayed until midnight, huddled in chairs we couldn't leave, surrounded by lit candles to ward off the mosquitoes. But the story of *The Wedding of Zamfira* is what impressed me most deeply.

August 23, 2018

Nonsense

Most of my opera-loving friends chose not to attend the December 12 broadcast from the Metropolitan Opera of the new production of Verdi's *La Traviata*, on the grounds that they had already seen it many times. Correct, one of the most beloved operas in the international repertoire, *La Traviata* is present on all the stages of the world, and although it has registered a century and a half since its premiere, it continues to fill performance halls to capacity. It is understood that among them, many have seen the performance several times. I believe I have seen at least a dozen productions of this opera, one of Verdi's most beloved, because, after the tragic years of his youth, *La Traviata* helped him understand that many victims of society are unjustly condemned by the very society that produced them.

The new production at the Metropolitan is surprisingly different from everything I knew about *La Traviata*, through the freshness of the conception of Violetta, the opera's heroine, of the dramatic musical punctuation, sprinkled with small pauses to highlight certain moments, of a staging as inspired as the sets, and especially of the acting and the quality of the voices of the main characters. The musical direction belonged to Yannick Nézet-Séguin, the new musical director of the Met, a talented young Canadian, originally from Montreal, with the capacity to deepen the music, the text, and the true intent sought by the author.

Have you ever read *Cineplex* magazine? I leaf through it whenever I go to the cinema. In the December issue, a few articles caught my attention that, tangentially, create new paths for thought and reflection. Here, for example, is what the article on page 62 says about the film *It's a Wonderful Life*: "In May 1947, only a few months after *It's a Wonderful Life* appeared on screens, an FBI memo was written, indicating that this film contains evidence that 'Communists are infiltrated into the film industry.' In other words, the film portrays a venal banker, physically and spiritually corrupt, hated by everyone, which, as the monograph mentions, makes the banker a bad and dishonest character, which is upsetting for those in the upper class. But let not forget that, at that time, the Governmental Committee on Un-American Activities was in full swing, hunting down filmmakers suspected of communist sympathy and activity."

That was then. Since then, 70 years later, audiences continue to watch on screen the almost-by-heart-learned story of these common people, about the superiority of love, of family, of philanthropy, and of the honesty of the simple man compared to the rulers of banks and other institutions. But I do not know that it has sparked any revolution, uprising, or even a simple demonstration in the street, with placards and slogans incriminating the government. I do know, however, that this film has the soothing quality of a soul balm, which makes you wipe away an unnoticed tear during its viewing, but in the end, it helps you find yourself in the film's heroes—better, more confident, and much more optimistic. If only films like this were still made today!

Another article reproduces the interview given by American film star Natalie Portman to Marni Weisz in Toronto, regarding the new film *Vox Lux*. Related to the subject of the film, the heroine, victim of a violent mass shooting at a school in Staten Island in 1999, became, thanks to the attention given by the media, a musical "pop" celebrity. 18 years later, a terrorist attack takes place on a beach in Croatia, which seems to have been inspired by one of the heroine's videos from her youth. As a result, a reporter in the film asks: "What difference do you see between a terrorist and a pop star?" Her answer is what must be mentioned: *"I don't know, except for the fact that if you don't give us attention, we won't exist. At the same time, as long as you give us attention, as much as the media mentions to us, that gives us drive and strength. One of the ideas is, to whom do we give attention? Who is recommended as new? How many clicks do you get, and how much money is there? It's not about searching for the truth, it's about what story can be sold quickly, and if the story is about a shooting, or about a pop star's divorce, it all becomes the same, and that is the condition we live in now. That is the reality we live—the truth. Human relationships, human experiences, human suffering have value in dollars."*

To the interviewer's question whether the value of pop culture is in decline, Natalie Portman says: *"Everything is devalued, everything has become so accessible, that nothing matters anymore, nothing is sacred, nobody cares about anything. I am more pessimistic. But when you see some of the political scandals that appear and the crazy things people suggest and carry out, without leaving any trace, it's as if you say 'Oh!' When, around you, there is so much, everything becomes cheaper and less important."* In other words, we return to *Anything Goes*. We live in a consumer society, in which cheap, shoddy things are glorified, because they satisfy an immediate need. Things crafted with skill, which can endure for centuries, are no longer appreciated, because fashion changes quickly. Thus, we change as well.

Who still learns a poem by heart today, who still reads classic literature, who still cares about history, whether ancient or modern? The generation that comes after us places no value on any of these things. Paintings carefully preserved for generations, furniture inlaid by true masters of past times, and our libraries, to which we added everything most precious in human thought, will be given away for nothing to dealers of antiques and will rot with them. Artists of great value starve. Pseudo-artists, created instantly by the media, swim in money. And we keep ourselves busy with nonsense.

December 18, 2018

And God Gave Us Internet

Many years ago, I met a lady with a well-deserved respect, built on years of hard work in the service of others, who became my adviser at a time when I needed guidance, and also a hospitable host, where I was warmly welcomed by her whole family, in which her mother, brought from Romania, was the soul of the house. Moments like those cannot be erased from memory, and whenever I hear or see her name, the thought gladly revives those memories.

About two decades have passed since then, with only occasional holiday greetings or, rarely, a phone call. Her sister, my colleague in that huge enterprise that produced the "guts" of the automobiles in circulation, would sometimes update me on important family events, when we happened to meet at rare professional meetings. But the mill of time has ground down many of our old concerns. The years of withdrawal from productive activity came, and with them, many of our former connections gradually shrank to the family nucleus around which everything seemed to revolve.

And God gave us internet…

At first, I timidly watched the children swiftly handling all sorts of images on a computer worth as much as an entire month's salary. Then, when the little gray plastic box multiplied at an incredible pace on every desk corner, we had to learn the finger dance across the keyboard. No longer did we shuffle papers than from desk to desk, but we sent an e-mail. It was said that, by saving paper, we were saving trees, but when I was held accountable for not replying to an urgent matter, I discovered that for every e-mail I needed printed copies as proof. Today, every employee has whole shelves of printed, duplicated, and carefully bound evidence stored at every level of administration. On a national scale, our forests have been transformed into personal and collective archives, with the same ingenuity with which we are forced now to pay the luxury of receiving our bills by mail, at home.

But the true *boom* was discovered by politicians. Once every room was already pulsing with a tiny electronic chip, they found the right moment to slip in their own (dis)informative messages among the endless commercial advertisements, and thus we got used to fishing in the waters of this invisible river, called the web, in which ideas and virtual fantasies could be received and passed along. In addition to the flood of news from newspapers, radio, and television, the internet opened the hemorrhagic artery of the "real" news, no longer whispered quietly from ear to ear, as in the past, but trumpeted in all four corners of the world by well-wishers, not rarely paid to do so.

Thus, thanks to the internet, many contacts with people I had met in the past were surprisingly rekindled in images and live voices, through the vibrant ether of the new machines capable of swallowing the distances between us. Schoolmates, friends from youth who remained loyal to old places, and relatives we had voluntarily parted from, reappeared with nostalgic joy before our eyes, recalling memories. And, not least, I was happy to find again on the internet the lady who once guided me with useful advice years ago. Only now, the messages I received from her were no longer addressed personally but generously scattered on Facebook. The content of many of those messages saddened me.

None of us came to these lands without well-founded reasons. Whether it was poverty and deprivation, endured despite all efforts, or ancestry labeled as hostile reducing our civil rights, or the "dogs" of the secret police on our trail chasing us with false accusations, we paid the tribute of exile choosing freedom. The memory lingers of those early years when each of us still children at the time saw after the end of the Second World War, the dawn of a new era in which people would live in peace, understanding, and prosperity.

But it was not so. Freedom was replaced by the dictatorship of the proletariat, class struggle, nationalization, rationing, inflation, stabilization, collectivization, prisons to punish many for no other guilt than telling the truth. So, we found ourselves placed in a world of endless lines for food, clothing, and other necessities, a miserable world, where nothing could be obtained without a bribe and where one was forbidden to express his fillings, under the risk of being taken off and made to disappear.

We learned in the school of practice what socialism as a social order means. Because of it, within a few decades, an entire nation—the spiritual flower of the Romanian society—was transplanted from its soil, with roots deeply embedded in faith and traditions inherited from ancestors, into the superficial pot of Marxism, along with the weeds of anarchists at odds with the law, who assumed the right to teach others how to live. Thirty years have passed since the democratization of the country after Ceausescu's dictatorial regime, but the damage of communism continues to shackle the nation, still bound by the same lying, unscrupulous pretenders as before.

I began to write when symptoms like those experienced in Romania started to be visible in Canada too, where life had still unfolded peacefully, like in an idyllic painting. When the contrast between Canada's conservative, restrained politics, and Obama's demagogic-democratic politics on the far left—with chronic unemployment at 8% and millions of people dependent on food stamps—became striking, I was outraged by the articles in the press that criticized the conservative government while flattering the American president. And I am even more outraged today by the daily venomous fabrications against those who wants to redress the country in a positive way, hiding from the world the remarkable achievements conservatives obtained economically, politically, and internationally under Trump. In the 2020 electoral campaign, Democratic candidates fiercely declaim the same copied slogans, the same extremist-socialist reforms, ecological and full of unachievable promises.

The lady friend from past years, displays on Facebook, with candid innocence propagandists' democratic slogans identical with those used by communists in Romania, not knowing that she is serving those paid to spread them. On this continent, people do not know the horrors of socialism. We have a duty to let them know.

February 23, 2019

Clear View

I believe I am not the only person tormented by unanswered doubts in the face of the daily waves of information that crash over us like a tsunami, catching us unprepared to face them or to resist them. This continent, North America, looks like a fortified city, well-built and envied by everyone, yet it lets the wind blow freely inside, bringing the freezing blast of violent storms stirred up by hostile spirits, fabricated lies, and unfounded theories. Inside, the citizens are protected, lacking nothing, and mind their own affairs, but evil spirits scream relentlessly that the sky will fall on them, that the city walls are rotted by mold and must be torn down, and that everyone must share what they have with the rest of the world.

Readers of *Observatorul* journal have the fortunate opportunity to read the articles of Mr. Gabriel Watermiller, a learned scientist and renown Romanian-Canadian writer, who gave me an essay to read: *The 77-Year War and American Hegemony*, from which I want to reproduce a few ideas that clarified my overall view of the current historical moment.

Drawing on the idea from the book of the same title by the great scientist and historian Neagu Djuvara, Mr. Watermiller describes the historical evolution of many civilizations of the past, and arriving at the distinction of American society, he stops at the observations of the French author Alexis de Tocqueville from 1835, who said that two tendencies in America support each other: the religious spirit and the spirit of liberty. Religion sees nobility in human freedom, while liberty regards religion as the protector of morals, laws, and democratic governance.

A third element was the commune, a social nucleus, sovereign, of the American people, independent of the state and led by annually elected officials through secret ballot, controlling the administration. Interestingly, both authors—Djuvara in the 1970s and Tocqueville nearly two centuries earlier—saw global hegemony ultimately belonging to the Americans: "The American's conquests are made with the plowman's plow, the Russians with the soldier's sword. The former has liberty as his shield, the latter, slavery," wrote Tocqueville.

"The common feature of civilizations," wrote Mr. Djuvara, "is that over many centuries they have followed the same political evolution: all emerged at some point, played their role, and disappeared according to a similar scenario." Essentially, everything in the universe is born, evolves, and then dies, death being not a complete disappearance but a transformation.

Mr. Watermiller's essay also discusses many ideas put forward by the American author Samuel Huntington. He argues that the main causes of global conflicts after the Cold War are religious and cultural in nature. Observing that Western civilization has reached an impasse, Huntington admits that the United States can neither dominate the world nor withdraw from it.

Analyzing the causes of the decline of Western civilization and the United States, Huntington lists rising antisocial behaviors (crime, drugs, violence), family decline (divorces, underage pregnancies, the increase of single-parent families), declining education standards, and more. The Italian professor Giuseppe Sasco believes that the hemorrhage of investment capital to China is harmful, leading to a situation today where Americans have little to sell to the Chinese, while the colossal U.S. external debt weakens and questions its status as a hegemonic power.

From a demographic point of view, the Western world is in continuous decline in birth rates, below the number necessary to maintain the existing population, the only one capable of preserving religion, culture, and customs established over centuries. The recent increase in immigration to Western countries intensifies problems, as newcomers resist assimilation, demanding legal recognition of their religion, culture, and native customs.

It is hard to believe, but it seems that the greatest enemy of democracy and freedom is freedom itself. Today, not dictatorship but freedom carried to absurdity is the great danger. The two components of American identity, religion and liberty, are fiercely attacked by a small but affluent group of intellectuals and publicists, promoters of multiculturalism, claiming special rights for minorities of race, religion, or sexual orientation over individual freedom. Rejecting the creed and Western civilization would mean the end of the United States, Huntington said.

Mr. Watermiller identifies three forces currently assaulting the gates of Western civilization: India, Islam, and China. All three have demographics exceeding the most optimistic projections for natural population growth in Western civilization. India, despite its surprising economic development, is held back by multiple internal, conflict-laden issues regarding its cultural-religious mosaic. Islam and China are serious contenders for the next hegemony. Islam, through aggressive attempts at global Islamization by Muslims, as we witness. China, through its human potential, the enthusiasm with which it absorbs Western culture, and the unconscious facilitation by the West that allowed it to rise to the status of a major world power.

Djuvara's essay concludes by predicting that U.S. hegemony will be short-lived, followed by major upheavals. Gabriel Watermiller believes that the phase of the struggle for hegemony in Western civilization is not yet over. Even if American hegemony proves to fail, it will likely only mean the regression of the North American branch of Western civilization. "It is a painful admission for us, the generations sacrificed to the Marxist-Leninist slavery experiment, who suffered and hoped to see the light of freedom, whose beacon has always been, even in the darkest moments, the lady with the torch on Liberty Island."

I have attempted to briefly convey the content of Mr. Gabriel Watermiller's essay, which summarizes studies of many renowned international authors on world civilizations over the last six millennia. Today, we are at an important crossroads in history, and instinct suggests that something is about to happen soon. What exactly, no one knows, and that is why the confusion, unease, and concern for what will happen to children and future generations is so overwhelming that it is hard to bear.

Mr. Watermiller's essay has lifted slightly the shutters of the unknown, letting us glimpse a small fragment of the uncertain future.

March 23, 2019

The Secrets of the First Writings in the Romanian Land

A documentary book about the history of the earliest written records on our country's territory was made accessible to me by engineer D. P. Popescu, who let me borrow *The History of the Book and Printing in Oltenia*, authored by Gh. Pârnuţă and Nicolae Andrei. The result of years of research in documents and charters from monasteries and libraries spread both inside and outside the country's borders, this work is of great importance to us, lovers of the written word, because it helps us better understand the character of our nation and allows us to know those who effectively contributed to the transmission, enrichment, and writing of the Romanian language.

Leaving aside the three clay tablets found at Tărtăria in 1961, dating more than 3,000 years before our era, we learn that at Ocniţa (Ocnele Mari) fragments of pottery were found, inscribed with Latin letters, three Dacian names dating from the first century A.D. During the first Dacian-Roman war, 101–102 A.D., Trajan received from the Dacians a message in Latin written on a mushroom, advising him that peace would be wiser. This moment is depicted in a scene on Trajan's Column in Rome.

Emperor Diocletian also received from Decebal a letter in Latin, proving that the Dacian king had a chancellery with skilled scribes. Numerous monuments, temples, public edifices, and funerary stones are marked with capital Latin letters, as are the names of potters signed on vessels dating from the second century at Sucidava. Also, in the first century, on the Grădiştea Hill, inscriptions with Greek letters were found on stone blocks, evidence that the Geto-Dacians knew both the Latin and Greek alphabets.

After the conquest of Dacia by the Romans, Latin inscriptions greatly multiplied. From 1369, we have the Latin letter of Vladislav-Vlaicu, ruler of Wallachia. But in Dobrogea, Prahova, and other places, inscriptions in Slavonic and Cyrillic letters, dating from the ninth–10th centuries, have been found. In the village of Mircea Vodă, a stone inscription was found: "jupân Dimitrie" ("Lord Dimitrie"), written in Cyrillic letters, from the year 943. Before the founding of the principality of Wallachia, numerous religious texts were copied in monasteries, the oldest of them in Slavonic, from the early 11th century. Likewise, some manuscripts were produced in our lands starting in the 11th century.

The writing of the Romanian language with Latin letters was used as early as the 12th century. From Ilinca, the daughter of Pătraşcu Vodă, we have many letters written in Romanian with Latin characters. But the Cyrillic alphabet was used for a long time. Ion Heliade-Rădulescu, Iancu Văcărescu, many scholars, and numerous inhabitants fought for the replacement of Cyrillic with the

Latin alphabet. On July 18, 1859, the Public Instruction Board requested Prince Alexandru Ioan Cuza to issue a decree requiring all public authorities to use only the "ancestral letters," Latin. The decree was published in the *Official Gazette* in August of the same year.

Manuscript books and the art of letters appeared in our lands between the 14th and 16th centuries, in the monastic world. In 1359, in the synodal letter of the Patriarchate of Constantinople, Iachint was appointed Metropolitan of Wallachia, with the mission of organizing church life. During the reign of Vladislav Basarab, who founded a new diocese in Severin, a chancellery functioned there, employing calligraphers who labored to copy manuscripts in Slavonic, Greek, and Latin, the common languages of that time.

At the end of the 14th century, Voivode Vladislav Vlaicu laid the foundations of Vodiţa Monastery, at the request of the monk Nicodim, an Orthodox missionary who carried out, for three decades, an untiring political-religious activity in Wallachia. In the monasteries of Vodiţa and Tismana, Nicodim served as spiritual guide and teacher, urging his disciples to sustain an active work of copying old texts, theological writings, and the first book preserved to us, written by him in 1404–1405: *The Gospel Book of Nicodim*. A veritable masterpiece of calligraphic art, with decorated letters, colorful frontispieces adorned with gold, and wooden covers bound in gilded silver, it is the oldest illuminated manuscript preserved in Wallachia.

Bistriţa Monastery, founded at the end of the 15th century, was also one of the great cultural centers, where many manuscripts were created and preserved, including a gospel, an anthology, and a book from the early 16th century containing religious sermons, and another anthology including classical thinkers—Pythagoras, Plato, and Aristotle.

In this scholarly environment, at Bistriţa, the future ruler of Wallachia was formed, leaving behind the famous *Teachings of Neagoe Basarab to his Son Theodosie*, which gather eight moralizing texts of religious culture.

At Cozia Monastery, we must note the activity of the monk Filotei (Filos), former high chancellor of Mircea the Elder, author of the work *Pripealele* ("The Refrains"), written between 1400–1418, considered the oldest Romanian musical creation and the first known literary manifestation by a Romanian. It spread widely in our country and among neighbors, and was printed in Venice in 1536, being the first work of a Romanian printed abroad. Further editions appeared throughout the 15th–17th centuries, up until 1943, continuing with new editions in Slavonic and Romanian. Filotei of Cozia spread through poetry the Romanian spirit in the Slavonic world and even beyond, being regarded as the oldest scholar of our lands' early centuries, with the merit of intuitively recognizing the chance of survival through creation.

In the *History of Romanian Literature* (1954), there is mention of two Byzantine-style church hymns in Slavonic, written by two authors: *Pripealele* in honor of the Mother of God by Filos, the high chancellor of Voivode Mircea, and *Praise to Michael the Confessor* from the 16th century, by Simion Dudulovici, treasurer at Târgovişte.

Paraphrasing the humility of those calligraphers whose works were transmitted to us, I end these lines with the note:

I, the sinner and the least of writers, David Kimel, have written what is set forth above.

May 20, 2019

The Impact

The tree by the roadside stood as an unnoticed witness to the traffic on the road. Once, in its youthful years, the roadside tree watched the slow passing of carts traveling in both directions, and carriages of hurrying boyars urging their horses with cracks in the whip. Sometimes, people would pull their cart to the roadside, giving their animals a rest, and sit in the shade under the tree for a bit of coolness and a bite from their food satchel.

But today things are no longer the same. The animal-drawn carts have disappeared. The road is now crossed ceaselessly, day and night, by noisy cars that thunder past, leaving behind clouds of smoke, dust, and frightening noise. And behold, one of these machines veered at full speed directly into the trunk of the roadside tree. The impact nearly split it.

A similar impact struck me not long ago, during a friendly discussion with some young people on current political issues.

Like the roadside tree, I too have been an unnoticed witness to the historical changes that dominated the last century. Powerless and ignored, I had to endure, with humility, all the laws and command from above, which suppressed our right to protest and opposition. I endured with stoicism the poverty and imposed humiliations, listening with envy to rumors about the possibilities of those in the West, who could live, breathe, and speak freely what they thought.

When, only upon arriving among them, I could finally see the difference between servitude and freedom. Forty years of diligent work in the factory, in the full vigor of my youth, in my own country, did not help me pay even the monthly installments on a prefabricated apartment bought from state. Here, in the land of freedom, in Canada, without knowing anyone, without speaking English, within a few years I was able to buy a house, paid off after only a few more, raise and educate my children, and travel the entire world. It was a good time. Similar stories still happen today. Many acquaintances, who arrived here in recent years, found jobs, built new households, and are proud of their achievements. Yet the world is cornered by pessimism.

Despite general prosperity, since 2001, people have gotten used to living in fear. In so many places worldwide, and even here, isolated elements commit acts of terrible barbarism against innocent citizens caught in wrong places, or wrong time. Groups of militants of all kinds impose their views upon the population through noisy demonstrations, proselytes in power, intimidation, and the media.

Organized movements at the highest forums have created a united front to convince the world of imminent ecological disaster if the energy consumption of coal, oil, and natural gas is not immediately stopped. In education, young people are converted to the latest progressive-religious canons, which exclude the expression of opposing views and arguments.

In my discussion with my young friends, I was told that I should not worry about the future, because many young people are eager for progress. My generation, the past one, had the chance to shape the world as it saw fit, for better or worse. Now it is the right of the young to do the same. Even if their solutions are wrong, it will be a good lesson—they will learn from it, just as the past generation made mistakes, the consequences of which they bear today.

I look into the eyes of my young friends. They are attractive, intelligent, educated. They belong to a generation we can be proud of, as I am of my own children. They are right, they will be the ones to push the wheel of history forward. The question is: on what road? Where to?

I have the impression that the road they want to take is familiar to me. I have walked it once before, and the more signs I see along the way, the more convinced I am. It is called socialism. That worries me.

The roadside tree does not hate the machines—it accepts them. It knows the time of horse-drawn carts has passed and will not return. New technology has made life more beautiful, easier, and has given people more time to think, to see the world, and to care for their loved ones. But the new technology has also brought invisible eyes into every corner.

I fled Romania because of these invisible eyes, which watched, from hiding corners everything we did, everything we said, and where we were heading. These invisible eyes were, during communism, the armies of secret police informants, scattered through homes, phone lines, and all workplaces. Oh, if only the communists had had today's technology!

Orwell described in his *1984* book the role of video cameras, widespread everywhere, meant to track what each person was doing. The leaders of Ingsoc, The Big Brother, to maintain infinite power, needed control over every individual in society. But George Orwell could not foresee the level technology has reached today, and how limited our freedom of movement is now, when every room, street corner, or nook is scrutinized day and night by electronic eyes, when the smartphone records every conversation and notes where we are at any given moment, and when Facebook, Google, Instagram, and others assume the right to decide who can post and what on their platforms.

Why are these measures necessary? Who watches us from the shadows, and for what purpose? Young friends, do not be deceived. Like atomic energy, technology can be a double-edged sword and must be kept under strict control. Otherwise, others will control me, you, and everybody else.

The roadside tree, silent witness to the events around it, became victim of the impact of a road car. A similar impact struck me. You, my young dear friends, be different!

June 25, 2019

Spiral Slope

Ticuţă, my childhood friend, whose father was a carpenter, one winter day—I think it was after Christmas—showed me a wooden airplane, nicely polished. It had a propeller that wound up a rubber band inside, and when you set it on the floor, the airplane moved by itself to the length of the room. That was the role of the propeller: to screw itself into the air, pulling along the wooden toy. The clock's hands seem to copy the role of Ticuţă's toy propeller: pulling us, in time, with an inexhaustible screwing force, into the unknown moment that follows.

Winding the propeller one way, the airplane moved forward; winding it the other way, the airplane could not move backward. Nor can the hands of the clock do that; time is irreversible. But we can crisscross time with our thoughts. From legends, documents, and archaeological excavations we can reconstruct the past.

Two thousand years ago, a child came to the world, a child whose name would change the entire world: He was called the Christ, that is, the Messiah. He harmed no one, gave parables, and was Himself a parable for all. Multitudes followed in His footsteps, as in a continuous procession, eager to listen to Him and witness the miracles He performed. But prying eyes spread hostile slanders about Him in the world, and He was crucified.

A century later, Rome was shaken at the news of the assassination, in the midst of the Senate, of the man who had pushed the empire's borders beyond the shores of the Mediterranean, across the English Channel, and to the Euxine Sea, giving Rome a brilliance never regained since—Gaius Julius Caesar.

Another bold figure, an officer of inferior rank with a Corsican accent, Napoleon Bonaparte, born in the foam of the French Revolution—when the starving people overthrew the nobility under the blade of the guillotine—took in his firm hands the baton of a brilliant leader: the army, which he led to memorable victories. With enemies in all directions, including within his own government, he was arrested, taken to the island of Saint Helena, and poisoned.

The New World was the magnet of attraction, the refuge of the downtrodden, eager for a better life and the freedom to worship the Lord without papal intermediaries. They copied the ordering of the old world but created laws to ensure that no one would claim rights different from those of the other citizens, and they called these laws the American Constitution.

Instead of kings, they chose a president with a short term and powers limited by law. Thus, Abraham Lincoln, elected in 1861 as the 16th president at the critical moment when the Union threatened to break between North and South, tried to maintain balance through a policy of reconciliation, disapproved equally by those who wanted slavery maintained and those who militated for emancipation. As a result, many stirred up accusations, humiliated him by calling him "timid and ignorant," a man "without education," and he was slandered by opponents in every newspaper of the time.

His speeches, including the *Gettysburg Address*, received little attention in the press, and in 1864 almost the majority of members of Congress and even of his own cabinet were unfavorable and even tried to prevent his participation in the elections for a second presidential term. As the Confederate forces weakened and neared capitulation, which occurred on April 9, 1865, Lincoln was assassinated by John Wilkes Booth during a performance at Ford's Theatre, on April 15, 1865, only one day after the speech inauguration his new presidential term at the White House.

William McKinley was the last president who had participated directly during the Civil War, afterward serving as lawyer, member of Congress, and governor of Ohio in 1891. In 1896 he was elected the 25th president of the United States. In 1897, he initiated protectionist fiscal measures by introducing the Dingley Tariff on imported products that disadvantaged American producers. A rapid economic growth followed, to which was added the American victory in the war with Spain in 1898, because of which the United States gained control of colonies in Puerto Rico,

Guam, the Philippines, and Cuba. In 1900 he was reelected president, but on September 6, 1901, an anarchist assassinated him.

The same fate befell John F. Kennedy, the 35th president of the United States, elected in January 1961 and assassinated on November 28, 1963, by Lee Harvey Oswald. He stood firm against the maneuvers of communist states in the Cold War, initiated the founding of the Peace Corps, and supported the civil rights movement. He oversaw the continuation of the Apollo space program, and after his death Congress enacted his proposals for the Civil Rights Act and the Revenue Act of 1964.

Life is a slope rising in a spiral, year after year, to another level and a new vista, like a Babylonian tower vanishing into the mist of the clouds. On this slope we catch our breath, repeating past mistakes, with the addition of fashionable spices that lubricate the process of screwing the present into the future.

Apparently, humanity has never been able to distinguish between good and evil. In two thousand years of history, no one has understood that only those without merit are shielded by hostile inventions, while those most criticized are, in fact, the heroes who made important contributions to the age in which they lived. In these two thousand years, the worthiest of praise among people have been slandered, accused, and crushed out of envy, helplessness, and through lies. Some of them perhaps lacked the talent to make themselves understood, perhaps they had hidden sins, as anyone does, but they were sincerely driven by a desire for justice—and for that, they paid with their lives.

Today, when more than ever antagonistic forces separate us into opposing camps, incited by the embers of flaming accusations, ready to eliminate their opponents on the pyre, let us not repeat the mistakes of the past.

November 28, 2019

About Religion

The Offensive of Wrong Ideas

Only a few weeks ago, the ship of some American missionaries was captured by pirates in the Gulf of Aden, and all four travelers were killed. The ship carried as its cargo numerous Bibles, meant to be distributed to those who wished to know the Word of the Lord. Their example is inscribed in the Book of Martyrs for Christ.

In front of me lies another book, written years ago by Pastor Richard Wurmbrand, *Tortured for Christ*. In it, the author bears witness to years of suffering and torture in the prisons of Romania, for his underground church activities during the country's communist regime. At a time when the official church was subjected to the control of party organs and priests were forced to report on the problems and presence of parishioners, the underground church carried out its activities in private homes, attics, basements, or in forests, in small groups, where handwritten Bible lessons and prayers were shared with the faithful.

At these gatherings simple people, young and old, factory workers or peasants took place, but also some government officials, the police, or loyal believer from the army. The underground church was present throughout the country, not always led by qualified priests, but faith, fervent prayer, and personal example inspired the devotion of those who needed moral support in times of hardship. Many of these propagators of faith were denounced, imprisoned, and tortured for long periods of time. The country's prisons were full of zealots of faith.

Beaten, tortured, starved, locked in freezing chambers until frozen to death, revived and frozen again, they resisted pressure and torment, but did not renounce their faith. Many were killed, declared missing, and never heard of again; the book is filled with such examples.

After serving 14 years in prison in two terms—one of 6 years and another of 8—Pastor Wurmbrand was bought by a Norwegian Mission and the Judeo-Christian Alliance for the sum of $10,000 and allowed to come to the West. There he began to advocate for the release of all believers imprisoned by communist regimes, speaking before the United States Senate, the United Nations, and other international organizations. His testimony, however, expressed his deep disappointment and suffering, seeing the spiritual emptiness of the churches in the West. He claimed he suffered more in the West than he had in communist prisons, because Western civilization is dying.

The writer Oswald Spengler wrote in his book *The Decline of the West*:

"I see in you all the characteristics of the stigma of decadence. I can prove that your great wealth and your great poverty, your capitalism and your socialism, your wars and revolutions, your atheism, pessimism and cynicism, your immorality, your destroyed marriages, the abortions that bleed you from below and kill you from the top of your brain—all prove the death signs of the old civilizations: Alexandria, Greece, and neurotic Rome."

These lines were written in 1926. Since then, half of Europe has gone through social transformations, wars, and unprecedented dictatorships that affected the lives of millions of people, while the West, for the most part, continued to sleep. Unfortunately, the same thing is happening today. Millions of immigrants fleeing communist countries or absolute dictatorships, renouncing everything they had accumulated over generations, bear witness to the miserable life, persecution, and injustice, while their host country continues to flirt with communist authorities, whether from China or the Middle East. Even more, ultraprogressive left-wing organizations, local socialists, and communists, together with the unions, are trying to force the replacement of capitalist society in the West with a new social form—liberal-communist (or even a Sharia state).

The attack takes place on many fronts. Missionaries everywhere spread the Bible in African countries, Cuba, China, and other places where it is forbidden, while here, at home, in

America and other Western countries, politicians have removed it from schools, exterminated it from public life, and impose fines on those who dare to mention the name of the Lord. The well-known journalist Rex Murphy commented in the *National Post* that there are rampant efforts by some local authorities to remove from municipal buildings all Christian symbols—crosses, crucifixes, Bible quotations, and public expressions of patriotism. To this it is added the prohibition of erecting the Christmas Tree, as being offensive to some citizens.

In Saguenay (Quebec), the Human Rights Commission decreed the stopping of prayers before the opening of local council sessions, and not only that; it ordered the payment of $30,000 to the "victim," the offended person who brought the lawsuit, for the suffering caused. Will we again be forced to hide from the authorities to say our prayers?

August 2009

The New Expansion of Islam

The dilemma of these days has divided the world into two camps: pro and anti-Israel. Almost all newspapers, large and small, are caught in the fever of debates about the war in Gaza, whether just or unjust, and the results have been no less discussed. From Romania, I learned that Babeş-Bolyai University in Cluj-Napoca issued a declaration of the Romanian Israeli Cultural Society regarding the situation in Gaza, which, in its six points, stated that Hamas had taken power by violence, attacking the Palestinian organization Al Fatah as being ineffective, and then attacked the State of Israel with rockets. As a result, Israel intervened in Gaza on December 27, 2008, intending to destroy the Hamas infrastructure, an act considered irresponsible and unpardonable. In conclusion, the declaration maintained that terrorism is not a solution, and that states recognized by the international community must be protected with unshaken security. The cultural contribution of peoples must be cherished, and Israel's cultural heritage is among the most precious of humanity. The fate of Israel is the responsibility not only of the Jews, but also of the Judeo-Christian world, of Christianity, and of civilized humanity.

Paradoxically, Gaza was handed over to Palestinian control by the government of Ariel Sharon, in the hope that with its own autonomy it would prosper to the benefit of its inhabitants. That was not the result. In reality, the Arabs have shown, repeatedly, that they have little interest in forming a Palestinian state. The opportunities were many: in 1937 the Peel Commission recommended the partition of Palestine; ten years later, in 1947, the United Nations recommended the same thing, and as a result, the state of Israel was born; later, over two decades of peace initiatives by three American presidents—at Madrid, Oslo, Camp David, or the Road Map—the chances for the formation of a Palestinian state appeared, and each time were squandered.

The Arab world was not interested in the Palestinians having a state of their own. Their interest was in thwarting the creation of Israel, destroying it, and eradicating this state from the maps of the world. All the energy and wars waged over six decades aimed at the destruction of Israel. The same goal was pursued from the very beginning by the PLO, led by Yasser Arafat. The same goal is pursued by Hezbollah and Hamas, and the same goal is reflected in the rhetoric of Syria and Iran. I wonder whether all this commotion amounts to nothing more than that.

Increasingly it becomes clear that behind the Muslim world, the most radical elements of Islamic culture have managed to dominate the masses of Muslim believers through intimidation, terror, and a totalitarian ideology based on the precepts of the Quran. A striking example is Lebanon, once the only majority-Christian state in the Middle East. After 1940, when it gained independence from the French, it became a democratic country with universities recognized worldwide, attracting students from everywhere because Lebanon had open borders. Culture, trade, and the arts experienced a flourishing renaissance. Over time, as the demographic balance shifted, the influence of Islam became the uncontested power of the country.

The same seems to be happening today in Europe. Recently, while visiting Italy, I was surprised to see at almost every street corner the cars of the Carabinieri and police everywhere. Local guides take tourists around the cities, except into certain neighborhoods where not even the government police enter. If you ask to go there, you are advised to avoid them. The same is true in Paris, London, Amsterdam, or Innsbruck. In these neighborhoods, you find yourself in a different world, with shops, language, and attire all different, where women appear on the streets hidden behind cloaks that deform their bodies, their heads and sometimes even eyes covered, with a throng of children around them, walking behind their husbands like shadows.

More frequently, large mosques appear at road intersections, and periodically, during Muslim holidays, the area is flooded with worshippers and cars that block everything. The number of Muslim worshippers is continuously increasing, and municipal plans provide for the construction of additional mosques, while the local Christian churches have ever fewer faithful. Cities like Amsterdam,

Marseille, or Malmö in Sweden are already a quarter Islamized. The young Muslim population, under eighteen, predominates in many cities, and, interestingly, the satellite TV dishes in their neighborhoods are not directed to local stations, but to their places of origin. A statistic in the Netherlands showed that in 1909 there were only 54 Muslims; in 1960 there were 1,399; in 1994 there were 458,000; and by 2004 they numbered 944,000. In Europe, in 2007, there lived more than fifty-four million Muslims. But that is not the disturbing problem. The real problem is that they refuse to integrate with the local population. Their loyalty to the country and regime that received them is inferior to their loyalty to Islam. A third of Muslims in France do not oppose terrorist actions. In England, more than a third of Muslim students believe Universal Caliphates should be created, and half of Dutch Muslims were tolerant toward the September 11 attack. Faced with this growing multitude, European politicians easily accept the complaints of the Muslim population, which defies local laws, demonstrates in mass, and provokes acts of intimidation under the shield of political correctness. Thus, in England, Sharia law has been legalized, and in the Netherlands, politicians believe it should be legalized as well. In France, not long ago, the revolt of the poor neighborhoods of Paris left many victims and material damage. Worse still, many are forced to leave their homes, their neighborhoods, even their country, to find peace elsewhere. Unfortunately, Israel has remained isolated on the front line of defense, facing Islamic jihad, just as West Berlin was during the Cold War. Many democratic politicians suggest it would be better to abandon Israel to its fate, to appease the Arab world. Will it be appeased? If Israel collapses, Muslims will see in this a victory and will be encouraged by the weakness of the Western world, marking the beginning of the final conflict for world domination.

From a demographic standpoint, Islam is winning. Liberal politicians see immigration growth as a victory of their economic system, which attracts poor masses from underdeveloped countries, and as an opportunity to keep unskilled labor wages at the lowest level. Academia, the Arts, Unions, and other Civic Organizations believe in the theory of superior civilization, multiculturalism, and tolerance. Anyone who dares criticize the system is stigmatized by the media with labels like Extremist, Radical, or Xenophobe. In this way, those who should have defended millennia-old culture and traditions, civilization, national heritage, especially Judeo-Christian values—the politicians of society's elite—are hastening their ruin and destruction. Beyond Europe, Islam maintains struggles in various regions of the world against all that is not part of its faith— against the infidels. Surely not the entire Muslim population is extremist, but unfortunately the voice of moderates—whose religion has been hijacked by the ultra-zealous—is not heard. It is understandable that in Middle Eastern countries they have no right to openly oppose those who continually incite to hatred and murder. But in free countries like America, Europe, Canada, and others, they should rise together with the rest of the world that does not want a return to medieval methods—but they do not.

In the world there are over 1.2 billion Muslims, but only 15–25% (180–three hundred million) of them are radicalized. More than nine hundred million are moderates, and yet they do not take part in protesting against terrorist actions, even though they see that in this way they themselves become suspected as participants. And what is even more interesting is that in mosques in Europe and the United States, inflammatory literature is distributed, encouraging anti-state actions. Their imams preach a dogma according to which all religions except Islam are false, and that it is the duty of every Muslim living in infidel countries to hate, undermine, and oppose the laws. Justice, Democracy, and Freedom are proclaimed as the main causes of evil in the world, and every Muslim must eradicate them. The results of these preached doctrines lead to conflicts such as those in the West Bank, Gaza, Bosnia, Albania, Sudan, and, increasingly, in Europe. It is our duty to stop the spread of evil!

August 2010

The Water Must Be Clear

To glimpse the depth of the river down to its bed, the water must be clear, otherwise one sees only the yellowish haze of insoluble molecules carried away by the current toward unknown destinations. In its depth, water is the predestined carrier, which has, since immemorial times, transported along its path particles detached from the mother soil, plants and logs whose roots have lost their grip on the eroded banks, seeds of fruits carried by the wind on its surface and which will sprout or perish in other fields. Often, grains of golden sand, which will never lose their starry brilliance, lie at the bottom of the transparent riverbed. Water is a source of life, of burden-bearing, and of meditation.

So, it is with time.

Like water, time sometimes wears the clear robe of sunny mornings, in which hidden distances beyond the horizon can be discerned, or the gray haze of fog, which isolates you from the surrounding world, which only by sound makes itself somehow known. Like water, time carries on its irreversible path the destinies of so many peoples, countries, and lives whose experiences have enriched history and led to the making of the contemporary man, as reflected by today's events.

Time is the creator of our conception of life today, for no one will return to the theory of the flat earth in the 21st century. Time is the vehicle of scientific and technological discoveries, and in its monotonous course, gigantic steps have been achieved, which have elevated not only progress itself, but also human longevity and the quality of living. In time, the perspectives of future life hold the potential of miracle, through new discoveries in medicine, science, and explorations in other realms and depths. But this potential can be realized only under conditions of peace and total freedom.

Water is sent to earth from heaven through rain and snow, but these do not fall evenly everywhere. There are places with abundant rain and places where not a drop appears for years. Where there is no water, life is precarious; where there is too much water, life may be in danger. Yet water, as a factor of life, has enriched the earth with goodness and man with ideas and knowledge.

So, it is with time.

Like water, time has not created everywhere, uniformly, the destinies of men. There are places where time seems to flow more slowly than in other parts of the world. The progress of some continents would have remained completely unknown to those with a slow tempo, without the contribution of explorers from the advanced world.

Inequality does not seem to disturb those left behind; rather, "Progress" seems to frighten them. The advanced, with the most honorable intentions, want to help, trying to send doctors and medicine to heal their diseases, food to feed them, and houses to shelter them. In vain. Spirits rooted from the beginning of time continue to resist. Time cannot be pushed from behind.

Like water, fire too was sent from heaven.

Man learned to transform fire into light. With the help of fire, man transformed rock into iron, made tools, machines, airplanes, and conquered the skies toward the most distant planets. Man, also invented the weapon to defend himself. The weapon has attracted man as a tool of play. Children too are drawn to weapons, just like the man from unadvanced places. He does not want "Progress," but he wants weapons—and weapons he has obtained. Now he takes revenge on the bringers of Progress. Is this a joke of Time?

In ancient times, people defended themselves from enemies by building fortresses with high walls, surrounded by water and defensive towers. It was hard to penetrate these fortresses, and that is why legend still venerates clever Ulysses, who devised the Trojan Horse.

With the help of this horse, the Greeks penetrated the city of Troy, introduced there by the naivety of the Trojans. For ten years they resisted the Greeks, but now they believed they had been left a gift. With a handful of men inside the city, Ulysses opened wide the gates to the Greeks, who destroyed entirely one of the most advanced cities of the time—Troy.

The Trojan Horse of our times is called liberalism. Our fortresses have demolished their walls of defense, so the Trojan Horse is no longer even needed. Modern technology has placed in everyone's palm an instrument of communication, cheap, fast, and secret—between people. Those who hate Progress with death make use of its fruits skillfully and efficiently, right from here, inside the fortress where we raise our children. The vulnerability of the Trojans is our vulnerability too.

A few days ago, on September 21, in Nairobi, Kenya, a group of terrorists belonging to the Al-Shabab organization broke in, simultaneously, through three entrances of the Westgate Mall, at lunchtime, an hour of heavy crowding. By detonating grenades and shooting into the crowd—mostly civilians and children gathered for a cooking competition in a remote area of the shopping center—they created panic and terror among the people. Armed with sophisticated weapons and wearing bulletproof vests, they took captives, who were divided into groups of Muslims and infidels. The Muslims were allowed to leave, while the others were shot or held as hostages.

At the intervention of security forces and later the army, they resisted the fight for three days, turning the entire mall into ruins and killing more than sixty victims (believed to be well over a hundred), including two Canadians. Thanks to text messaging, many of the terrorists had the ability to organize defensively and even to leave the scene of the massacre unhindered. Today it is known that the action had been prepared and planned; they had familiarized themselves with the topography of the building's four levels by renting a commercial space, which they turned into an ammunition depot. Unfortunately, the defense authorities' response had no chance of such prior preparation.

Water washes stones, fire is covered with ashes, and time soothes pain through forgetting. To glimpse the depth of the river down to its bed, the water must be clear. Clarity is not attained by keeping your eyes closed or by burying your head in the sand.

Clarity is sometimes painful; it obliges you to make sacrifices, keeps you awake and clear-eyed, forces you to give priority to truth: if we cannot rebuild the fortress around us, then at least let us keep our eyes fixed on the Trojan Horse.

September 28, 2013

The Eternal Story

Last night, tired after a day in which I did not accomplish much of what had to be done, longing for relaxation, I sat in front of the TV box, which opens a window to the world. And the window transported me again to the border with Mexico, where tens of thousands of children continued the exodus, a flood that could sink America, already partly drowned in debt and with millions unemployed. But no one knows what is to be done to save these children from the claws of the humanitarian crisis aggravated by this exodus.

A moment later, the window opened an eye into Ukraine, where the remains of those killed in that deathly field are still being found, after the downing of the Malaysian plane MH17 by the Russians. And before anger could stir the blood in my veins, I saw the darkened sky of Gaza, where the place of stars had been taken by the trajectories of shells crossing each other in the night, sketching on the vault a hyperbolic dome of a pagan Gothic temple. Below, at the base, hell opened its wide arms of fire, surrounding the city in a circle of flames, without the appearance of winged angels rising to the apex of the dome. I saw nothing sacred in this spectacle, and I switched the channel to PBS, where I was somewhat luckier.

Lucky, because I came upon the broadcast of Verdi's incomparable *Requiem*, with the San Francisco Orchestra, under the baton of the angelic-faced Venezuelan conductor, Gustavo Dudamel, transmitted from the Hollywood Bowl Amphitheatre in California. After this concert of nearly two hours, I remained pinned in my armchair, to collect my thoughts, and thus I stumbled upon Charlie Ross, moderating an interview about Afghanistan and the Middle East—and I think then a hallucinatory headache seized me, making me close my eyes.

I found myself with my wife at the window of a room opening onto an inner courtyard. All around, many cheerful faces at the windows, looking down into the courtyard full of bulls enraged by being stabbed in the back with sharp pitchforks. At one moment, a man clad in a red tunic was pushed from the stairs into the herd of bulls, which rushed with their horns into the body, from which the tunic seemed to drip in red blotches onto the courtyard dirt. Horrified, I stepped back from the window and ran to the door to give him aid, but two bearded thugs grabbed me, pushed me into a room with walls lined with tiles inscribed with Moorish script, and forced me to put on a red tunic.

"No!" I protested, "I am not a Jew! My wife is a Christian!" I saw in the eyes of the thugs their disdain, as they left me alone in this room, from which there was no way out. Suddenly, the entrance doors swung open, and the hall filled with people in red tunics. We were all locked here, in this hall, without a window, seemingly waiting, in terror, to be thrown at the raging bulls outside.

I retreated into a corner near a low door, which silently opened. On the other side, in a large hall, there was a party; people in groups, standing with drinks and plates of snacks, did not seem to notice me, and I hid behind a wall, pressed against it. Noise, commotion, laughter. Through the large doors appeared the thugs, passing by me without noticing, and the party went undisturbed.

I deduced that if I did not wear the red tunic, I might blend into this crowd, and I took it off. The tunic slid to my feet, and I noticed other tunics on the floor, between the feet of the crowd. I moved along the wall, toward the opposite end of the hall, watching to see if anyone followed me, spotted on the left a dark corridor, and hurried into its shadow. I turned a corner into another corridor, where, at the end, there was a small, barred window. I found a door, opened it, and huddled inside. It was a low room with a Turkish toilet, and I crouched there to catch my breath, drenched in sweat. From here, there seemed no way out. Hanging on the back of the door, I caught sight of a greenish tunic, on whose lapels shone the emblems of the SS.

When I opened my eyes, a doctor was giving a lecture on television about the benefits of positive thinking. Nothing seemed more absurd and grotesque to me than this lecture about the art of thinking positively, today, when only a short while earlier, the most terrible images of war had made me relive the moments of terror from my childhood, when planes sowed death with every bomb dropped on Bucharest.

Even now I tremble at the memory of the rancid smell in the shelters where we tried to save our lives, of the whistling bombs falling around us, and of the explosions that made the ground quake beneath us indifferent to our tears or prayers.

Charlie Ross's interview about the resurgence of anti-Semitic demonstrations in Europe, disguised under anti-Israeli slogans, still echoes in my ears. Beginning with the Human Rights Council of the UN, which voted to condemn Israel for genocide before analyzing the causes that led to this war. It is overlooked that Hamas launched from Gaza more than 3,000 long-range rockets into Israel, infiltrated terrorists through tunnel networks built under the border to commit murders in Israel, and used schools, hospitals, ambulances, and crowded places from which to launch rockets—knowing that any Israeli armed response would cause human losses and provide a welcome public relations campaign.

But who cares to seek the true aggressor, when it is only about some hapless Jews, who escaped by luck from Hitler's claws. In Turkey there were demonstrations in front of the Israeli embassy, with slogans inscribed "May the Lord bless Hitler" and "The Muslims will completely annihilate the Jews." In France, anti-Jewish violence was grave, and only the intervention of the gendarmes prevented a miniature edition of the Nazi *Kristallnacht* in Paris. For days, Jewish neighborhoods were the target of violent attacks—homes, shops, synagogues broken into, and intimidation. Such attacks continue throughout Europe, in London, Brussels, Germany, and in Sweden, at Malmö.

The Jew, his eternal story as scapegoat, continues even today.

August 2, 2014

Let Us Not Forget!

To be honest, my little writing laboratory for commenting on current events is reduced to a few notes scribbled in the margins of a Sudoku book, which sits on the coffee table in front of the television. When memory, inspiration, and clippings from newspapers no longer help, I leaf through the pages of the Sudoku book to see what notes I made over time. This time, I know I cannot forget the bitterness that overwhelmed me as I sat in front of the television, when the announcer reported, just the other day, that at Garisa University in Kenya, 147 students were pulled from their dormitories by terrorists from the Al-Shabaab group (affiliated with Al-Qaeda) and killed, because they were Christians.

Earlier, ISIS had beheaded 21 Egyptian Coptic Christians who had gone to Libya to work, kidnapped by terrorists. Before them, we had witnessed other executions by beheading, for the same reason—they were Christians. But their crimes are not limited to Christians alone: in Iraq, near Tikrit, eleven mass graves were discovered, containing the bodies of at least 1,700 Iraqi cadets who had fallen prisoner to ISIS.

Numerous terrorist acts with bombs, cars packed with explosives, and machine guns fired into crowds are reported daily in public places, and the list includes countless similar examples.

While I was writing this article, a video surfaced in Egypt from Libya, showing two groups of Christians from Ethiopia who had gone to work (apparently on their way to Europe), captured by ISIS. They were massacred—one group, in the province of Barqa, executed by beheading, and the other, in Fazzan province, executed by gunfire. The total number of victims is still unknown.

My bitterness is not provoked only by their heinous crimes, because from barbarians we cannot expect more honorable deeds; my bitterness is deepened by the sight of the drowsiness and general indifference in the face of such savage acts. How is it possible that, after watching these scenes, after listening to the radio news or reading their reproduction on the front page of newspapers—how is it possible, I ask myself, that we continue our existence as before, as if nothing has happened? How is it possible to change the TV channel to something more cheerful after such horrors? How is it possible to kiss our children on the forehead before sending them to bed, without shuddering at the thought that overnight, other children, just like ours, living on different meridians, will pay with their lives for our problematic peace and ambiguous safety? What kind of people are we, if our blood does not boil at the hearing of these atrocities? How can we remain mute and indifferent, when a handful of wretches can so freely unleash so much pain, terror, and tears, just like during the barbarian invasions about a millennium ago?

At the Vatican, on Easter Sunday, Pope Francis brought again into discussion the fact that, in the last days of the Ottoman Empire, the first genocide of the 20th century was carried out, through a "calculated effort of mass extermination" of the Christian population of Armenia.

"By omitting to call genocide by its true name"—the Pope said, "we create a climate in which it becomes easier for executioners to persecute those who place their hope in faith and in Christ, to be odiously killed in public, beheaded, burned alive, or forced to abandon their native lands."

By drawing attention to the genocide in Armenia a century ago, Pope Francis appealed to world leaders to recognize that genocide as such, to prevent similar atrocities. His appeal underscores the fact that the Christian world today suffers because of faith, and he stands as one of the first world figures to raise the issue of recognizing the danger represented by Islamic terrorism. But unfortunately, there are too few voices condemning the barbaric acts committed by ISIS, both in the territories it occupies and beyond them.

The free world, said an article in *National Post*, needs a leader who, under current conditions, does not exist. The resonance of John F. Kennedy's words, at his presidential inauguration on January 20, 1961, still echoes clear and convincing:

"Let every nation know, whether it wishes us well or ill, that we shall pay any price, bear any burden, meet any hardship, support any friend, oppose any foe, to assure the survival and the success of liberty."

Where today is the person capable of speaking such words, of inflaming souls with optimism, inspiring them, uniting forces with the rest of the world, and leading us back into the light?

"What the world urgently needs today is a dose of Kennedy's spirit" - the article said - *"because the legitimacy of the democratic system can be lost quickly, once its representatives lose faith in pursuing the right path."*

But who can give us that spirit? Obama? President Obama is too deeply entrenched in his own utopian vision of a world in which military-like uniformity, and the equal distribution of material goods—not according to the individual's contribution to creating them, but as in a primitive commune, where everyone gets an equal share—prevail. His conception, pushed to extremes by adopting ecological slogans and vilifying those who have more, has led to the stagnation of the American economy.

On the external front, nothing proves more the President's insensitivity than his amorphous reaction to the abusive actions of China, of Russia, and to the effervescence of the Islamic world. Because of the inept policies of the White House, millions of refugees have left their homes, possessions, and occupations, flooding countries not yet penetrated by terrorists, especially Europe, which is on the verge of sinking into a new cycle of refugee aid, risking prolonged financial crisis, food shortages, unemployment, inflation, and popular discontent.

Then who can inspire us with a spirit like that of John F. Kennedy? The answer can only be found as a result of the elections for the new president in 2016. Our hopes, and those of the entire world, are directed toward that episode, in the expectation of the verdict of the American electorate, which this time, we believe, will be the right one.

April 20, 2015

The Holy Land

It has only been a few days since I returned from the place where the Lord gave His first children a spot under the sun, in which to forge their life. For thousands of years, this land has been sanctified through sacrifices, blood, and tears; merciless wars have scorched settlements and fields, the sun has turned farmland into deserts ravaged by storms, and water has nestled in hollows from which salt is extracted. The people chosen by the Lord to inhabit these lands were scattered across the world like dandelion fluff in the wind. Yet a handful of people preserved the Law, and the Divine Presence has remained in these places, from the most distant times until today. This place is called Israel.

Driven from their homes and country, the people of Israel were persecuted continuously, and generation after generation of Jews, expelled from one place to another, because of their unusual traditions and customs, could not settle permanently anywhere, though nothing they wanted more than to be considered like everyone else. Politics, poverty, and the need for scapegoats inflamed anti-Semitism, instilled hatred, and created persecutions. Hitler's rise to power in Germany unleashed the ugliest genocide known to history, in which more than six million mothers, elderly, and children were killed with industrial ingenuity, following long-prepared plans.

In this situation, the return of the Jews to the Promised Land became an immediate necessity—not, as in the past, a millennial dream of homecoming to the Holy Land. The horrors of the Second World War convinced many, especially the youth, that the only solution for the Jewish people was to return to their land. But opposing forces blocked their entry, setting annual quotas and rejecting, with the force of bayonets, those who exceeded the sum. Refugees crowded on ships were pushed back to sea or diverted to Cyprus, where, interned in camps surrounded by barbed wire and soldiers, they relived the years spent in Nazi camps.

The Declaration of Independence of Israel, on May 14, 1948, provoked the immediate reaction of the Arab countries, which formed an armed coalition of Egypt, Jordan, and Syria, with Iraq's participation, invading Jewish localities. The war lasted less than ten months, ending in Israel's victory. But the experience was to repeat itself continually, at intervals of a few years, until today.

Shortly before President Kennedy's assassination, Israel's Prime Minister, Golda Meir, had a personal meeting with him at his residence in Florida.

"I tried to explain to him why we were so desperate to obtain weapons from America," Golda Meir recalled. *"At first, I reported on the current situation in the Middle East. Then, suddenly, I thought that this intelligent young man might not understand very*

much about Jews and what Israel means to them, and I decided I must explain. So, I said: Mr. President, allow me to tell you why Israel is a country different from others. For this I must go back a long way because the Jews are an ancient people. They have existed for more than 3,000 years and lived alongside nations that disappeared long ago. In ancient times, each of them was subjected to oppression by foreign powers, at one time or another, but in the end, all accepted their fate and became part of the culture of the dominant power. All, except the Jews. Like all those peoples, the Jews too had their land occupied by foreign powers. But their fate was different, because—of all nations—only the Jewish people were determined to remain what they were. The other nations stayed in their land but abandoned their identity, whereas the Jews, dispersed among other nations in the world, left their land but never lost their determination to remain Jews—or their hope to return to Zion." Returning to the threat of a new Arab invasion, she continued: *"If we lose our sovereignty again, those of us who survive—and there will not be many—will be scattered as in the past. But we no longer have the great reservoir we once had, our culture and our religion. We lost much of these when six million Jews perished in the Holocaust."*

Kennedy listened without blinking. He leaned forward, took Golda's hands in his, looked her in the eyes, and said solemnly:

"I understand, Mrs. Meir. Do not worry. Nothing will happen to Israel!"

His promise was respected by all U.S. presidents to this day.

Today Israel presents itself to visitors as a country where urban planning, civilization, and technical progress blend with the beauty of parks, the multicolored variety of shop windows, the hum of pedestrians, and restaurant owners serving lunch at tables placed on sidewalks. The cities vibrate with continuous hustle and bustle, day, and night, for the real boutiques of Jaffa and Ha-Tachana—the old 19th-century railway station, restored—begin to buzz with people only after nightfall.

As someone who has had the chance to travel through many of the cities of the world on five continents, I can testify that what I saw in Israel equals, in equal measure, the most beautiful of what I have ever seen. Returning to Israel after an absence of four decades, the changes recorded there shocked me in a way hard to explain. Nothing from the past could be recognized; the tallest building in Tel Aviv, Kolbo-Shalom, has now become an anonymous sight compared to the forest of high-rises spread across the horizon. The country is covered with a new network of highways, only one of which is toll—and in Jerusalem, the roads cut through tunnels drilled into rock, making circulation accessible. And, on the way to the Western Wall, a sign draws visitors' attention:

"You are approaching the holy site of the Western Wall, where the Divine Presence dwells at all times."

With devout thought, I approached the wall and, after a short prayer, placed, like all visitors, a small note with a wish between the stone slabs of the wall.

May Divine Peace remain a permanent presence!

May 23, 2015

Darkness at Noon

I think that, growing old, I have become irritable. It is hard for me to align my views with those of my own daughter, my daughter-in-law, and many times, even with my son, with whom I share the office space of the business he created back in his university years. As for my wife, I won't even mention. To avoid clashes, we strategically choose certain corners of the house where each of us reigns, mulling over our grievances in silence. On the other hand, perhaps the fault is not mine alone. Maybe each of us has contributed something to this rise of the mercury in our bile, causing eruptions that are hard to contain.

I worked hard for eight decades of my life to accomplish everything I have. My achievements were due to the stubbornness to match the knowledge and skill of those around me through both physical and intellectual effort. Even if I did not always succeed in this, the fact that I tried to learn new things at different stages of life bore fruit in the end, and probably most of all in the years after immigrating to Canada, when I had to find new technical solutions for projects during my last twenty years of service at Magna International. After retiring, believing I was too young to lay down my arms, I accepted my son's offer to work with him part-time.

A passion from my youth drove me to write some verses collected in a volume, *Simple Seeds*, and later the book *A Foggy Sunrise*, in English, so that it could be read by my children and grandchildren. These works grew significantly for me, becoming my most important achievement, second only to my children. In them I poured my heart, feelings, and all my hopes. I recreated the portrait of life in my homeland during my childhood years, so I could leave to my descendants an image of their ancestors, from whom I severed them by coming to Canada. The pains, the love, the horrors of war, their struggle for necessities when nothing could be found, and the terror of persecutions in the communist era can all be found in these books. But none of those close to, neither relatives, wife, children, or grandchildren have understood this. None of them made any effort to recommend the books to someone, to comment on them positively, or even to post a note about them on Facebook. Many of them did not even read them. That hurt me, but it cannot be said. Lack of understanding can create discord and sorrow.

Around me, the whole world has become quarrelsome. Everywhere there are complaints and demands. Each of us harbors reasons for resentment, long suppressed, which now seem to have found the right moment to burst out in these days. The entire globe seems to have turned into a giant volcano, ready to erupt. In some places, the eruption has already begun to pour out lava, bringing devastation and death among people unprepared to face it. The hideous eyes of Perdition watch from dark thickets, menacing and hungry for instant action at daily intervals, catching us off guard. In our souls' nest distrust, fear, and darkness. Darkness is terrifying.

On May 19, 1780, parts of southeastern Canada, New England, New York, and New Jersey were bathed in the morning by a brilliant sun in a sky of azure, without a single cloud. Around 10:30, the sunlight grew pale, and by noon it had disappeared completely, turning day into night. On the streets, darkness made roads impassable, in houses lamps or candles were lit, chickens went to roost, and frogs croaked as if it were midnight. People stopped their activities, withdrew into taverns or their homes, not knowing what to think. The phenomenon lasted the rest of the day and part of the following night. As communication at that time was primitive, the explanation of this frightening phenomenon led many to believe that the "day of final judgment" had come, and, shivering, they sought in the Bible for similar precedents. A good portion of the inhabitants found in Scripture references to the signs of the second coming of the Savior, such as *the sun will be darkened, the moon will not give its light, and the stars will fall from heaven.*

Even today, scientists continue to debate the causes of this phenomenon, which excludes both solar eclipse and volcanic eruption, leaving open only the possibility that burning forests in Algonquin had produced the dense smoke of so vast a region that it covered half the eastern seaboard bordering the Atlantic. In recent years, we have witnessed forests burning over millions of hectares, but never have we seen the sun completely eclipsed by smoke. Could it truly have been the sign described in the Bible in Matthew 24:29? I do not want to ask whether we are spiritually prepared for the second arrival of the Savior. I do wonder, though: if the Lord were to descend today, onto the earth, how would He be received? Coming among us in all His glory as peacemaker and teacher of goodness and humanity, who would follow Him and how many would scorn Him, just as happened in the past? And how many would hurry to demand His condemnation to death for a second time?

I do not justify my thought by any allusion to any person, movement, or political party, but I am horrified by the malice, cruelty, and incitement stirred in the name of demands justifiable, under social, political, class, racial, or religious pretexts. There have been, in the past, people who, under the impulse of divergent opinions, reacted with vocal violence and threats, but rarely did they resort to homicide. Yet there were cases, in the 1960s–70s, where murderous hands pulled the trigger, as with the two Kennedys, Martin Luther King, or Reagan, but most of the population disapproved and condemned those crimes. Today, media, television, and the noise of the masses are deaf, insensitive, or even complicit. The darkness at noon has nestled within us.

June 20, 2016

About Politics

A Palestinian from Jerusalem

In the *National Post*, which appeared today in Toronto (July 11, 2009), there is an article signed by Robert Fulford, entitled *"The Palestinian's Man in Jerusalem."* In this article, the author reproduces the ideas and feelings of an Arab Israeli journalist, Khaled Abu Toameh, who has been working in journalism for over 20 years and whose views differ greatly from what the world expects to hear from someone coming from his background.

He came to Toronto last week and spoke with several journalists. He is an Arab Muslim from a family in which his father is an Arab Israeli and his mother Palestinian. He studied journalism at Hebrew University in Jerusalem, after which he went to work at the PLO's newspaper, *Al-Fajr*. Disappointed that all he was asked to write was propaganda, he wanted to become a correspondent from Israel for the foreign press.

For the past eight years, he has worked at the *Jerusalem Post* as a specialist in Arab affairs. *"I am an Arab Muslim, and the only place where I can write honestly is in an Israeli newspaper,"* said Khaled Abu Toameh.

In his view, Abu Toameh considers that the peace process, which began in Oslo in 1993, was a tragic error that produced only a few promises and collapsed into war. Both Jews and Arabs were disappointed: the former because the security of the state became even more illusory, and the latter because they did not obtain the promised independence and no honest government was created.

At present, Palestinians are divided into two opposing camps: Fatah, which maintains a fragile force in the West Bank, and Hamas, which controls Gaza. The conflict between them has cost Palestinians nearly 2,000 lives, with no signs of ending. Fatah holds in prisons over nine hundred Hamas operatives, arrested mainly to show the world that they are fighting terrorism.

The world considers Fatah to be a moderate political organization, opposed to the radical Hamas. Abu Toameh believes that neither can be considered moderate. Fatah may sound moderate in English, but in Arabic it is just as virulently anti-Semitic and anti-American as Hamas. Both factions suppress any moderate opinion coming from anywhere. In his opinion, *"this is not a fight between good and evil. It is a fight between evil and evil."* It would have been desirable for the fight to be for what is best for Palestine and the Palestinians. *"But they fight only for money and power,"* said Abu Toameh.

The free world spends fortunes supporting Fatah in exchange for a few benign rhetorical speeches, but inside, Fatah does not enjoy popular support. The thefts of Fatah officials are only occasionally reported in the West, while the inhabitants of the West Bank have begun to take existing corruption as something normal.

The world believes that the chance for peace is limited by the new Jewish settlements built on occupied territories. Abu Toameh disagrees: *"I would have wished that the new settlements were the problem,"* because the Jews would have solved that problem long ago. If settlements were the problem, then Gaza would have had peace since 2005, when the Israelis withdrew their forces. But the result was war: war between Palestinians, war with Israel. *"The real obstacle to peace is not that Israel builds new settlements, but the inability of the Palestinians to have a government. Is there a partner on the Palestinian side to negotiate peace? No!"*

What is to be done? Abu Toameh believes that Israel must wait until Palestinians stop killing each other and create a credible political entity with which to negotiate. Only then will peace be possible.

July 2009

The Dance of the Stars

Do you still remember, years ago, how radiant the names of many European countries sounded, when our chances of seeing them with our own eyes were illusory? I recall the corner of our group in the 1960s, in the Technical Service Hall of our Plant, gathered around engineer Oniga, the only one who had the chance to travel abroad in his youth. As a student, he took a cruise on the Mediterranean Sea, circling the southern coast of Europe. Nostalgic in his recollections, in his orange lab coat, with white hair and black-framed glasses behind which his eyes cast a fatherly look upon us, he would unravel his memories.

Places he had visited, people he had met, unusual happenings were wrapped in an almost unreal aura in our imagination. Most of us were young family men, who knew that soon after finishing work we had to rush through markets, shops, and queues to buy at least some of the items on our lists of necessities for the home and children. Without doubt, from books, stories, and films, places like Germany, France, Italy, England, and others fascinated our imagination as the very peak of civilization, culture, and well-being. The testimonies of those who had had the chance to see them after the war ignited hidden curiosities and desires, whose attraction dispelled any lingering doubts about their truth.

In retrospect, today, many years after the start of the new millennium, I see myself boarding onto a kind of universal roller coaster, catapulted into unknown spaces and directions, torn from the whole past world and experience to which I do not wish to say goodbye. In fact, the rupture from that conventional life had not just happened now—it had taken place years earlier when we stepped into the year 2000.

It began with Y2K (the year 2000), when all computer users rushed in panic to buy new equipment, fearful that already recorded data would be wiped out in the old systems. Then came Israel's withdrawal from Lebanon, the death of Syrian president Hafez al-Assad, succeeded by his son, and on October 12, 2000, the USS *Cole* attacked by terrorists in Aden. President Clinton threatened vehemently, but both his and Bush's administrations were criticized for not responding militarily to this action. Encouraged by the lack of decisive retaliation, the attack of September 11, 2001, followed, destroying the World Trade Center and part of the Pentagon. That was the moment that changed the face and politics of all humanity.

A few years later, the entire world became unrecognizable: China had become a dominant global economic force, North Korea was threatening America with nuclear weapons, Europe—united under the EU—was struggling to escape the claws of economic crisis through austerity measures contested by the population, while better-positioned countries like Germany refused to continue bailing out states threatened by bankruptcy (Portugal and Spain). Students in London rebelled against tuition fees increased by 400%, smashing shop windows, burning cars, and attacking the heir to the throne. Greece, Sweden, and Ireland were shaken by large demonstrations, while in France, strikes continued in chains.

In Bucharest, the situation was no better. Russia, playing roulette with a completely inexperienced and naïve player, Obama, gained advanced positions over America while secretly helping Iran obtain uranium for the atomic bomb. Meanwhile, thousands of innocent people were being killed randomly, in the name of a misunderstood religion, by drug lords insatiable for maximum profits, or unscrupulous politicians. The stars of the Western constellation had ceased to shine on the darkened sky of humanity.

What will come next? If America, the Morning Star of Democracy and Freedom, disappears from the firmament, toward whom will people like us—those who have felt its warmth—turn their hopes? If America is erased as a world power, from whom will the people still live under the yoke of totalitarian politics and slavery hope for liberation? And if America ceases to be America, as we know it, then who will guarantee every human being the right to liberty in the pursuit of personal happiness proclaimed by the Constitution?

At this hour, stepping into the second decade of the millennium, there are only a few stars still flickering on the dark night sky, and many of them are false.

Our hope is turned toward a new miracle, the appearance of a new star—like that of the Magi, over two thousand years ago in Bethlehem—to show us the way.

November 2010

The Glasses Are to Blame!

Back when I didn't wear glasses - Lord how long ago that was - everything I saw matched exactly what everyone else saw: a white horse was a white horse for everyone, and a striped cat was nothing but a striped cat for the rest of the world. Now, when every second year I get a new prescription, I no longer see eye-to-eye even with my wife, who has such a collection of glasses that it would put Hakim Optical out of business. I don't know what opticians put into the glass of those lenses, but some people see one thing, and others see something else. Even that striped cat, some see it white, some see it black, and few see it as it is: striped. And in politics it's the same: some see one thing, others another, and when something needs fixing, nothing gets done, as if we were to find our way out of the distorted mirror maze. That's why things go the way they do. Utterly laughable. And the blame, I think, lies with the glasses!

A knowledgeable friend explained to me that certain things can be eliminated from reality by putting a filter in front of the lens. That's how the first Technicolor films were made. They added filters to the cameras for each color, filming with black-and-white film. Then, in the laboratory, they superimposed the colors one over another, and thus the color film emerged. In everyday life, knowingly or not, each of us has our own filter, but we lack a laboratory to superimpose these filtered images in such a way that we could have a complete and true picture.

Take newspapers, for example; put side by side all the papers that appear on the same day and you will see how much difference there is between what one and another write about the same topic. The same goes for television broadcasts; compare the news and commentary between CNN and Fox News: what one sees as white, the other sees as black. That's why, when you see how much difference can be created through a filter, and how much reality can be distorted through filtering, we must realize that in the absence of a laboratory to build the true image of life, that laboratory must be ourselves.

Only we can extract truth from the totality of exaggerations presented by the media through their narrow-angled filters, which magnify certain facts or individuals while diminishing the significance of others. Only within us lies the strength, the hope, and the solution for correcting the situation, letting ourselves be less manipulated by lies, disinformation, and political antagonism. Upon more serious analysis, I began to see that fighting is being waged against us, using the media as a means of communication. Because our standard of living is superior to that of much of the world and, especially because our system, culture, and freedoms have spread far beyond this continent's borders through television, films, and the internet, with the help of new technology, younger generations in other parts of the world can be attracted to Western culture. Thus, it becomes a danger to the systems in countries with deep-rooted religious traditions in the Middle East and Africa. The first measure of intervention there was the introduction, from primary school, of religious indoctrination and the virulent hatred of everything non-Islamic, especially of infidels.

While democracy created "tolerance" and "multiculturalism" for us, religion there created fanaticism and religious terror. Sharia, their law, is as zealous as the laws of the Inquisition. Today, our tolerance has become the tool of our own terrorization. Where else lies the explanation for all the terrorist attacks that have shaken humanity in recent decades—the hijacked planes, the bombed trains and subways, the attack on New York on 9/11, the Boston Marathon runners, the televised beheadings of prisoners—if not in the hatred of those involved, fueled by religious-fanatical dogmas with which they were indoctrinated? Against these, we are disarmed through our professed acceptance, tolerance, and the myth of multiculturalism. But more importantly, we are disarmed by our own abandonment of ancestral precepts of ethics and religion, allowing unacceptable changes in the laws of family, marriage, abortion, and the education of our children at home and in schools.

I wrote, in 2008, an article published in *ACUM* (Now), from which I reproduce a few passages, for its truth may determine the choice we make:

"I find the example of Lebanon eloquent. It was the only majority-Christian state in the Middle East. After 1940, when it gained independence from France, it became a democratic country, with universities recognized worldwide, attended by students from everywhere, because Lebanon had open borders. Culture, commerce, and the arts flourished in a period of rebirth. Over time, as the demographic balance began to shift in favor of Muslims—as is happening today throughout the world, due to the polygamous culture of Muslims, where any man may have four wives and countless children—their influence became more significant, though the situation remained under control.

After 1970, when King Hussein expelled the Palestinians from Jordan in the horrific Black September, killing thousands of them, the only country that gave them asylum was Lebanon, due to its open border policy. Once established in Lebanon, the Palestinians joined radical Islamist elements from Syria, and Yasser Arafat created their military camps against Israel. What he failed to achieve in Jordan found fertile ground in Lebanon.

At the same time, with Syrian support, Muslims created paramilitary organizations directed against the Christian population and the Lebanese national army. They created checkpoints on all national highways, persecuting Christians methodically, driving them from their homes and towns toward the southern border with Israel. By 1974, Christians in Lebanon had become prisoners in their own country, with limited freedom of movement, living mostly in underground shelters, deprived of food, light, heat, and means of survival.

Lebanon's territory was increasingly used for terrorist actions—raids and bombings against the population in northern Israel—and in 1982, when the Israelis entered Lebanon, advancing to Beirut, the propaganda machine financed and organized by Syria, Iran, and other Arab states misinformed the entire democratic world and gave rise to anti-Israeli demonstrations. Lebanese Christians, however, briefly returned to normal life, for which they remained grateful to Israel.

Today, Lebanon, the country that had compassionately received Palestinian refugees, has been transformed into an Islamic state. Its land has become a training ground for terrorist actions under the guidance of the Syrians, and Hezbollah has become the uncontested power of the country. Lebanon's past fame as a peaceful country, a land of light, nicknamed the Little Paris of the Orient, has faded away."

Do not put filters on the glasses. Let true light record unfiltered images of our things, facts, and our lives.

April 29, 2010

Why Don't I Get Along with My Daughter

My daughter considers me conservative, reactionary, homophobic, and racist. I am fortunate that we don't live in the same city, otherwise the list of epithets might not have ended there. Twice graduated at York and with a master's degree at Toronto University, she believes that if she sees the world through red lenses—fashionable in academia—the images will turn rosy and life will suddenly become blissful.

If I weren't a Jew, the son of a printer, born before World War II, growing up in Bucharest Grant neighborhood among the children of railway workers, if I hadn't been followed everywhere by the ghost of my origins and humiliated with the nickname "kike," even after the communists came, maybe those epithets above would not have offended me so deeply.

Like her, I too was once inflamed by socialist ideas, believing they would bring better days. I hoped that one day justice would prevail, that no differences would be made between people, and that every person would be happy. For many years I waited to see the fruits of these ideals, for which we were asked to make ever greater sacrifices, but with each passing day, life became harder, injustice deeper, and the cancer of corruption devoured the last natural bonds between people: kindness of heart and understanding.

The well-being of the people, trumpeted daily in the press and on the radio, through measures meant to raise our living standards, materialized in ever harsher laws and decrees, suspended freedoms, and scapegoats for every hardship. Meanwhile, the people's representatives in government positions, lived in nationalized villas or new ones, feasted at gatherings and congresses, and relaxing hunting on former dispossessed estates. All this in the name of social equality in Socialist Romania, where most of the population waited in endless lines to feed their children, unless they had to bribe some acolyte in a key post for the smallest favor. The much-proclaimed care for the people's well-being uprooted from our ancestral land of plenty and drove us among strange people and strange lands in search of horizons brighter than the ones at home.

How can I explain all this to a child who had the chance to arrive here at preschool age, who does not know what it means to live through winter in a house without heat, who has never stood in a line, and who never had to travel clinging to a tram bar in the rain or wind just to get to school? Certainly, when she compares her life with the lives of less privileged children—even here in Canada—I understand her compassion and her sincere need to act somehow to eradicate poverty and social injustice.

But everything she sees happening is only the effigy on the visible face of the coin; she does not know, does not see what lies on the other side. She is too young to remember the horrors of life in the society from which I pulled her, where freedom was absent, rights to choose, to speak, to act on personal convictions did not exist. We, however, know and remember.

She does not know and cannot know the effort parents made to learn English, the effort to find work, accepting unskilled and underpaid jobs, sometimes delivering newspapers in the middle of the night for an extra buck, without thinking to rely on social assistance, to complain, or to claim entitlement to more. We knew we were immigrants, newcomers in a country that helped us rebuild our lives, and we did not expect to receive everything for free.

It is not the same today. The newcomers are different. They know the language and even the laws in force about immigrant rights. Not all newcomers arrive here to escape absolute dictatorships that created suffocating conditions of life. Many come simply to escape poverty, without doing anything about it. Canada is a rich country, where life is good, and as a result, they have brought the rest of their relatives—parents and grandparents who can benefit from social assistance, housing, and free medication. It is striking that many pensioners, who contributed more than twenty years of work and taxes to the Canadian economy, receive smaller pensions than elderly people living off social assistance who contributed nothing to this country's wealth.

A good part of the new immigrants is not as delighted, as we once were, with the beauty, wealth, and generosity of Canada. They want it different: with women veiled in black from head to toe, turbans in the army, police, and government agencies, with children carrying daggers at their belts in class, and with laws to legalize their holidays.

What is hard to understand is that pressures are being applied by many leftist organizations, unions, and some municipal bodies for changes in civil rights, culture, religion, and national customs. Overriding the will of the voters, politicians at various levels of government introduce, abusively, anti-popular personal agendas— such as carbon taxes, more aptly called "the smoke tax," as in the times of serfdom at home, and theories about climate change.

More often municipalities have acquired a taste for "Bylaws" rules—unprinted, unpublicized, but obliging citizens to pay hefty fines if violated. The food industry is quietly reducing the weight of prepackaged products day by day, thus increasing their price without notice.

In education, local school boards facilitate the introduction into classrooms of materials unauthorized by parent councils and contrary to the traditional moral principles that guided this nation's existence over the years and on which this country was founded.

How can I explain to my daughter how deeply worried I am to see, even here, the same abuses and dishonesty that made me give up my country, family, and friends years ago, in search of luck in the wide world? How can I make her see that every coin has two faces, that what you see on one side is not the same on the other, and that the noblest intentions do not always bring the desired results?

April 2011

Debt

Rarely does a film let you glimpse certain aspects of life that, too often, you feel are not right, but you don't realize exactly what. Such a film, which I recently rewatched, made in 2009, *The International*, with Clive Owen, Naomi Watts, and Armin Mueller-Stahl, helped me see, through the thicket of tangled threads of world politics, the goal pursued by those at the top of the social pyramid. Below, I reproduce the dialogue of a scene from the film, between the two investigators (Naomi and Clive) and the director of an international arms company:

"Mr. Calvini, we'd like to know why IBBC, a bank, would invest hundreds of millions of dollars buying missiles and control systems from your company?"

"IBBC bought missiles worth millions of dollars from the People's Republic of China. We resell them to clients in the Middle East. Along with these missiles, they were equipped with the Vulcan guidance system. My company is one of only two in the entire world that produces Vulcan equipment."

"But why would a bank be compelled to invest such a large capital and other resources just to resell these missiles?"

"It's an experiment. Small arms are the only weapons used in 99% of the world's conflicts, and no one has the capacity to

produce them faster and cheaper than China. What is sought is to make IBBC the exclusive agent of Chinese small arms in the Third World."

"Billions of dollars invested just to become an agent? Surely, all this energy doesn't generate much profit for them. No. It's not about profit from selling weapons. It's about control. He who controls the weapons, controls the conflict."

"No. No... IBBC is a bank. Their objective is not to control the conflict; it is to control the debt that the country produces. You see, the real value of a conflict, its unique value, is in the debt it creates. If you control the debt, you control everything. Do you find that disturbing?"

"Yes."

"But that is the very essence of the banking industry: to make us all, whether it's a nation or an individual, slaves of debt!"

Here lies the entire secret: to be transformed, nation or individual, into slaves of debt. The best example: Romania. With how many sacrifices, an entire generation reduced to a life of unimaginable deprivation, to pay off the last penny of the country's debt, only for today's new leaders to sink it even deeper into debt, after they sold off everything that could be auctioned. A generation subjected to slavery by a schizophrenic dictator, fallen into the hands of other predators, even more devoid of the most basic scruples, whose only concern is hoarding at the expense of their fellow citizens and without fear of the One above, making us slaves once again.

Another example: Greece. Revitalized after joining the European Community, it overestimated the advantage of bank-offered credits, spending more than it produced, and today, when it can no longer pay even the interest, we see the results. Next in line, slipping down the same slope, are Portugal, Spain, and Italy.

By reducing interest rates to almost zero, banks encouraged easy loans, which tempted many to make debt upon debt, buying houses and living beyond their means. Nations or individuals profited from this false prosperity until the first drop in housing prices, or the first layoffs caused by economic stagnation. When the debt can no longer be paid, the bank throws you out of your house.

The dilemma hangs over Europe and the entire world, like the sword of Damocles. Who will be able to save Romania, Greece, or the rest of Europe?

Closer to home, the United States is not in a much better situation. With sixteen trillion dollars of debt, an amount equivalent to the national product and still growing, if there is no immediate (radical) change in economic policy, the situation in Greece will be replicated in the USA.

By making debts of such a nature, with an appetite for even more debt, people are beginning to lose confidence in the capacity and honesty of those who govern the country, especially now, when, in five months, they will have to decide who will receive the keys to the White House.

In Canada, a country that does not lack a wide range of elements advocating socialist ideas and propaganda, to which is added a number of artists, environmentalists, and anarchists, the question arises whether all of these together, when they pound their chests saying they fight for the many, when they demand equality with those at the top of the pyramid, do so out of sincerity, foolishness, or betrayal? When the government raises taxes, imports oil from OPEC instead of cheaper Canadian oil that would also create more jobs for Canadians, making new debts every time, I ask: is that a patriotic act, or a betrayal?

Because now I understand the essential point of the banking industry. Now I know that politicians are bought by the banks to make us all, nation or individuals, slaves of debt.

May 26, 2012

The Giant and the Magic Mirror

The first morning of September this year surprised us with a thick blanket of fog, through which the silhouettes of the houses on the other side of the street could barely be glimpsed. The car's steering wheel trembled hesitantly in choosing the right path, because in the fog, any shadow takes on ghostly proportions with frightening consequences, if you are not careful. I feel the same way today, watching daily events, which, with each passing day, become more worrying. It is not so much the events themselves that are the reason for concern, but the fact that no one can predict what lies ahead of us. Groping through the fog, you cannot recognize the road, you lose direction, and wander into the unknown.

In just a few years, too many things have completely changed, and everything we thought was solid and stable has begun to shake like jelly. Insecurity is a frightening thing. Without security, man becomes paralyzed and everything around him stagnates. Who has the courage to change jobs for one with better pay, when, all around, many companies are closing? Who dares to buy a house when he doesn't know if tomorrow, he will be laid off? And who can invest their savings in a business when other businesses around are collapsing? Through the fog nothing can be seen, only sounds piercing through, and too often, these sounds signal sorrow.

In the United States, presidential elections are at the doorstep. The whole world watches with tense attention what is happening there, because for almost a century, everyone has seen in America the only proven force that could, through decision and strength, bring things back to normal. But in recent years, since 2008, the strength, decision, and firmness of this country have weakened beyond recognition. This weakening has become so obvious today that anonymous nations, whose names were almost unknown, have begun to rise with threatening bursts of violence, demanding rights more or less imagined. The world looks on in astonishment at the change, waits with bated breath to see what the response will be, but nothing happens. The American giant, the great fighter for freedom and democracy throughout the world, the symbol of hope for liberty for all those still living under the despotic heel of totalitarian regimes, seems to have fallen into a lethargic sleep. The giant sleeps.

Many ask: what is the cause? It is not in the American tradition to be indifferent to someone's insolence. It is not in the American tradition to be careless in the face of injustice, of threats, or of underhanded blows. And it is not in his tradition to stand with folded arms, waiting for charity to provide what is necessary. Or rather, it was not in his tradition. Now, it seems things have changed. In the last almost four years, it has become part of tradition to wait with an outstretched hand for welfare aid, unemployment checks, and food stamps. It is part of the wealth redistribution program, and it has caught on.

It is true that the economy is down, it is true that there is no work to be found, it is true that the debt has surpassed sixteen trillion dollars and continues to grow, but "Father Obama" said that in the next four years things will improve, and so everything is OK. And the giant turned over on his other side and took another nap.

In fact, he is not even sleeping, he is only dreaming. Not even dreaming—he holds in his hand a magic mirror, with miraculous powers. On its surface he sees everything he wishes, he sees wonderful places where his feet have not yet walked, he sees, vividly, events he has never heard of, he sees stories from the past and prophecies about the future. He sees what he never even imagined, and he is completely absorbed. The magic mirror brings him into contact with friends he has not seen in a long time, and he can exchange a few words with them, he can follow the road at a distance, and he can laugh at the antics of imaginary heroes. The magic mirror is inseparable from giant's hand; it has become part of him; from the moment he wakes up until he goes to bed. He cannot even conceive of parting with it, not when he eats, not even when he is in bed.

Since he discovered the magic mirror, he no longer sees what is happening around him, he no longer hears what is spoken in the family, he no longer participates in discussions, he almost doesn't even speak anymore. As if enchanted, everything he knows he has learned from the mirror, because the giant no longer reads the morning paper. The last book he read was an eleventh-grade assignment, and even that in summary form. But he is up to date with the latest gags about celebrities, pop music, and fair maidens in the nude.

Meanwhile, the forest is burning. The fire devastates everything and draws us closer to it. Action is needed, but the mirror does not say it is urgent. The mirror assures that there is still time, that we should wait a little longer. Maybe the rain will come, and the fire will extinguish itself. The mirror lies. The giant admires another fair maiden.

The fire crackles behind the house.

September 23, 2012

Dreams

"It seems curious how much is written in the Bible about dreams. I believe there are approximately sixteen chapters in the Old Testament and four in the New Testament in which dreams are mentioned... If we are to believe the Bible, we must accept the fact that, in ancient times, God and His angels appeared to people during sleep and made themselves known in their dreams."

These words belong to Abraham Lincoln who, according to Bill O'Reilly's book *Killing Lincoln*, told a circle of friends on the evening of April 11, 1865, about a dream he had, in which he awoke from sleep to the wailing of a crowd. Going to see from where the cries came, he entered the East Room, where in the middle of the hall lay a catafalque surrounded by candles. Three days later, on April 14, Lincoln was assassinated during a performance at Ford's Theatre in Washington, D.C. The assassin, John Wilkes Booth, an actor affiliated with the Confederacy's segregationist politics, had listened to Lincoln's April 11th speech, which laid out the plan for abolishing slavery in America and granting equal rights to Black people. That speech, delivered from the second-floor window of the White House, came just two days after the surrender of the Confederate armies under General Robert E. Lee to the superior Union forces commanded by General Ulysses S. Grant.

The assassination of the president was the final act of the American Civil War, which lasted more than four years and took the lives of tens of thousands of people.

Ninety years earlier, in April 1775, the revolt of the population against English troops had begun at Lexington and Concord, suburbs of Boston, because of taxes imposed on tea in 1773. In protest, the people sank four English ships in Boston Harbor that were carrying crates of tea. Thus "The Tea Party" was born, and this was the signal for the people's war against the English armies, which led to the proclamation of the Declaration of Independence of America on July 4, 1776. These intertwined dreams—the dream of Independence and the dream of Liberty—brought forth the America of dreams, as a symbol of democracy in the world and a magnet for all other dreams everywhere.

Dreams are important. I do not know to what extent we can draw guidance for everyday life from dreams, but each of us has dreams, desires, hopes that demand to be fulfilled, and I know how hard it is to face the disparity between reality and what we dreamed. Especially for us, who had to leave our country, our family, and our friends to fulfill our dreams and give our children a better life. We cannot and must not abandon their fulfillment in the face of torrents of pressures that seem aimed at nothing else but bringing us back to where we started, even if the geography has shifted a little. We, the population in general, are simple people, living simple lives and having simple dreams. We do not dream of becoming millionaires, we do not want to live in palaces, nor to be surrounded by servants; all we want is to be left to live our lives as they were given to us, in peace and quiet. But if someone dares to rob me of what is mine, obtained with difficulty, with sweat and effort, then God is my witness, they will have to deal with me! And God forbid I should catch someone with his hand in my pocket!

Unfortunately, things no longer match, we are plundered and robbed with or without our will. It is not done by one or another, but by those at the helm, in the name of the law. They do it knowingly, through false promises and smiling faces. They do it because we are too busy to give importance to the news (already limited, or even overlooked) that appears in newspapers, giving more importance to humorless clowns and television sports programs. They do it because we have become accustomed to ignoring the actions of those in charge, believing that there is not corruption. They do it from the shadows, weaving the spider's web of deception with which they want to ensnare us. Deception has been transformed into both political weapon and art. It is easy to create a problem, to bring a few corrupt witnesses with university diplomas to confirm the problem, frightening the crowd—and the people, terrified, will follow the indicated path. Some will embrace the new theories, even when they make their lives harder today than yesterday, reduce their freedoms, and push them into poverty. Others will profit, promoting "salvation solutions" through which fabulous profits can be made. Some will believe fanatically in the new theory and will sabotage any attempt at rational dialogue. And the lie begins to take on the proportions of a contagious plague, where there is only one victim, struggling to catch its breath: the people.

In essence, one of these theories much spoken of is climate change, just the other day, the United Nations issued a new report on this subject. All recent climate changes are listed as being caused using fossil fuels and carbon dioxide emissions. Many argue that in the recent natural calamities of this year, there is nothing special compared to other disasters that took place decades ago, at a time when fossil fuels were used only in small proportion. And, in fact, the major fuel consumers in the world introduced CO2 reduction laws more than a decade ago.

In Ontario, the population is subjected to an unprecedented regime of energy reduction through tariffs and taxes. And since there is no limit to the constraints imposed upon us, the White House is considering introducing this year regulations on methane emissions. The scope of these regulations goes beyond that of carbon because methane is emitted not only by industry but also by living beings, farms, and especially the extraction of natural gas and even oil pipelines. These regulations will again raise the bar of price increases in the near future.

Dreams, desires, hopes. Over our heads, those living in the Olympus of Queen's Park (the Ontario Parliament) decide our destinies, forgetting that they too are mortals. Soon their time will come as well to scrutiny and us, the people will be able to decide their destinies. Election day is approaching!

February 2014

The Killing of Democracy

There were cold days that made me turn on the heating system. Then came days with gentle sunshine, guarding from the heights of the azure sky the joy always welcoming this brief gift of fine weather, after a year not too generous with good days. I went outside, onto the small terrace at the back of the house, to warm my soul in the mild light of late September. The trees themselves trembled with joy, little birds, with sharp beaks such as I had never seen before, circled around a flowerpot on the terrace, in which a few stalks of orache, heavy with seeds, were growing, while the carpet of soft grass, like velvet, seemed to reproach me that, once again, I had delayed the mowing for too long. In moments like these, the mind is reconciled with being, peace seems to embrace the universe, and the soul is flooded with complete harmony, where no room remains for any other desire, thought, or need. Only that pleasure is short-lived.

From house, I hear my wife answering the phone – oh Lord! these phones always ring at the least welcome moment – and I must talk with the publisher where my next book will soon see the light of print. When I return to the garden, I bring with me the morning paper, and Leonid, my next-door neighbor, greets me, as usual, with a remark about the beauty of the weather.

For over thirty years, with my neighbors on both sides I have established relations that made it unnecessary to fence our properties, so passage from one to the other is free. Just as "back home" we used to visit with our neighbors. In this way, my children and theirs had room to play, could kick the ball around on the wide lawn behind our houses, and we often, in the evenings, could sit down for a chat, which was frequently accompanied by a glass of wine.

This time, the conversation started with the latest news in the paper. It seems that many in Harper's government want to bring forward the date of the next federal elections, because otherwise it would give the Ontario Federation of Labor time to launch a campaign like last year's, against the Conservatives, in which they spent more than ten million dollars on negative TV ads. The unions are determined to use their entire political arsenal to remove the Progressive Conservative Party from government, and for this purpose they created last year the UNIFOR organization, by merging the Auto Workers' Union with the Communications, Energy and Paper Workers' Union. According to Conservative members of parliament, the Ontario Federation of Labor would have at its disposal in this campaign around 40 million dollars, to be used not only for promoting Justin Trudeau's Liberal Party, but more as a sort of shadow political party, with its own strategic campaign arsenal, field organizers, professional agitators, and a political command center. The Liberal Party, once in power supported by such an organizational apparatus, will be obliged, whether it wants to or not, to introduce without reservation the platform prepared by the union leadership, with or without the approval of union members. In this way, the direction of the policy of this federal government would, inevitably, be guided not by the nation's elected representatives through democratic principles, but by the interests of some from the leadership of the unions.

Not long ago, I asked myself in an article whether it is possible for a democracy like ours to be so easily captured through manipulation by organizations that were originally formed with the purpose of helping the underprivileged. The historic role of unions is undeniable, as they fought fearlessly to raise the standard of living of workers forced to work 12 hours a day for a miserable wage, insufficient to feed their families. Their children were sent to work from a very young age, in harsh conditions of cold, dust, dampness, and many risks of accidents. By organizing strikes and popular demonstrations, they managed to attract many sympathizers to their cause, students, and a number of thinkers among the socialists, who helped them force politicians to improve the economic and social conditions of the working class.

Today, the results of these struggles are evident everywhere, and especially in this part of the world, where every wage earner lives in comfortable conditions, most in modern houses with many rooms, owning cars, and guiding their children to obtain diplomas from the most important universities and academies. Layers of intellectuals from among the working class became professors, obtained top positions in institutions and universities, distinguished themselves as authors of important works, and many succeeded in politics.

The ideological substratum, however, has divided the world into two camps. Not all wage earners benefit equally from the same rights. Large enterprises and corporations, including the government, employ tens of thousands of workers, who are organized in unions. Small businesses, with a limited number of employees, which produce more than two-thirds of the economy, fluctuate daily depending on market demands, have limited capital, pay high interest to banks, and negotiate wages at the lowest level.

The difference between the salaries, benefits, and compensations of those unionized and those in the private sector is shocking. Under the protective umbrella of the unions, the leadership of a unionized enterprise has no right to fire someone with derisory performance, cannot punish acts of indiscipline, and must pay for numerous sick days, whether the person was truly ill or not.

Not the same is true in the private sector. Unfortunately, all these measures imposed by unions are passed on to the population in the form of higher prices, increased taxes, inflation, unemployment, due to jobs lost in the private sector or moved elsewhere in a foreign country as uncompetitive.

That is why Harper's government began negotiating with the unions to reverse some of their privileges, a fact for which Unifor wants to ensure the removal of this government in the next elections.

Which brings us again to the question: is it possible that our Democracy could be stolen right before our eyes by groups seeking only to satisfy their own interests? It does seem so! With the help of millions raised from membership dues, it is certain that it is possible to influence public opinion in the press and on television programs, bringing defamatory presentations, disinformation, and empty promises.

We saw how they managed this in the elections in Ontario, in New Brunswick, and no less in the United States. But more than that, we have our own experience "back home." In Romania. We know how easily promises are forgotten and replaced by unpopular reforms and laws.

Let us not allow it to happen again.

October 1, 2014

The Clique

In all of Canada there is only one classical music station – FM 96.3 – which has a curious slogan: *"Beautiful Music for a Crazy World."* Crazy world? Nothing could be truer!

Endless discussions on television and in the press about the constitutional abuses of President Obama, who seems to have assumed the right to decree laws, completely ignoring the resolutions of the two legislative chambers: Congress and the Senate. The facts are so well known that they are hardly worth mentioning. But, out of curiosity, I leafed through President Barack Obama's biography, only to discover that he graduated *magna cum laude* from Harvard University, specializing in constitutional law. More than that, he taught Constitution at the University of Chicago for twelve years. Therefore, all these abuses are not born of ignorance but carried out with full knowledge. Hence the question: What drives him to break the law and to what end?

A little-known fact takes me back to an analysis of the situation in Russia during the time of the last tsar, Nicholas II, who is known to have been a very gentle man, deeply rooted in religion, somewhat lacking in energy, and lazy in thought. His decisions were taken at random, usually following the advice of the last counselor he had spoken with. He was so absent-minded and devoid of vigor that his own mother tried, at the death of Tsar Alexander III, to pass the right of succession to the throne to the younger brother, Michael, but it was not possible. When Nicholas was regent and a member of the Council of Ministers, he was presented daily with petitions that required resolution, but after two or three a day he grew bored and threw the rest into the fire.

The end of the 19th century and the beginning of the 20th were marked by the rise of industrial capitalism, and the great landowners and nobility, who still used serfs, were concerned that all these socio-cultural changes would undermine patriarchal Russia and push it into revolution, as in France. Fearing that they would lose their wealth and power, hating the evolution of the new society, those in the tsar's inner circle made a clandestine coalition with the secret police, known as the *Camarilla*. Within this organization, secret police agents were infiltrated into the revolutionary movement, with the mission to stir up conflict. In most cases, they carried out acts of terrorism and assassinations among cabinet ministers, which were then attributed to the revolutionaries.

Considering the revolutionary threat, they persuaded the tsar to enter Manchuria in 1904, claiming it would be an easy action that would increase his prestige. But the Russian troops, poorly prepared and inadequately armed, were defeated by the Japanese, who retaliated vigorously and destroyed the entire fleet. Shame, hunger, and revolt engulfed the country. At the urging of Father Georgy

Gapon (later revealed as a police agent), the people gathered on January 9, 1905, with a petition, icons, and portraits of the tsar, asking for protection for the problems of the common people of the empire. The Camarilla warned the tsar that there would be trouble and advised him to leave the city. The commander of the St. Petersburg garrison ordered fire on the crowd, and more than 1,000 demonstrators, many of them children, were killed in this "Bloody Sunday."

The tsar was not an anti-Semite. He saw himself as the ruler of all of Russia, including all nations. The Camarilla, with the help of the secret police, distributed anti-Semitic pamphlets and incitements to local pogroms throughout the suburbs. To quell the revolts, Nicholas appointed Stolypin as prime minister, about whom Stalin would later say, in the *Short Course on the History of the Communist Party (Bolsheviks)*, that the infamous *"Stolypin's Tie"* (the gallows) was used to stifle the revolution. What Stalin omitted to mention is the fact that, one day, two "visitors" exploded a bomb in his summer residence, killing his entire family. Through very harsh measures, Stolypin reintroduced order in the country and, until his assassination in 1912, Russia flourished economically, culturally, and politically, arousing the envy of European countries.

In Parliament (the Duma), on October 15, 1912, following an investigation, the conclusion was reached that: *"It has been proven that, in the last decade, we have had a series of crimes by Russian officials, implicating the political police. It was everywhere, organizing illegal printing presses, clandestine bomb-making enterprises, and acts of terrorism, and it became a weapon in the war between individuals (the Camarilla) and factions within government circles."*

I stop here with the analogy concerning the Camarilla and the role of the secret police in Russian politics, with results so well known throughout the world after the October 1917 Revolution, such as the assassination of the tsar and his family. We know the role of the secret police from our own experience in Romania, and we still cannot erase or heal the wounds it inflicted on its citizens.

But the question arises: is there still today a Camarilla interested in dictating, by any means, our life and activity? I do not know, although the evident organization of all the demonstrations in the country and abroad indicates the existence of some professional "guides" coordinating them from the shadows. Anyway, it is easier to ask a question than to give an answer.

The last few years have put us face to face with situations as unforeseen as they are dangerous. The whole world seems to be submerged inside a boiling volcano, and no one is trying to find an exit. The economies of large and small countries alike are collapsing before our eyes; war has engulfed two continents and seems to be reaching the countries of Eastern Europe. Iran is emerging as the fourth world power, with the support of the White House.

On the domestic front, maneuvers are being made, with the support of the unions, to remove from power the Conservative government led by Stephen Harper, in the same style and with the same arguments that raised the Liberals to power in Ontario. Many individuals and organizations from abroad operate under the shield of charitable centers and send mercenaries to stir up the crowds, as was seen at the *G8 Conference in Toronto, Occupy Wall Street*, or *Idle No More*. Anarchy seems to be the fuse of their efforts, and it is not difficult to foresee the goal.

In Ferguson, plotters from the shadows showed their odious face, stoking racial hatred, while the president, the chief agitator from the White House, encourages the torrent of demands from people of color, which threaten the legal authorities and the socio-democratic economic structure of the United States.

Following the worsening international situation, the influx of refugees from Iraq and Syria, Iran's hegemony in the Middle East, and what is happening in Russia, it appears that World War III could not be avoided, which might not exclude the possibility that it is exactly what Obama seeks, in order to benefit from a new presidential term.

March 29, 2015

There is Hope

About an hour away from Vancouver lies a small town called *Hope*. A picturesque settlement located where the land begins to ripple progressively toward the eastern mountain range with its eternal snows, it has carved its name and reputation into the palette of local surprises that dot British Columbia through the mastery of wood sculptures. These guard about every street corner; true works of art chiseled into the mighty trunks of trees. There, Hope sealed the final impression before leaving this province, with the certainty of its beauty, hospitality, and reconciled spirit, realizing that hope (*Hope*) truly exists.

Few remember today that J. F. Kennedy was awarded the Pulitzer Prize in Literature in 1957 for his book *Profiles in Courage*, in which he highlighted aspects of the lives of many Americans throughout history who, through their unyielding acts of bravery, contributed to shaping what America is today.

"In the days ahead," wrote Jack Kennedy, *"only the very courageous will be able to make the hard and unpopular decisions necessary for our survival in the fight against a powerful enemy... and only the most courageous will be able to keep alive the spirit of individualism and liberty that gave birth to this nation, nurtured it like a child, and carried it through the most severe trials until it reached maturity."*

This is, I believe, the secret that defines a hero of the *"silent majority"* the new term used by the candidate for the presidency of the United States, Donald Trump.

It is undeniable that Trump manages to attract, with an extraordinary magnetism, immense crowds of voters who drop everything to come and listen to this billionaire. He became famous long before his announcement as a presidential candidate, through the buildings he raised everywhere and especially through his television shows. Out of curiosity or interest, people of all ages, professions, and social classes come to hear him before other candidates, who cannot manage to gather even a fraction of the same crowds, because this builder of grand palaces has the gift of speaking plainly, saying what each person considers important and urgent. In Trump's speech, there are no pompous texts, no trendy slogans, no promises to the middle class. He doesn't read from a teleprompter, like others, and he does not shy away from calling things as they are, even knowing that many will use his words against him. His speech pulses with a fearless strength; his energy is unmatched, and from his mouth bursts a truth that is clear and convincing, as it already exists in the minds of those who eagerly absorb every word.

Trump has risen in the darkened sky of politics like an extraordinary star, a unique phenomenon, watched with interest from every corner of the world and, above all, as the only chance to repair the damages caused by the current administration, which—whether knowingly or out of incompetence—has managed to alter the historic course of America, turning the land of triumphant freedom into a world plunged into discord, confusion, and disorder. In direct confrontation with a seasoned politician like Hillary Clinton, Trump is seen as the only presidential candidate with enough tact, talent, instant responses, and counterattack arsenal. The reason for Trump's popularity lies in the fact that he is not a career politician, with hollow credibility, accustomed to twisting the threads of intrigue through the corridors of Capitol Hill, but rather a businessman, knowledgeable of the laws governing the road to prosperity. In general, he embodies the hope and chance of the *"silent majority"* for positive change.

Like Trump, Dr. Ben Carson—a famous neurosurgeon, the first to successfully separate conjoined twins joined at the head, author of many specialized and social-political articles—has never held public office but is now running for the highest office, President of the United States. Affiliated with the Conservative Party, Dr. Carson opposes the concept of profit in healthcare, advocating for removing public health from the political arena, including Obama Health Care. A man of integrity, with a positive stance on the disintegration of family within American society, especially among African Americans, he is the founder of a one-thousand-dollar scholarship program, which has so far benefited more than 6,700 students. He is also a supporter of introducing a single tax rate, which he calls a *"proportional tax."* His balanced attitude, answers flowing from a deep conscience nourished by a strong belief in justice and religion, place Dr. Carson in the first ranks of presidential candidates, in the eyes of voters.

Carly Fiorina is another candidate for the White House, who has never held public office, but who, over the years, has managed to climb the entire ladder of experience—from a modest secretary to CEO of Hewlett-Packard, becoming the first woman elected to lead one of the top 20 companies ranked by *Fortune* magazine, with over 150,000 employees. In the opinion of voters, Carly Fiorina represents the conservative counterpart to the Democrats' candidate, Hillary Clinton, whose honesty has become questionable, in the historic race to become America's first female President. The rise in popularity of these candidates, who have never held government positions, shows that a large part of the population is tired of giving their votes to professional politicians, many of whom profit through influence peddling.

Among the other conservative presidential candidates, the most favored politicians with chances of becoming the 45th president of America are Marco Rubio, Chris Christie, John Kasich, Ted Cruz, Jeb Bush, Scott Walker, and Mike Huckabee. Although the U.S. elections are still more than a year away, the courage of some candidates in tackling issues and proposing solutions is to be appreciated. The common subject in their discussions—undeniable to all of them—is that the current situation cannot continue and that radical changes must be made, both domestically and internationally.

When worry is fed daily with increasingly worse news, all that remains to people is only hope. Hope that someone, maybe one of these candidates, will be endowed with enough courage, willpower, and determination to bring America back once again to its historic path, as a symbol of freedom in the world.

August 31, 2015

Who Do I Vote for?

The other day, our great Romanian actor, Dan Puric, presented a pantomime performance about the unhappy life of an emigrant in the diaspora and his journey back home. The performance was moving in every respect, and Dan Puric's portrayal of the hero highlighted this actor's extraordinary talent, the creator of a unique show in terms of subject, mobility, and expressiveness of movement, which far surpassed the tableaux of Marcel Marceau and even Charlie Chaplin's little tramp. It was an unforgettable evening, especially since, after the performance, Dan Puric talked with the audience for a long time, until almost midnight, sharing memories, thoughts, and anecdotes.

Unlike Dan Puric's hero, the Romanian emigrant in the diaspora has evolved; he is no longer the same man who came trembling with fear, not knowing whether he would be able to find his place among strangers after leaving behind at home everything that defined him: family, friends, and colleagues. Thanks to intelligence and a thirst for work, he succeeded, integrated, and today is proud that what he could not achieve in his own country, due to incompetent leaders, he has achieved here, among strangers. Many of these emigrants today hold positions of responsibility in large international companies, have distinguished themselves in the professional, social, and political environment, and enjoy well-deserved respect in the mix of society. Our unanimous pride is justified by the fact that we are active participants in strengthening the Canadian economy, our second homeland, and at the same time, we show sensitivity to the evolution of problems inside and outside the country's borders.

Many of us, especially the younger ones, follow with deep concern the problems that still burden each of our lives, wishing with every fiber to personally contribute to the improvement and change of unresolved issues. The concern with which they speak and their sincere desire to improve shortcomings in various social areas such as hospitals, schools, and public transport are praiseworthy and deserve to be noted. Among them, my own child, who came to Canada at only eight years old in 1975, is outraged that the government does not provide adequate funds for medical care in hospitals (the field in which she works), in schools, and in other sectors. A studious nature with initiative, she has risen to lead a group of social workers in the hospital where she works, introducing better methods of caring for patients and their families. I understand her disappointment that she cannot accomplish more because of the lack of funds, but at the same time, I myself am disappointed to see her change in lifestyle, from modest to excessive, with inclinations toward imported products, while she criticizes others, the government, for not providing enough money to those with fewer resources (a phenomenon that seems contagious among many in our community). Undoubtedly, there are many problems to be solved, and not a few consider that the authorities act far too slowly.

Canada is not an isolated island in the middle of a calm ocean, without waves and storms, as if on an isolated island, even though fierce battles for survival are being fought all around us, in a world haunted by poverty, famine, unemployment, and war. If we separate the island from the rest of the world, all those who accuse the government of the shortcomings they have signaled are right to do so. But, considering the events that continue to rage furiously over the entire world, the prudent man seeks shelter until the storm passes. In short, Prime Minister Harper supports nothing more than the application of this principle in governing the country, which, so far, has managed to keep Canada away from the dangers that have harassed and continue to haunt the rest of the world.

The same precaution is not reflected in the electoral platforms of the other political parties. Before the elections of October 19, the stalls of the electoral fair were filled with the megaphones of lies, revived with pamphlets and TV commercials, trying to buy voters by disparaging the positive achievements that led to a modest budget surplus last year, although the government maintained and reduced income taxes for employees, retirees, and small private businesses. With their eyes on victory in the elections, both the NDP and the Liberal Party want to change the course of the

Canadian economy by proposing uncontrollable spending, higher taxes, and increased national debt, which will cause everyone to lose, especially the future generation, which will have to pay the bill.

I attended the debates of the three leaders of the federal political parties on Thursday, September 17, 2015, organized by *The Globe and Mail*. I do not understand why only CHCH from Hamilton broadcast the debate? The Canadian Broadcasting Corporation (CBC), funded by public money, should have broadcast the debate on all stations across Canada, a debate important to every citizen interested in deciding whom to choose, but undermined the occasion, replacing it with a second-rate film. Who, at CBC, CTV, or other national TV stations, in their chase for ratings, has the right to assume that voters would not be interested in federal elections, on each party's platform, and in the future of the national economy?

From the chaotic clash of the three candidates, who kept interrupting each other and often spoke over one another, firing accusations, it would have been hard to find a winner except by analyzing the reasoning behind some answers. Justin Trudeau maintains that since interest rates are so low today, the Liberal Party, in its desire to stimulate the economy, wants to invest billions in the next three years in infrastructure, public works, roads, bridges, and transit, through borrowing and raising taxes on corporations and high earners. Tom Mulcair (NDP) says he wants to keep the budget balanced for the next four years, reduce taxes on small businesses, while the minimum wage will be increased, contributions to the Canadian Pension Plan and Employment Insurance raised, and corporations will pay 3% more in taxes.

Many will probably be attracted by this kind of promises, but upon deeper analysis, none of these measures ensures sustained economic growth or an increase in jobs, as long as taxes are increased, the country once again plunged into exorbitant debts and blindly led down the same path in which many European countries such as Spain, Portugal, and Greece have failed. That is why my vote will go to Harper.

27 September 2015

Fight for a Place in Elysium

The Elysian Fields, first mentioned by the great Homer in *The Odyssey*, were destined for mortals favored by the gods, for the virtuous and the greatest of heroes. These fields were located at the western edge of the earth, near the stream of the Ocean, where life is easier for man. There is no snow there, no storms, not even rain, only the westerly breezes of the ocean that could cool man. In other words, the first of the great writers known to humanity, in his blind existence, was able to see heaven, not the one revealed in Genesis, from which man was cast out, but the one created by man 3000 years later, on the western edge of the ocean, in the New World. But the Elysian Fields have lost, over time, their former brilliance, as if they had drifted away from us into impenetrable spheres; few know their name today, although the names of the immortal dwell there, while many of us jostle fiercely to make a place among the immortals.

Let us imagine, for instance, the disappointment of Mrs. Hillary Clinton, who could hardly wait for the eight years of President Obama's administration to pass, the man who dethroned her in 2008 in her historic attempt to be the first female president of the United States, simply because before him, none of the presidents had been black. But now, in 2016, the situation is completely different. No one disputes that it is her turn at the presidency; her nomination as the Democratic Party's candidate will be a kind of triumphant march through the primaries, after which the coronation will be a festive formality, following the crushing of the Republican candidate in the November elections. Who could have foreseen that from within her own party, an old man past retirement age, a septuagenarian socialist, would arise, stirring storms with unrealizable promises, poured out through the spray of spittle at the tribune of his fiery speeches, attended by thousands of people? And who could have foreseen that from the opposite camp, a billionaire, a man who had already acquired everything one could acquire in life, would decide, for amusement, to try his luck in politics? And from one side, and from the other, people continue to be drawn, as if by magic, to their rallies, which surpass all records of participation in political speeches, while she, the famous Hillary, former First Lady, former Secretary of State, and baptized in liberal creed from her school days, finds herself increasingly isolated in a circle of only a few hundred loyal listeners who have not yet abandoned her.

From both sides the rain of accusations and attacks continues without interruption, calling into question her very nomination, despite the 541 superdelegates, the gift from the "elite" – the shadow leaders of the Democratic Party – who decide, from behind the scenes, who must win. With the immense popularity that Bernard Sanders has gained, especially among young people, the intervention of the Democratic Party leaders, by granting the 541 superdelegates to Hillary, puts in the balance the unity of the liberal movement and democracy in the party, which could have tragic repercussions in the fall elections. Thus, after all this, adding the latest events caused by the classified email scandal, the secret server in her own house, the Benghazi attack, and the imminent accusation by the CIA for negligence in keeping state secrets, Hillary Clinton has every reason to be disappointed.

Among the Conservatives, the situation seems to have stabilized at last, as Ted Cruz and John Kasich have left the arena, helping Donald Trump surpass the number of delegates needed for nomination, and at present he is, unofficially, the candidate of the Conservative Party. Many times, I have asked myself what reason Trump has for abandoning all his businesses – in which it is said that everything he touched turned to gold – and deciding to enter politics? Many do it for money and power; he has both. Destiny has been more than generous with him. It endowed him with exceptional qualities: charm, energy, intelligence, vision, and determination. He built and spread his enterprises and his name all over the world, accumulated wealth, beautiful women, fame, and respect. What is he missing?

All the years spent in school have no value if, in the end, you do not receive a diploma. The diploma is the unanimous recognition that you are educated. Based on a diploma, work and reward are assigned accordingly. The culminating point in the development of a person or a thing is called "apotheosis." In the ancient world, heroes or emperors were elevated among the gods, with honors and glorification.

In Washington, D.C., in the rotunda of the Capitol building, one can see on the dome ceiling a majestic mural painting created in 1865 by Constantino Brumidi, called *The Apotheosis of Washington*. Through this mural, the nation showed its eternal gratitude to its first president and commander-in-chief of the Continental Army during the American Revolution. The elevation of a person to such a divine rank is probably what Trump and others aspire to. Let us hope that these aspirations, translated into achievements, will convince mankind to grant him the glorification he seeks.

Less evoked these days was the farewell speech of Stephen Harper at the Conservative Party Convention in Vancouver, through which the former prime minister officially withdraws from Canada's political life. Without pomp, with his characteristic modesty, during his ten years leading the Canadian government, in difficult historic times in which many nations lost their balance and economic stability, he steered the country's destiny on a smooth course, sheltered from turmoil. Perhaps it is too early for eulogies, but surely history will secure him a place in the Elysium of our foremost leaders.

30 May 2016

The Rock

Years ago, on my first vacation in Spain, I toured all the towns along the Mediterranean coast, between Granada and Seville, with a car rented for two weeks. Among the splendors of the Alhambra, the tiered depths of the caves in Nerja—where nearby, I let my imagination float on the waves of the sea from the Balcony of Europe—and traveling further, on the road to Cordoba, through the historical vestiges of Malaga and the new tourist destinations of Torremolinos and Marbella, I was struck by the unexpected discovery of Ronda, where it seemed as if a gargantuan axe had split the settlement in two, leaving a massive chasm between them.

But I was unprepared to discover, after crossing "La Línea de la Concepción," that I had entered another country, with a different language, currency, and customs, as if I had suddenly landed in the land of Albion, beyond the English Channel. This was Gibraltar, a peninsula marked by the rock of a mountain rising more than four hundred meters high, considered in Antiquity one of the Pillars of Hercules, the creator of the strait that opens into the boundless ocean.

It was my first visit to this rock, which stretches over less than seven square kilometers, at the foot of which lies a fairytale-like town, neat and aligned along a single main street, with hundreds of dazzling shops and swarms of tourists. It was a place like no other, with a tumultuous history, passed like a trophy over the centuries among Moors, Spaniards, and Englishmen, still isolated from the world even today, stubbornly refusing to be incorporated into Spain, the only land connection with the rest of Europe.

The determination with which this small people (30,000 inhabitants) defend their independence, resisting for decades the pressures of assimilation by Spain, seems to be inspired by the very rock to which their lives are bound.

In the same vein, my thoughts turned to our own country, a small people at the foot of the mountains, surrounded on all sides by foreign tribes, languages, cultures, and beliefs, constantly under pressure of subjugation, Slavic influence, Catholic domination, and religious repression, yet who, throughout millennia, managed to preserve intact their identity, speech, and ancestral faith. The granite rock of the Carpathians became an integral part of the structure of Romanian souls, which cannot be displaced.

The result of the June 23 referendum in England made me reflect on the above. The Britons have been rooted on their island in the middle of the ocean since the mists of prehistory. They withstood the Vikings, the northern tribes, those of the neighboring islands, the Roman incursions led by Caesar almost half a century before their capitulation; they preferred to convert their faith in order to free themselves from the ordinances of the Vatican, and today they rebelled against the decisions dictated by the European Community, in which they had no right to speak. The incredible act of separation from the rulers in Brussels occurred, leaving the world shaken by the prophecies of the greatest seers of our time, of a merciless cataclysm, which so far has left no trace.

Humanity is in perpetual change. From one day to the next, actions and currents once unforeseeable take decisive shape in our days, with transformations imposed against the will of many, in the laws and relations among people, even within many families.

Through new ideologies with metastatic ramifications, antagonistic layers have been created within the population, while the ruling elite, the media, and academic circles exert pressure on society, advancing claims and rights for certain minorities, at the expense of the personal freedoms of those who represent the majority.

As the rich grow richer and the poor sink deeper into poverty, the discontent and resentment of the middle class at the state of affairs are rightly attributed to government leaders, the financial machinations of London and Washington, and the elite of parliamentary officials in Brussels who impose new laws. As a result of the open-border policy, which allows immigrants to absorb the already declining jobs in the economy, the standard of living has been reduced.

General dissatisfaction is greatly exacerbated by the fact that many of these immigrants do not integrate into the traditional British social fabric, forming compact communities (ghettos) in London and other major cities, where the language, customs, dress, and jurisdiction are replaced with those of the countries from which they come. By this, English constitutional laws are ignored or nullified, because of the decisions of judges inclined to give priority to political correctness. Politicians, lacking the courage to publicly oppose for fear of losing votes (seeing the pools), allowed the referendum to offer the British people the opportunity to assert themselves, opting for Brexit, national identity, and independence from the European governors and from those who seek global rule.

Rex Murphy wrote in a commentary in the *National Post* that *"the EU vote is the most dramatic illustration so far of how the ruling elite of many Western countries has lost the loyalty and trust of the population."* He further added: *"...they (politicians) contemptuously dismissed the concerns of ordinary people that the EU project drained their own national identity, dissolved the democratic system established centuries ago, and forced their country into total submission to unelected foreigners with no accountability from the Brussels supragovernment."*

This is the feeling of many of the twenty-seven countries still in the European Community and, if something does not change soon, it is possible that the discontent of some of these nations will lead them to adopt the British exit model.

It is interesting how Colby Cosh views the problem from a Canadian perspective:

"It costs us, every day, a lot of money because we are not the 51st state. We keep the Americans at bay, preserving our freedom to make trade and defense arrangements based on mutual agreements and sovereignty. We do this, even though we share a common language with the Americans, and they are much more similar to us, culturally and ideologically, than an Englishman is to an Estonian."

"Vox populi, vox dei," the Romans used to say, and this motto must be inscribed in golden capitals on the frontispiece of every building in which public officials, whether elected or appointed, must not be allowed to forget it. Brexit is a warning!

July 2, 2016

Dilemmas

Never have I been so overwhelmed by the torrent of information traffic on the internet, which proves that people everywhere are filled with anxiety, trying to untangle the threads of current politics. Against the backdrop of the American presidential elections, where on both sides the label of corruption is shamelessly hurled, each of us seeks to extract a thread of truth, sorted from tons of lies. Articles, essays, and YouTube videos reveal daily data and realities that the official press either ignores or deliberately buries, while newspapers and television run campaigns of slander and vilification against everything that invokes conservative principles, opposed to political correctness, both domestically and internationally.

The entire mechanism of influencing minds is described, in unsurpassed detail, in the new book by Radu Cinamar, published in Romania and on Amazon, titled *Future with a Death's Head*. The author, or authors behind this name, have so far published four books with deconspiratorial content, exposing the entire machinery of backstage machinations of international freemasonry and the Bilderberg group. Starting from the idea that society is divided into two antagonistic social classes: rulers and the masses, with the temptations of money and power, the masses can easily be manipulated through the financial levers available and by controlling the mass media. The clarity of the objectives pursued by these groups is surprising, explicitly describing many of the unanswered phenomena of our day.

Among other things, paradoxically, it has become evident that the exodus of immigrants from Africa and the Middle East, which continues to create chaos in most European countries—something that, to each of us, seems like a relatively new phenomenon—was foreseen and planned not long after World War I by Coudenhove-Kalergi, recognized as the father of the European Union. His goal was to create a mass of mixed-race individuals with sub-intellectual characteristics, which are easy to manipulate. In his book *Practical Idealism*, Kalergi indicated that the future of the United States of Europe would not be the people of the old continent, but a kind of slave-like population, produced by multinational mixing, with no other quality than being ruled by the elite. He further proclaimed the abolition of the right of self-determination of European states, from which democracy would be eliminated. Leaders elected by the people would have no decision-making power at the national level, while the population would be blended with other races, so that national identity would be annihilated. These themes are beginning to become apparent today in everything we see happening in many European countries.

The aim of ultraprogressive currents, of many governments (including Canada's), and of the constant calls of the UN, which insistently recommend that we accept millions of refugees to offset the declining birthrate in European countries. Canada, and America, is to transform its identity into a mass of individuals without ethnic, historical, or cultural cohesion. The Kalergi Plan is, without doubt, the program for establishing a single, totalitarian government in Europe and the entire world.

Ilie Şerbănescu, in a recent online article explaining Greece's economic problems, writes that Aristotle, the great Greek philosopher (384–322 BC), said: *"Democracy is the easiest road to tyranny."* He also noted that *"democracy is one of the most corrupt forms of state organization, since the state becomes captive in the hands of small interest groups, easily able to manipulate the masses for personal enrichment, while the population is kept in abject poverty."*

In this context, going back to Cinamar's book, one of the Bilderberg group leaders, Massini, declares: *"To better conceal the political and financial maneuvers we unleash, we use the most spectacular, but at the same time the most ludicrous idea we have managed to infiltrate into the masses over the last two hundred years. This is probably one of our most valuable acquisitions, which has brought us many benefits and is proving very effective even today. You will be surprised, but it bears a very familiar name: democracy. The notion itself is worthless; nevertheless, it is the most suitable cog in our machinery, which is very successful with the masses... What do we achieve through so-called democracy? In most cases, it leads, first and foremost, to division among different social categories that make up a people, and to confrontation, often open, among populations around the globe. The idea we offer the world, but through which we cover up our true intentions and actions with everyone's consent, is to create the illusion of free choice for everyone. But when it comes to tens and hundreds of millions of different, stressed, and perverted people, their so-called free choice can easily be directed through different methods."*

Mr. Massini did not forget to add: *"It is a system that has proven its efficiency amply over time. If someone opposes it, eliminating him from the political stage or as a social personality is generally not a problem, thanks to the many connections we have, the corruption, and the financial system we control. In more particular cases, such as that of the United States, we cannot afford mistakes or actions outside those we have foreseen. That is why each American president is nothing more than a choice and emanation of our Masonic goals, and he must, obligatorily, be a prominent member of our lodges."*

That is why, probably, the circus in the American political arena has such great significance.

August 14, 2016

Veritas

Another year has passed over us, sprinkled with joys and troubles, another year endured stoically, as witnesses to the stormy electoral debates in the South, and now that things have somewhat calmed, we are curious to see what joys (or troubles) the new year has prepared for us. After eight years of political dominance with an extremely leftist platform administered by President Obama, the contrast could not be more evident between what was and the political promises of the newly elected president, Trump.

Although the air is still thick with fog, millions of people in America and everywhere watch the change of tenants at the White House with hope that a brighter and sunnier horizon will open across the sky. With a little luck, this change may begin with eliminating the divisions among people linked to race, gender, color, or sexual orientation, which have been and still are promoted by Democrats. Perhaps climate change will no longer occupy the first place on the new president's agenda, freeing energy consumption from the stranglehold of over taxation that forces ordinary people to choose between food and heating their homes in winter. And perhaps this new government will be fairer, more honest, and more open with those who elected it, calling things by their name: the truth.

It is said that in Roman mythology, Veritas was the goddess of truth and the mother of Virtus (Virtue). It is also said that she lived in a deep cavern on earth, from which she could barely rise to the surface. The Greeks considered her the daughter of Zeus, but at the same time, a creation of Prometheus. The great fabulist Aesop said that Prometheus, who molded the first man and gave him fire from Olympus, decided to make from clay a statue of truth as a model for mankind. While he worked on it, he was summoned to Zeus and told a servant named Deception to watch over the house. The servant, eager to prove his skill, began to make a statue himself, copying in detail what Prometheus had done. But when he reached the feet, the clay ran out. Prometheus marveled at the resemblance between the two statues, baked them in the oven, then breathed life into both. The original, Truth, set out walking with measured steps, while the servant's copy, called Falsehood, remained rooted in place. Since then, people have seen that Falsehood can successfully begin something, but, having no feet, Truth ultimately prevails.

We, however, do not live on Olympus, and Truth only rarely surfaces. In place of Truth, Deception and Falsehood have multiplied by kinship with Fabrication, Calumny, Rumor, and Cowardice. In a world where anything and anyone can be bought; Money has conquered Olympus and become more powerful than Zeus. With money, virtues have been bought and sold like harlots to those wishing to gild their crest.

Politicians, journalists, professors, scientists, and even priests have been surprisingly bewitched at the sight of gold and, to obtain it, have disowned their calling. The torch of truth, which was supposed to lead us to light, has fallen into dishonest hands, and nations stumble forward in darkness.

It is no secret to anyone today that there are so-called "illuminated" groups in the world who long to become rulers of the entire globe and are no longer satisfied with starting small, local wars. The idea of global domination has existed since ancient times. Everyone, from Alexander the Great to Caesar, Napoleon, Hitler, and others dreamed of extending their power over the whole world.

Today, however, the situation is different. In place of resolve, strength of character, and military genius, the illuminati have money. With money, no corner of the earth, no political area, and no aspect of their interest remains untouched. The vast number of groups and individuals supported, bought, and influenced by them seems unreal. From climate change, mass immigration of refugees from Asia and Africa, the occupation of Wall Street, and Black Lives Matter—all are projects funded by these shadowy schemers, hidden behind cohorts of ministers, politicians, agitators, and media figures who mask their actions under the guise of protecting democracy.

For a long time, there has been talk of George Soros. Many believe he runs America from the shadows. An immigrant upstart from Hungary, who managed through stock market machinations to amass a huge fortune, he is determined to reshape the world according to the visions pursued in the darkness of his mind. He is the creator of the Open Society Foundation, has funded countless left-wing nonprofit organizations in the U.S. and other countries, including Canada, which do everything possible to obstruct the normal life of free society, financial, scientific, or economic activities, and push in Europe the idea of reintegrating Transylvania into Hungarian territory.

To achieve his goals, Soros undermines the democratic order on this continent, financing activist movements such as Black Lives Matter, with demonstrations not always peaceful, accusing the police of being a tool of white reprisals against people of color. In this way, many police officers, demoralized by the fear of prosecution, prefer to turn a blind eye to criminal acts that affect society as a whole.

The direct interventions of organizations funded by Soros in the internal politics of states, including Canada, are not limited only to racism and public order, but extend to other fields of activity such as education, energy, immigration, provincial and even federal elections, pollution, and climate change. Internationally, Soros and the other illuminati exploit the mass migration of refugees from Syria and sub-Saharan Africa to undermine the national identity, faith, and cultural values of European and North American countries. But their main goal is to undermine governments and public authorities to ease the way for globalization.

Veritas, the goddess of Truth, must not be left forgotten by the world and by fate at the bottom of the cavern destined for her.

December 4, 2016

Democracy

"There has never been a democracy that did not commit suicide."

John Adams

You can tell me anything; I am capable of believing any theory, even the one that claims Trump is a diabolical plague in the current history of the United States. But you will not be able to convince me that all the protests against him, since his inauguration as the 45th president, have been and still are spontaneous manifestations. I cannot believe that, the very next day after the inauguration, on January 21, millions of women across the continent went out into the streets to protest against Trump, simply out of an instinct of female solidarity. Of course, the ninety million dollars allocated from Open Society funds (George Soros' organization) for these demonstrations, were only a mere coincidence.

Nor can I believe that the worldwide protests against the decision to suspend entry into America for citizens from seven Middle Eastern states with majority Muslim populations were also unorganized. And I cannot believe that the gangs of hooligans who entered, armed with fireworks, Molotov cocktails, and irritant sprays, into the University of Berkeley in California to stop a conservative lecturer from addressing students were not financed, carefully planned, and knowingly carried out by certain extremist circles in the Democratic camp.

I suspect there is something in the air about democracies in this world, where nothing seems to be more sacred to humanity than the idea of democracy — which, the more often it is invoked, the more illusory it appears.

There have always been strong characters in the history of the United States who influenced and determined the political profile of the Union, which ultimately led to the creation of the two parties. When Congress unanimously chose George Washington in 1789 as the first president, the idea was not that each party should have a candidate for this office. Candidates could be from any group, and whoever gathered the most votes would be president, while the runner-up would be vice president. The first vice president was John Adams.

In George Washington's cabinet, two men distinguished themselves with traits that shaped the governance concept of the new state: Alexander Hamilton, Secretary of the Treasury, and Thomas Jefferson, Secretary of State. In fact, these two men could not have been more different in both, thought and decision. Hamilton, with great popularity in the northern states, supported the creation of the first national bank, trade with England, and industrial development. Jefferson advocated for a government with limited powers, represented the southern plantation owners and farmers, and defended the interests of those living on the frontier.

Around them, influential men organized themselves into antagonistic clubs, which began to crystallize, during the 1792 elections, into two distinct parties: the Federalists, embracing Hamilton's ideas, and the Republicans, siding with Jefferson.

The divergence of interests between the northern and southern colonies, due to the nature of their main occupations, was the essential part of discontent with government policies and foreign relations, in the context of Europe's political fluctuations.

In 1792, General Washington was elected for a second term, with John Adams as vice president and the Republicans holding the majority in the House of Representatives. Four years later, in 1796, George Washington refused to run again, because of the Republicans' fierce criticism of the outcome of negotiations with the English over Jay's Treaty of 1794, and he retired. John Adams (Federalist) was elected president and Thomas Jefferson (Republican) vice president.

John Adams did not change the composition of Washington's cabinet, which was entirely influenced by Hamiltonian Federalist convictions. This led to the proclamation of draconian laws in 1798, such as the Alien Act and the Sedition Act. The Alien Act gave the president the power to arrest and deport undesirable persons, while the Sedition Act could punish anyone found guilty of writing, publishing, or transmitting any false,

scandalous, or malicious news against the government.

This law was directed against the Republican opposition, and because of it, many people were sentenced to years in prison and fines up to 5,000 dollars. Together with abuses of power, over taxation of the population, and dissensions within the Federalists, they lost voter support in 1800, which led to the election of a new president: Thomas Jefferson, with Aaron Burr as vice president.

The totalitarian inclinations of progressives are analyzed in Jonah Goldberg's book *Liberal Fascism*, in which he speaks of Woodrow Wilson, under whom more dissidents were arrested and thrown into prisons in just a few years than Mussolini managed in his entire career. It is estimated that 175,000 Americans were arrested for failing to demonstrate their patriotism, far surpassing the witch hunt of McCarthy's time — another Democrat — who established the terror of anti-American activity. Like Alexander Hamilton, Wilson introduced the Sedition Act to silence criticism of America's war policy, forbidding the writing and publishing of any disloyal announcement about the United States government and army.

Today, events confirm that a new offensive of these totalitarian inclinations of progressives is taking shape, trying to undermine, through demonstrations, slanders, and criminal acts, President Trump's program of national renewal. There is no doubt that behind these actions are instigating forces that go beyond the borders of the United States, pursuing the globalization of the entire world into a field of obedient executors, deprived of analysis and rights, meant to serve a group of potentates who will dictate the course of history. Any attempt to oppose this globalization plan is met with revolts manipulated by armies of mercenaries, well paid, who will use all propaganda means — media, television, and art — to mobilize as many "rebels" as possible, until the government is forced to resign.

America still has the chance and must resist those who want to change it.

4 February 2017

Breaking News

On the evening of April 6, a new chapter in world affairs opened with the decision of the new American government under Trump to punish with a drastic military response the genocidal action of Syrian president Bashar Assad, who used chemical weapons against his own people, killing about 80 people — many of them children — in unimaginable agony, by Sarin gas poisoning. Humanity is shaken by the televised images of this barbaric act committed by the Syrian dictator, who had already used this form of repression against a population dissatisfied with the conditions in which they were forced to live.

But although public outrage was widespread, the politicians of the world were deceived by the indulgent attitude of President Obama in 2013, who left the action unpunished, contrary to his warning that *"crossing this red line"* would not be tolerated. As a result of the former Democratic president's policy — undeserved Nobel Peace Prize laureate — who was afraid of provoking an international wave of protests through a military response in Syria, the executioner-dictator of this people caused the death of half a million innocent men, women, and children, forced the exodus of more than five million refugees in search of a safe place for their families — suffering in poverty far from their country — and resulted in new alliances and conflicts in a region already shaken by endless political and military hostilities.

The new U.S. administration's response was marked by a judiciously limited proportion, meant to issue a competent warning to those involved that their future activity is being closely monitored, that any violation will be paid dearly, and at the same time to address a larger number of pretenders who believe Americans are weak and therefore entitled to certain demands.

But things seem a little different now. Among those warned are North Korea and Iran, open aggressors and inveterate enemies of the United States and the democratic world, pursuing special compensations through nuclear intimidation. The Trump administration does not seem intimidated. Russia, on the other hand, is carefully weighing its next move, unwilling to enter into a battlefield conflict with a better organized and prepared America.

The surprise attack on Syria was served as dessert at the official dinner offered to Chinese Premier Xi Jinping by Donald J. Trump. The matter seems simple: either China restrains North Korea, or America will. As a result, negotiations between the two countries are expected to thwart North Korea's provocative activity, while mutually advantageous trade cooperation and good relations of friendship are anticipated. Both domestically and internationally, the echoes raised in public opinion by the American president's retaliatory strike on the Syrian air base were positive, received with relief by most people around the world, who see in this act the beginning of a new era in international politics — a rebirth of American prestige as defender of democratic principles and human rights. This response will not be long in convincing many allied countries to reintegrate into a common effort to eradicate the common enemy, ISIS, and its extended tentacles everywhere.

In just eleven weeks since his inauguration, Trump has amazed the world with his almost gargantuan energy, introducing a series of measures meant to improve the economy, create new jobs by reopening enterprises already moved to other countries, and curb the illegal entry of unvetted immigrants. He held numerous meetings with political leaders from various countries, many of them disillusioned with the former administration's policies, on whose support they had relied. But all these achievements were followed only by a part of the population, who rejoiced in the accomplishments realized in such a short time. The other part, blinded by the unexpected electoral loss of their candidate, Hillary Clinton, unleashed a grotesque campaign of defamation, personal denigration, and accusations against President Trump, his entire administration, and his entire family. Most television stations and newspapers, including those in Canada, carried out a strong campaign of disinformation, fabricating stories often proven false, letting loose the floodgates of illusory commentary to produce calls for his expulsion from the White House and public trial on invented charges without any evidence.

As if bad news must be buried, none of these newspapers and TV shows mention the acts committed by the old administration at President Obama's order, concerning the illegal spying on Trump campaign members before and after the elections. The same person who launched the false claim that the Benghazi terrorist attack — which killed the ambassador and three staff members — was due to an obscure TV film, Susan Rice, is now involved in this episode, having ordered the illegal unmasking of the names of civilians from the Trump campaign and their dissemination in the media, with the intent of publicly discrediting him. With the same natural innocence, the press forgets to inform the public that Mrs. Clinton and her illustrious husband benefited from three-quarters of a million dollars donated by Putin and Russia to the Clinton Foundation for the sale of 20% of American uranium, plus a speech given to the Russians.

Upon leaving the White House, the former president asked the Democrats to resist at all costs every action of the new president. Every day, with dogmatic fanaticism, Democratic Party supporters in Congress, the Senate, and the press oppose fiercely — without distinction between good and bad — every step, intention, and law introduced by Trump's cabinet.

A diligent worker, Trump hopes that, in the end, the people will appreciate the effort he has put in.

7 April 2017

Lies Were Born in Paradise

It is said that in a land where the sky is eternally clear, the sun pours gently rays over meadows soft as velvet, and the birds of the sky sing from morning until evening, a man and his son ruled over a garden unique in beauty, which they called Paradise. Diligent servants took care that the master's peace was undisturbed, ensuring order and harmony reigned in every corner. Among them, the most beloved was a charming young man, with bright eyes, speech flowing like music, and cherubic curls, named Lucius.

More handsome than any, Lucius enjoyed the master's parental affection and even that of the son, who had allowed him privileges denied to the other servants. Confident in the gifts he possessed, Lucius wanted favors equal to those of the son, whose modesty and moderation were known and admired by all. But since he could not ask the master for such a desire, he began to spread among the servants the idea that it would be better if all members of Paradise were equal to their superiors. Was it not a sin that, in a place as harmonious as Paradise, where LOVE was venerated and considered the law, some had different rights from others? Some began to take his words seriously, others dismissed them as a joke, while Lucius insisted, he spoke only out of love for justice and true harmony.

The master saw what was happening in Paradise but considered it better to let things take their course, until everyone could, on their own, see Lucius' true intentions. Under the deceptive veil of love for justice and for those around him, he argued for freedom and equality for all, insinuating that if he were chosen to lead Paradise, things would be completely different. At this point, the master banished him from Paradise along with all his followers. Thus, we may say that lies, deception, and corruption were born in Paradise.

On a fair stretch of land, with mountains and meadows like in heaven, and riches coveted by neighbors hungry for power, lived hardworking people who did not dare covet others' goods. But fate placed this land at the crossroads of winds, and man had to face their exhausting furies, which never succeeded in making him abandon his ancestral home.

Tribes of barbarians swept like locusts over these lands, burning and consuming everything in their path. Then, the Porte sent foreign dignitaries to squeeze gold from the sweat of impoverished people. And enemies never ceased to trample the ancestral soil, from all directions.

Then from the East appeared, benevolent, warm, and protective nation, to help them with fine words and brotherly guidance. They sent teachers and advisors, and while they struggled learning their lessons, trains departed loaded with their best goods, until not even seed remained.

Thus, they learned that lies, deception, and corruption were perfected on Earth. That land was called Romania.

After man's children finished exploring the land where they were born, seeing that the riches of the Orient were taxed by the Pasha's collectors and by bankrupt Italians, they set out across the seas in search of new routes to the source of silks, brocades, and spices. After months sailing toward the sunset, when they found land, no one realized at that time that a new age of history had opened with the Birth Certificate of the New World.

Today, we count ourselves among the hundreds of millions of inhabitants of this world, which has become a magnetic center of attraction for those impoverished in their homelands, for those terrorized for praying differently, and for those threatened with the loss of freedom for expressing their desire to be free. The first to come to this world were themselves persecuted in their fields by local rulers for the purity of their faith, followed by the multitudes who could not feed their children, those terrified by the diseases and wars of the Old World, and many seekers of better fortune.

When the question of government arose, those who hated tyranny opted for a republic, while the traditionalists remained loyal to the crown, and as a result, they separated — some to the north, others to the south. Today, more than two centuries later, these nations, sharing fate and common aspirations, continue to live in peace and harmony, with neighboring hearths, like brothers.

But the world has changed. The horrors of the last world war created the need for vigilance in preventing new wars, promoted by some as sources of enrichment. The lucky ones everywhere found a new way to profit from the confusion of those seeking an easier life. Social inequality in the old European world made many believe the solution lay only in socialism. Those who have not lived under socialism cannot understand the mistake.

The richest of the rich found socialist ideas as a deceptive picture, behind which it is easier to carry out their plans for a globalized world. A first step on this path is the European Union; a legislative body composed of bureaucrats appointed by the governments of member nations. From among these bureaucrats, the rulers of the European forum are chosen. They can draft laws that each country is obliged to obey. Bureaucrats are not elected by the people; those elected democratically by the people are the parliamentarians, deputies, and ministers of the nations. Yet all the laws passed in each country have no value if they contradict the laws made by bureaucrats of the European Union.

The schemes of the world elite are masked by illusory slogans, speeches meant to show fraternity with the victims of the wars they themselves finance. At the same time, nations are bombarded with threats and declarations in the press and on television, with frightening conclusions from charlatan scientists, politicians, and professional agitators, predicting the most horrific world cataclysms, if their solutions are not followed. Our present days are affected by zealous politicians who decide for us our present and our future.

Today, Americans are making a 180-degree turn away from globalization. We in Canada, continue still on the road that, so far, has produced nothing but more poverty. People feel deceived, but not knowing whom to believe, they vent their anger on anyone.

Lies, deception, and corruption choke out our last hopes.

25 July 2017

Pawns of Sacrifice

In an interview given in July to the independent American website *Journal Review*, Romanian General Ion Mihail Pacepa said that, for someone who has lived two lives (in which, I dare to include each of us — one in socialism and one in capitalism), it is clear that *"the virus of Marxism, disguised as socialism-progressivism, and the Stalinist cult of personality"* has infected the shores of his adopted country, America. The first symptoms, he said, appeared already during the 2008 election campaign, when the Democratic candidate, Barack Obama, declared: *"I am the one the world has been waiting for!"*

After Obama's inauguration as president, the political magazine *Newsweek*, on February 7, 2009, published in capital letters on its cover the message: *"We Are All Socialists Now."* Only two years later, the American economy confirmed, with indisputable statistics, the results of this government's measures: 14 million unemployed, 41.8 million recipients of free food coupons, millions of other Americans driven out of their homes, Gross Domestic Product (GDP) fell from 3.6% to 1.6%, with a significant increase in public debt to 13 trillion dollars.

Thus, it is evident that the mirage of socialist ideas, repeated this time as in all other countries infected with the same virus of Marxism, proved infertile in every field of activity — except poverty. Even so, the chimera of socialism continues today to blind millions everywhere, because the idea of social justice is efficiently promoted by certain groups eager for advancement in the social and political arena.

Most newspapers, magazines, and television programs, supported by certain personalities from academia and the arts, profess opinions directed toward a single goal: to focus the concept of social inequality — especially of those who do not belong to the white race, to reclaim injustices suffered by African Americans centuries ago, and to overtax those at the top 1% of society.

The fact that one of the most prominent representatives of this category — the very tip of the 1%, Donald J. Trump — was elected President of America grotesquely deepened the discord with the viewpoints demanded by the democratic media. As a result, a broad campaign of slander, defamation, and insubordination was extended and supported with hysterical energy across all political and informational channels against the new administration.

The hatred unleashed by the press poured into acts of popular violence, amplified to the maximum in all television channels and newspapers. Despite all attempts to dehumanize the president, the voters — those anonymous pawns, who ultimately decide the victor — continued to remain loyal to their chosen one.

The Internet has gained an important role in the development and dissemination of ideas; among the younger generation, it has become the only source of information. Based on this phenomenon, the founder of the Facebook platform, Mark Zuckerberg, a Democrat whose fortune exceeds seventy billion, can influence the outcome of presidential elections at the White House, knowing he can rely on the "millennials." With Facebook media as a propaganda tool, sufficient funds for the electoral campaign, and strategists from Mrs. Clinton's defunct campaign, it is not excluded that he might succeed.

Along with Facebook, Amazon, Google, and other giants in the field of cybernetics, they have accumulated the entirety of circulating information in the world — in science, technology, finance, art, and geopolitics. As unique sources of information and expertise, they hold a monopoly on ideas which can easily be controlled, promoted, or filtered by these platforms according to their goals. Most governmental and private institutions increasingly depend on the technological and security capabilities of these Silicon Valley giants for planning, strategy, and execution decisions.

Collaboration between institutions and tech companies, although it may accelerate major innovations in all fields, also presents the risk of competition between these companies and their clients. These tech giants, exploiting the advantage of expertise, will be able to decide freely whom to serve or not, and who may be replaced in the future. Many banks and financial institutions are already viewing with concern the possibility of such a scenario now that Facebook can facilitate banking transactions and Amazon is perfecting voice-activated financial transactions.

If the most important institutions in the world of finance — banks, stock exchanges, and insurance companies — foresee the danger presented by Silicon Valley, how much more are we, the anonymous consumers across all meridians, entitled to regard with concern the power accumulated by these giants, who hold the monopoly on information and the ability to control it.

History, culture, and ideas can be easily distorted and channeled as authentic truth, if the interests of some demand it. We already see what is happening today: social media from Silicon Valley, indoctrinated in the vanguard of progressive-democratic ideas, is effectively engaged in politics, as was the recent case of the dismissal of a Google employee for writing an article claiming that women are not interested in a high-tech career.

Just as our country, Romania, was dominated for more than 40 years by a communist ideology that entirely falsified the nation's history, and today we still struggle to restore historical truth, this danger is now amplified globally. It is not enough that progressive politics in recent decades has encouraged the disintegration of families, alienated children from parents, and attacked our religious beliefs by banning the Ten Commandments in public; now they want to destroy the last national-cultural vestiges as well — the statues of personalities from national history, as a final attack on our identity.

For those too impassioned to see what we lose through the destruction of statues or their removal from pedestals under cover of darkness, it is enough to remind them that the civilization of the world, with all its beauties, was built through human sacrifice. With the exception of Athens, all other ancient cities were built with slaves, yet not even the barbarians destroyed them.

On the chessboard, pawns defend the aristocracy and are often sent to sacrifice. We were born and remain pawns of an unjust world, where lies are the main argument.

Our mission, as pawns of the world, is to keep watch.

25 August 2017

Myopia

"When I'll strike once to blow

the rock will split by axes' force

and streams of water clear flow.

Boys! This is art, a lighting torch!"

Mihail Beniuc

Myopia, in popular language, is called *"short-sightedness"* and illustrates the man forced to bring an object close to the tip of his nose to distinguish it. Scientifically, however, myopia is defined as a vision disorder, characterized by the inability to distinguish objects at a distance — the incapacity to see things in their full complexity.

For a long time, I have been troubled by the thought that the errors of our generation are due to some ecological — or perhaps astral — phenomenon, which diminishes our ability to see things clearly at a distance and in perspective. How else can one interpret the fact that, despite the efforts of the last decades to create decent living and working conditions for humanity, the results achieved are below the initial level?

Perhaps things would not be so strikingly obvious if — in contrast — America had not developed a current with different visions, which, in a short time, managed to correct the downward economic trajectory, like a chronic global malady, and turn it into one of continuous ascent. With a few decisive measures, met with massive and unjustified reaction from those identified with the previous leadership, the new government set to work, removing many of the obstacles in the way, thus clearing the path for smoother traffic in all directions — and they succeeded.

In only one year from the inauguration, President Trump instilled a robust optimism in tomorrow, and, like a true magician, the things around us took a different turn.

This was due especially to the annulment of many regulations from the previous administration, of the influence peddlers from Wall Street, and of other special interest groups swarming through the Capitol's halls. Likewise, through the introduction of tax-cutting reforms for individuals, small businesses, and companies with international market output, using all existing energy resources — including coal — and ensuring border security, the economy was able to record a new boost.

It is not too hard to remember that, before Trump, economic experts in Democratic political circles affirmed that modest economic growth was *the new normal* in the world. In 2014, the International Monetary Fund established that developed countries had entered the *era of secular stagnation.* In 2017, the World

Bank drafted a report highlighting the *"Fragile Recovery"* after the 2007–2008 crisis, repeatedly mentioning *"the new normal,"* and concluded that America under Trump would grow at a slower rate than under Obama. It must be noted that in Obama's eight years of presidency, the American economy never reached 3% GDP growth, achieving, on average, only 1.5% per year.

Just days ago, at the World Economic Forum in Davos, Switzerland, the annual meeting place of the most influential people, politicians, and financiers across the globe — the very center of the international elite — among the last speakers was President Trump, who said: *"Putting America first does not mean America alone."* Rightly so, alongside the fact that the American economy had shown 3% growth in the last three quarters, securing over two million new jobs and lowering unemployment to 4.1%, thousands of employees received $1,000 bonuses from companies pleased with the tax cuts. The overall optimism was also greatly fueled by the stock market, which has risen, from January 2017 until now, by more than 30%.

But not only in America. The American economic engine has the power to drive the economies of the entire world. When America prospers, most countries in Europe, Asia, and the Americas enjoy similar prosperity.

"As President of the United States, I will always put America first. Just as every leader of other countries should put their

countries first," Trump said. But how many of those present will be willing to follow this exhortation?

At home in Canada, let us be honest, things are not as good. Prime Minister Trudeau said at Davos that Canada too is open for business, as an attractive place for investors from around the world. Yet, despite this, foreign investment in Canada has dropped to only 11% of GDP, ranking 16th out of 17 OECD (Organization for Economic Cooperation and Development) member countries. This is partly due to the low level of investment in productivity, which amounts to about 50% compared with other high-productivity countries. On the other hand, after the United States reduced taxes from 34.6% to 19%, Canada now charges 21%, up from 17.5% in 2012. To all this must be added the rise in energy costs, the ever-increasing carbon taxes, and finally, if one adds the rise in minimum wages in many provinces, the balance no longer seems as attractive as the Prime Minister presented.

Letting the results speak, the conclusion is simple: a prosperous economy is a free economy, untangled by bureaucratic laws and regulations. At Davos, the forum's president, Klaus Schwab, asked Trump to what extent his business experience helped him make decisions as president. The answer, like his success in his first year as president, speaks for itself.

In Ontario, the last businessman to head a conservative government was Mike Harris, elected in 1995 thanks to his platform called *"The Common-Sense Revolution."* He introduced significant tax cuts (income taxes by about 30%), balanced the budget, and reformed social benefits. His measures greatly helped reduce spending, except in public health, created superior economic performance, and managed to cut eleven billion from provincial debt, balancing the budget.

Unfortunately, the background noise of opposing voices is so deafening that the best intentions of those with clear vision and well-determined goals for the public good are, most often, obstructed. Myopia makes some unable to see beyond the tips of their noses.

28 January 2018

Caution

I remember, I was a young boy then, that at the Giuleşti Theater the play *The Living Corpse* by Leo Tolstoy was performed, with Ovidiu Brădescu in the main role. Such a spectacle cannot be forgotten. Protasov, the hero of the play, married to Lisa — a woman he loved and adored above all else in the world — believing her unhappy in their marriage, and in love with the family friend, Karenin, suddenly disappears from their lives. He is faking his own death, leaving his papers and clothes on the bank of a river. Divorce would have brought him public disgrace, while suicide required great courage. After his death was legalized, Lisa eventually accepted marriage with Karenin. Months of loneliness and wandering passed, and in a tavern in the Russian taiga, Protasov poured out his memories to a stranger over a glass of vodka. At the next table, a scoundrel overheard the story and threatened to expose the affair unless he received payment from Lisa to keep the secret. When Protasov refused, the man revealed the truth: Lisa was accused of bigamy and condemned either to separate from Karenin or be deported to Siberia. In a final act of heroism, Protasov committed suicide on the steps of the courthouse, while Lisa mourned him, saying he was the only man she had ever truly loved.

In the most oppressive days of loneliness, whether in the trenches of the front, in captivity, or in the army, how often have we not witnessed such sincere recollections, with proof in letters or photographs, sometimes filtered through the purity of tears that cannot be restrained, giving way to a longing as deep as the ocean. It is a strange yet normal phenomenon, and no one can imagine that some would take advantage of it.

I have met newcomers from Romania, trying to find a legal gateway through counselors and lawyers, demanding exorbitant sums for a work visa in Canada, and who, like Protasov, showed me photos of their house, wife, and children left behind. They are unfortunate people who want a better future for their children.

Mr. Puiu Popescu, editor of the *Observatorul* magazine, wrote in the previous issue that *"each of us desires something in life. Some seek to possess material values, big houses, expensive cars, serious accounts, etc."* Others *"dedicate their efforts to the accumulation of knowledge, to the contemplation of the world's beauties, to the pursuit of wisdom, and to the attainment of glory."* Em Sava tells us that among us there are many who deny their origins, wanting to rid themselves of it like an old coat they are ashamed of. A reader, Nick Tănase, writes that *"within each of us there exists a longing to depart. A longing for blue, for fresh green, for another world that pushes you to cross borders"* Our desires, however human they may be, are not all the same.

In the play *An Ideal Husband* by Oscar Wilde, I found the following quote: *"When the gods wish to punish men, they grant them their wishes.* " The evidence of this truth is unlimited: from the example of a parent warning his child not to touch the stove, lest he get burned, to the joy of the child discovering the jam jar when his mother is away, to the intoxication of speeding on the highway, until the policeman appears, and so on. From the Bible, we learn the story of the prodigal son, who squandered his share of his father's wealth and returned home repentant for his unworthiness.

But the moral of this quote is deeper, going beyond these examples and reflecting itself in history. I refer to that repetitive history, from the beginning of the world, from which no one wants to learn anything.

Revolutions have always been triggered by the need of people to bring important changes to the social structure, and the ideas of these changes have mobilized masses determined to accomplish them. But not all revolutions succeeded; many were crushed with brutal cruelty by authorities determined to preserve their power, flooding the confrontation squares with innocent blood. Some succeeded, but many were hijacked by string-pullers, who diverted the ideal and eventually brought more suffering than before.

The Spanish Civil War of the 1930s, nationalist Nazism, and communism, which spread like a plague to many parts of the world, illustrate the fragility of structures that cannot sustain themselves.

Canada, stretched like a giant polar bear between the two oceans, Atlantic and Pacific, pulsed with a single heart, Montreal, as a center of communication with the rest of the world. This city was the letterhead, the business card, and the parking place of those who wanted to do business here. But once the idea of separating from the rest of Canada came to life, banks, large firms, and thousands of Anglophones left Quebec, choosing other centers in the rest of the country. Today, Montreal's crown has lost its past luster.

Social media has today become the center of mass polarization around an idea, a political platform, and propaganda used equally by both the opposition and the government. Many opinions hold that in the Arab Spring of 2011–2016, social media had a critical role in mobilizing crowds, encouraging, and influencing opinions, and for this reason many governments rushed to block access to websites, the internet, and media.

Statistics show that during the Arab Spring, the number of those using social media, especially Facebook, increased considerably in most countries in the region. Mobile phones, Twitter, Facebook, e-mail, YouTube, and television spread news and images — true or false — and in this way contributed to the revolution.

Wars today differ from the past. We no longer have two countries confronting each other on the battlefield. They have become generalized, internal, penetrating our homes and families, and conflicts multiply, revitalized by what we see daily on television, in newspapers, and on the internet. In the storm unleashed by this avalanche of information, ideas, propaganda, slander, and apologies — although you don't know whom to believe — it is hard not to be swept away by the fury outside.

Only one instance remains to sort out the truth: our caution.

24 July 2018

From a Photograph

In Romania, Harvest Day is still celebrated; here, we got used to celebrating Thanksgiving with a golden roasted turkey. Back there, we celebrated Harvest Day with empty cellars, trying to stir our appetite with cheese and onions, since the main course—half with plain bread, half without meat—couldn't tempted us, neither the dog slipping under the table. But now autumn has burst upon us with rain and cold, Thanksgiving has been left behind, like a station in a provincial town passed by an express train, and we are in the full unfolding of the famous Indian Summers.

Without being a supporter of the Facebook platform, I began killing time browsing the posts of this clandestine marketplace of information, horrors, and gossip sold for free, from which everyone picks what they like. Photos, videos, cooking tips, erotic offers, election propaganda, and even some literary attempts configure this public bazaar, like an anonymous indicator of the present social psyche.

Yet sometimes a photographic image can stir the deepest feelings through the truth it expresses, often innocently or without intent, yet painful as such. One such photograph, accompanied by a short caption, I must recount here: Against the backdrop of a small country house, a lonely old woman stroked a cat in her arms, saying to it: *"It's so good that you didn't leave me!"* How much truth in those few words! It is said that between 2.5 and 3 million young people under thirty-five left abroad after 1989. It is heartbreaking to see the parents of these young people left alone at home, to guard the homestead where they raised their children in the belief that, in old age, there would be someone to care for them, to offer support, caress, and a little warmth. But it was not to be so.

Gone from the parental hearth, the children learned to speak foreign languages, acquired new skills, developed different tastes, built families wherever they settled, and when they came home, rarely, in haste, on a short vacation, accompanied by fussy children crying to go home, the pain pierced the hearts of these parents like a sharp dagger.

The fate of these parents is the fate of a country abandoned by its vital element—youth, vigor, and the natural energy of the young person capable of moving mountains. Leaving, they made room for good-for-nothings to gorge themselves greedily on the wealth accumulated by generations of a people eternally wronged by foreigner's century after century and now fallen into the hands of degenerate sons who auction off everything that remains, giving it away for nothing. Oh, where are you, Great Țepeș Vodă!

I am no expert in Romania's problems; I can hardly orient myself in this tangled labyrinth that seems to lead nowhere. And even if I were, I would probably refrain from commenting on what happens there, for distance does not always mean clear vision. But neither can I watch indifferently, with detachment, the drama of those left in the country, condemned to add, day by day, to a life of physical and spiritual wear, deprived of hope for something better, because, after 30 years since the overthrow of Ceaușescu, nothing they hoped for has yet come to pass.

The years of proletarian dictatorship led to the complete annihilation of the intellectual elite, those spiritual peaks that shaped and influenced national consciousness through remarkable contributions in politics, art, and culture, cultivating the inherited legacy of honesty, common sense, and faith in God.

Four and a half decades of communist ideology were enough to reverse notions of ethics, respect, and conscientiousness deeply rooted in our people's customs, replacing them with indifference, neglect, and a total lack of respect for anything that does not belong to oneself. Communist slogans, unpaid labor, collectivization, and socialization created a class of upstarts, secret agents, informers, and inquisitors whose mission was to strangle attempts at personal liberation from the rigid corset that stifled freedom of thought, communication, and conscience.

The result of these ideologies led to the rise of elements devoid of basic ethics—politicians concerned with quick enrichment at the expense of the population, or worse, sold to foreign interests. Easily bought with hard currency, they facilitate the cultivation of unpopular ideologies alien to our national outlook, to religion and ancestral customs, ideologies incompatible with their hidden goals of globalization and world domination.

Unfortunately, this phenomenon has become increasingly visible even here, in Canada. Many of those perched in positions of responsibility, in Parliament and even in the person of the Prime Minister, let foreign influences gain the force of law under the pretext of measures beneficial to the middle class. The most progressive ideas of the new far-left ideological wave, which paralyze the country's economic activity, are turned into laws with the approval of most liberals in Parliament and the noisy chorus of the press gallery. Thus, promises made to voters before elections are turned into laws contrary to those promises, but the press, social media, the intelligentsia, and unions continue not to notice these fundamental and unconstitutional deviations.

Trudeau seems more concerned with not losing his celebrity status in international progressive circles, a kind of star of the cosmopolitan world, affiliated with top globalists such as Obama, for whom nothing is more important than trumpeting contentless slogans with the resonance of social justice.

In his arrogance that he could give Trump a lesson—Trump having initiated a new trilateral economic cooperation treaty with

Mexico and Canada—Trudeau tried to introduce socialist-inspired conditions, such as open borders and a revaluation of the minimum wage, to please the globalists. Since Trump ignored his conditions, he waited, delayed, prolonged the time, and in the end had to capitulate to the one holding the reins. Thus, Canada lost the chance of a mutually beneficial agreement for both countries, ending up only with scraps of the bilateral treaty between the US and Mexico. On this occasion, Canada lost many advantages of the old NAFTA treaty from the past.

From a photographs' story, sometimes we could take a tour around the world in search of clarity.

5 October 2018

Angels and Demons

The last angel who lived among us, I believe, was Mother Teresa. I know claimants to the papal throne, prelates, famous connoisseurs of the Bible, and illustrious scholars, but I found nothing holy in them, except for the pleas of sermons from the pulpit. None of them bothers to help someone, none brings to their table a needy person or a child who has nothing to eat, and none touches the wound of a sufferer. Suffering has always been rich in victims; only mercy and personal giving are poor, almost nonexistent. Ultimately, many priests, preachers, and zealots of faith differ little from smooth-talking merchants who live off commissions from their sales.

Yet kindness has not disappeared completely. Ordinary people, from all layers of society, many with very little to share from their modest means, open their hearts and purses to help however they can—others, the sick, the elderly, the orphans, many from countries they have never heard of—doing so purely out of kindness and humanity. In our own country, their anonymous generosity was extended so broadly after the earthquakes, after the negligence of the Ceauşescu era, for the children in orphanages, and now for many pensioner families who cannot get by with what they receive from the government after a life of work and suffering.

Too often, the light of this generosity is filtered through the fingers of greedy officials who unlawfully pocket the goods destined for the needy. Because among us there are fewer angels than demons.

Angels and demons. Are all those who help other angels? Can we consider demons all those who lie and take a little from others' goods? Didn't the outlaws like Robin Hood robed the rich to give to the poor ? In that case, were they demons or angels? Can we separate in a person what is good from what is evil? What is the limit, where is the boundary between good and evil? That is the question that has troubled me in recent days.

I, the beneficiary of a life whose generosity has offered me more longevity than wisdom, blush at the memory of certain past actions (many with honorable intentions at their core), though in my life I have helped many. Then, where is my place? Among the angels, or…?

It is easy to judge others. It is even easier to drag them to the pillar of infamy, to mock them, to hang tin plates around their necks with scandalous inscriptions, and to splash them with the filth of human wickedness. We can do this if we are surrounded by a crowd that shouts, agitates, and does what we do. The crowd, the mob, gives us strength, gives us courage to believe we are right, makes us feel invincible.

The crowd, the mob, brought down the Lord.

In recent weeks, a man accused of all manner of crimes was brought to the scaffold before the eyes of the world. They brought accusers, witnesses, lawyers, and judges, and the mob began to savor in anticipation of the condemnation and execution of the wrongdoer.

The wrongdoer, however, has a legendary reputation, a biography enriched with extraordinary achievements, incomparable with most of those in his world, and nothing will prevent those after us from celebrating this hero who built remarkable works. His accusers would have been proud, in the past, to have had the honor of a simple handshake from him, but today they do not know how to diminish his qualities, so they ignore them. All that matters now are his flaws. His flaws, elevated to the rank of major crimes that cannot be overlooked without a punishment to match—the capital punishment.

His defenders, silenced by the refusal to call witnesses, still brought multiple proofs of innocence for each accusation, but as if none of their words resonated in the air, the accusers kept repeating the same charges, repeatedly, exasperatingly, believing that repetition would give them more weight. But this time they failed. The accused was acquitted.

His enemies, however, promised to continue collecting new charges, because their hatred of one such as him—whose brilliant effort exposes their struggles to seize power at any cost—cannot tolerate any delay. Their decision to destroy everything he has built and continues to build springs from their inability to confront, in direct combat, a stronger adversary, and so they must resort to low blows and other tricks. Their arsenal is large and spacious. If necessary, they will find other means.

How easy it is to be deceived and how easy it is to let ourselves be deceived, when we are surrounded by deceivers with languid voices painting promises of future paradises. Some do it from the pulpit while the donation basket is passed hand to hand among the faithful. Others did it on street corners, gathering curious passersby, but with new technology, today they do it using cell phones. The most dangerous are those who do it in Parliament. They believe themselves saints and want only good.

For our own good, they beat their chests that they will do anything, fight for us, make the impossible happen—only give them our vote. There are many of them, and the choice is difficult. Whom to believe? Can you discern the truth from words? Can you know in a man what is good or evil?

The last angel who lived among us was Mother Teresa.

Angels and demons. The struggle continues, as in heaven, so on earth. Good and evil confront each other unceasingly. Good and evil confront each other within us, leaving us to wage the battle of purification in the tribunal of conscience, without witnesses or lawyers. This tribunal is more just than all others and it is the only one that can truly dictate the direction of our next step and the choice we make.

4 February 2020

Books by David Kimel:

Simple Seeds – Poems

A Foggy Sunrise – A True Story

A Sweetless Love – A Novel

In Pursuit of Happiness – Short Stories

Domniţa and Tudor Avădanei – A Novel

From Faraway Horizons – Travel Notes